STOLEN BY THE MOB BOSS

A RUSSIAN MAFIA ROMANCE (BRATVA HITMAN)

NICOLE FOX

Copyright © 2019 by Nicole Fox

All rights reserved.

No part of this book may be reproduced in any form or by any electronic or mechanical means, including information storage and retrieval systems, without written permission from the author, except for the use of brief quotations in a book review.

❦ Created with Vellum

MAILING LIST

Sign up to my mailing list!
New subscribers receive a FREE steamy bad boy romance novel.

Click the link below to join.
http://bit.ly/NicoleFoxNewsletter

ALSO BY NICOLE FOX

Kornilov Bratva Duet

Married to the Don

Til Death Do Us Part

Heirs to the Bratva Empire

Can be read in any order

Kostya

Maksim

Andrei

Tsezar Bratva

Nightfall (Book 1)

Daybreak (Book 2)

Russian Crime Brotherhood

Can be read in any order

Owned by the Mob Boss

Unprotected with the Mob Boss

Knocked Up by the Mob Boss

Sold to the Mob Boss

Stolen by the Mob Boss

Trapped with the Mob Boss

Volkov Bratva

Broken Vows (Book 1)

Broken Hope (Book 2)

Other Standalones

Vin: A Mafia Romance

STOLEN BY THE MOB BOSS: A RUSSIAN MAFIA ROMANCE (BRATVA HITMAN)

Stolen by the Mob Boss: A Russian Mafia Romance (Bratva Hitman)

A mob boss killed her family. Now, he's sent me to finish the job.

Lucy is an innocent girl – orphaned by a terrible tragedy.

Then she sees me kill a man in cold blood.

I can't let a witness roam free.

But I can't bring myself to kill something so innocent and beautiful.

She wants revenge on the mob boss who stole her family.

I can help her... under one condition:

As long as she's here, I'm going to make her MINE.

1
LUCY

There's a fire on TV.

For a moment, I'm unsure what I'm looking at. The TV is across the diner, hoisted up in the corner of the room, but when I squint, I see that the news is reporting on a massive factory fire. I glance out of the window, and as expected, I see the black cloud ominously rising in the air. The fabric factory is quite a few miles away, yet I can still smell it from here.

The thought of it sends me back to a place in my memory. Not a happy place. Not a place where I ever wanted to go again.

I'm a little girl again, staring out with my nose pressed against the car window, watching as the smoke billows from the shattered windows of my home. All around us, lights flash, red, blue, red, blue, and I squeeze my eyes tight, trying—despite everything—to pretend that I'm not here.

I was too young then to understand what happened. At least, to *truly* understand what happened. I heard lots of words when I climbed out of the car and took off running toward the flames. I could hear the policemen shouting at me to stop. And Nana begging me to come back. But above it all, I thought I could hear my parents calling my name.

Only, they couldn't have been. My parents perished in that fire. A gas leak, that's what the detectives said. Mom and Dad never saw it coming. When Mom flicked on the burner to start dinner, everything went up in flames. Sometimes I wonder what that must have felt like. Did they suffer? Did they feel anything at all? Or was God merciful enough to make it quick and painless?

I remember falling to my knees on the front lawn, sobbing as two firemen pulled me away from the flames. My lungs burned and my eyes burned but more than anything, there was the unshakeable hollowness of loss. I'd spent my entire life in that home. Every year on my birthday, Mom would line me up with the doorframe in the kitchen and carve a little mark above my head. Every Fourth of July, Dad would invite Nana and all of his family over, and at the end of the night, my cousins and I would sit in my bedroom and throw tiny little poppers at each other.

I lost my first tooth in that house. I saw my parents' first fight in that house. And just like that, it was all erased, wiped from existence.

There was only one man to blame.

The police ruled it an accident, something that could've happened to anyone, but that never sat right with me. Shady real-estate dealer Abram Konstantin received only a slap on the wrist. A "Promise you'll be more careful next time?" My parents were burned alive and the only person that was punished was me? Bullshit. Nana says that if I hold onto this for the rest of my life, it'll eat me alive.

But the part of me that longs for justice says, let it.

Let this ache and sorrow consume me and drive me to find the truth about what happened that day. Let it bring Abram to justice and show the world that the disgustingly wealthy can't be allowed to get away with things like this. I want to make an example of him, to show that every life is precious and throwing money around doesn't negate the negligence that killed my mom and dad.

But the realistic side of me has to let this go. I can't function if I spend all my life holding onto it. There's no future if I'm stuck in the past. So, like I always do, I turn away from the television and take a moment to clear my head.

This is why I hate slow days. When the regulars are in, I can distract myself. I can plaster on a welcoming smile and be the best waitress Rudy's Diner has ever seen. When it's empty, I find my mind wandering away, crafting daydreams of vengeance.

It's exhausting.

I turn back to my job, cleaning the counters and rubbing down the cash register. Dirt and grime are no match for the chemical concoction that Madeline and I have created. After growing tired of keeping seven different cleaning products around, we spent one night creating the perfect solution to clean every last inch of Rudy's. Our manager, Rudy Bradwell, was impressed enough not to yell at us for wasting most of his cleaning supplies while trying to find the right balance.

If Nana knew these were the kinds of things I get excited about, she would be proud. All her life, she cleaned up after everyone else. She babysat me while Mom and Dad worked. Dad always told me that she was the strongest women he knew, next to my mother, and I understand why.

Even now that I've moved back to town since graduation, Nana still likes to argue with me about taking care of her. I don't know how many times I've heard the phrase, "I'm old, not dead." She's as hardheaded as ever, but every now and then, I feel her gratitude shine through.

While I was away at school, Nana didn't have anyone to talk to or keep her company. Most of her old friends have passed away, and while I was gone, very rarely did anyone stop by to say hello. Only a handful of neighbors checked in on her, and I'm thankful that they were able to care for her while I was gone because I don't know what I would do if anything happened to Nana. After everyone that I've lost, I don't think I could survive another loved one leaving me.

"Are you ever *not* daydreaming?" a familiar voice asks from behind me.

I turn to see Madeline approaching with a handful of dirty dishes, a mischievous smile on her face. She's one of the most gorgeous women I've ever seen. Perfectly dyed blonde hair, perfectly white smile, and the kind of curves any woman would kill to have. It makes sense that she's a model when she's not on the clock at Rudy's.

"Sorry," I say, blushing. I hate that I have a tendency to get trapped in my head because I usually end up becoming much more reserved. People often read that as either standoffish or awkward, so I've been trying to live more in the moment and spend less time with my own thoughts. But old habits die hard, or whatever they say.

"You know, I was thinking about what you said last week."

"What did I say last week?" I ask. Madeline disappears for a moment to drop off the dishes, then steps back out into the diner, hands on her hips.

"You told me no guys were looking in your direction when I asked whether you were dating or not."

I self-consciously brush a lock of hair behind my ear and turn my attention towards the counter, wiping it down. I hate when Madeline puts on her matchmaker boots and tries to set me up with different guys. I mean, of course, I appreciate her offer and the fact that she tries to introduce me to new people, but her taste in guys doesn't match mine. She likes older, obscenely wealthy guys that have connections. Not exactly my type.

"But," Madeline continues, "I think the truth is that you're sabotaging yourself. That guy with the red hair during breakfast today is proof of that."

"What are you talking about?" I ask, trying hard not to blush.

"You know exactly what," she says, laughing. "I saw the way he was looking at you and how he kept trying to get you to sit down and talk to him. He was hot! We both know that."

"He was ... attractive, yes."

"Why didn't you go for it then? Why didn't you sit down and talk to him?"

I sigh and turn around, leaning against the counter with one hip. "Because I'm on the clock and he had a tan line where his wedding ring used to be. He probably just got out of a marriage, and I don't want to deal with all that baggage."

Madeline clicks her teeth and shakes her head at me. "This is what I'm talking about. You keep finding reasons not to go for men. You're sabotaging yourself so you never get close to them."

"My god, it's like Dr. Phil is in the diner with me," I groan. I toss the rag behind me into a bucket full of other dirty napkins and wipes. "Maybe I just don't feel like dating right now. Maybe with everything going on with Nana and my writing and this job, dating just isn't high on my priority list."

Madeline shrugs. "Maybe. But I know you. I've seen you fawn over guys one minute and then find something wrong with them and turn your back the next. All I'm saying is, it couldn't hurt to give a guy a chance before you turn him away. I think you could meet someone really special."

Despite all of her nagging, I know Madeline wants to be helpful and this is her way of showing it. Other people might grow annoyed with her incessant nudging and prodding whenever an attractive man walks into Rudy's but it comes from a good place, so I don't let it bother me too much.

"Anyway," she says, glancing around at the nearly empty diner. "We should probably get started on cleaning up after the breakfast crew. Lunch will be here soon."

"Sounds like a plan," I say.

∽

When I close the front door behind me, the first thing I hear is a gasp from the living room.

Something's wrong with Nana.

My heart rate spikes. I drop my purse clattering to the ground and spring around the corner as dark thoughts race through my head. Maybe she fell, or had a stroke, or someone broke in and …

Nope. I race in the room to find Nana with her eyes glued to the television. One of her soap operas is playing, and it looks like someone just got shot by a masked gunman.

I let out a heavy sigh.

My body begins to unwind, and I scold myself for being so paranoid. I can't live every day anticipating the worst, but it's another one of my tough habits to break. After everything that I've lost, seeing Nana join that list might just be too much for me.

"Hi, sweetheart," Nana says without looking away from the television.

"Hi, Nana." I pull off my jacket and hang it up in the hallway, taking a seat on the big purple sofa next to her. It may be hideous, but the couch is one of the softest things I've ever sat on in my life, and though it doesn't go with anything in the room, I think that's how Nana likes it. Nothing in her home makes sense.

She has massive paintings on the wall that span various artistic styles, from modern images of puppies to pop art replicas of celebrities and surrealist landmarks across the globe. Her rugs range from faux fur to homemade crocheted ones, and all the furniture in the house was picked up from yard sales or gifted to her after friends passed away.

To say that Nana's house is a collaborative group effort would be an understatement. That's what I love about it. None of it makes any sense, but when it's all together, that kind of chaos is harmonious.

We sit in silence for a moment while the show's climax plays out on the screen before us. When it goes to commercial break, she turns to me, pats my hand, and smiles.

"How was work?" she asks.

"It was okay. Relatively slow, but we got a lot of regulars in."

"Did you see that fire on the news?" Her voice is soft.

I swallow hard and look up at her. I've never expressed the bit of PTSD I feel whenever I see things like that on the news, but Nana knows. Sometimes I wonder if she's been a mind reader this whole time. Rather than saying anything, I just give her a slow nod.

"Are you okay?"

The way she says it almost brings tears to my eyes. Nana has this distinct ability to be stern and strong and confident when she needs, but also uncomfortably tender and caring. It always throws me for a loop when she switches it up and cuts right to the point.

"Yeah," I say quietly. I pick at the tattered edge of one of her throw pillows, keeping my focus on anything but the soft brown eyes staring at me. "I don't think it'll ever be easy."

"It won't," she confirms. "But you'll learn how to cope better. You'll learn how to take it all in, feel it, but not let it overtake you and your thoughts."

That all sounds nice and dandy, but I don't know if I'll ever be strong enough to somehow do what she does. I can't imagine never feeling a twisting knife in my gut anytime I think about what happened to Mom and Dad. Not only is the wound still open from the fact that I lost them, but it's made even worse, salt sprinkled on top, because Abram Konstantin will never be punished for what he did.

Years ago, I sat down and tried to figure out everything I could about him. I wanted to know the man responsible for the death of my parents. I wanted to know who he was and why he was able to skate through life without any kind of repercussions for his actions. More frustrating than anything else was that he was essentially a ghost.

The only articles I could find about him in English were about his real estate dealings and all the businesses he ran in the city. His entire online identity was a sterilized wasteland of uninteresting articles and pictures posing with powerful people. Though my findings were limited, I took note of all the people he was close with.

Millionaires and billionaires, powerful people in town. He associated with the top of the top, and suddenly it started making sense. He didn't get away with negligence because the police truly found him innocent. He used a more precious capital, one that wasn't palpable but still carried more weight than cash. He had connections. He had people that could help him sweep the ash of my singed childhood under the rug, away from the public eye.

There's no way in hell I'll let this go. But for Nana's sake, I give her a small smile and a nod. "I'll try," I say. My answer seems to satisfy her because I watch as she leans back in her seat more comfortably.

"Are you doing okay?" I rise from the couch and take a step toward her, grabbing one of her pillows and fluffing it up. Recently, Nana had a health scare, and I've basically become like her mother, always doting on her and trying to make her as comfortable as I can.

"I'm fine, darling," she says. She pats my hand again reassuringly, and just like I lied to her about trying to let the fire go, I can see that she's filtering her words and holding back what she really wants to say. I can't blame her. Strokes aren't anything to speak lightly of, no matter how minor.

"I just want you to be okay. Even if it means taking more shifts at Rudy's so that I can afford your medicine. Whatever it takes, Nana," I say. There's nothing that I wouldn't do for her, and I want her to know that without a shadow of a doubt.

"Lucy," she says, almost sternly. I stop flitting around and look down into those deep blue eyes. "I'm the grown-up here. I'm taking care of you, baby. You shouldn't be worried about me. What you should be worried about is having fun and meeting a nice man."

It takes all my strength to hold back a groan. Two times in one day is a little too much for me. "Nana, I don't need a man."

"Nobody *needs* a man, Lucy. But they're fun to have around. And I want you to experience that. I want you to settle down with someone nice. At least try."

"Okay." There's no point in arguing with her about this, and I'm afraid that if I do, she'll get worked up and be sick again. "I'll make you a deal. As long as you take the next few days off, I'll go looking for a husband and we'll make some grandbabies for you. How does that sound?"

Her chuckle is sugar sweet, and I find myself growing warm from just her presence. Any time I start to feel anxious, I turn to her for relief. "That's my girl."

The commercials end, and just like that, her attention is now laser-focused on the twisty, complex storyline playing out on the screen. I've lost her to her stories, but that's okay. I have stories of my own to write.

I give Nana a heads-up that I've put lunch in the oven for her, then grab my laptop bag and head downstairs. There's a tiny little coffee shop a few blocks away, and with my headphones blaring my favorite song, it takes almost no time to make the trip. I step through the doors and give a small nod to the barista I see every afternoon.

While I get my laptop set up and go searching for the location that I saved my manuscript, I can't help but feel like such a stereotype. Nana getting sick was the biggest reason I decided to come back to New York, but another reason is the fact that here, my opportunities of having my work discovered are so much higher.

New York is full of possibilities for unpublished authors, and I know that deep in my heart, this is what I'm supposed to be doing. Storytelling was always my passion growing up, and when I got to college, I took my first creative writing class. There, I had the idea that I'm currently working on.

It's about a woman losing her child to a notorious murderer in town, and after years of looking, she finds the first clue that could lead her to find out what truly happened that night at the deadly lake behind her home. It's marketable, that much I know, but the hard part for me is finding the time to finish it.

Between working at Rudy's and taking care of Nana, I rarely have time to sit down and just be with my characters. At work, my mind wanders back to thoughts of scenes in my book, and with Nana, I think about what my protagonist would be doing if someone was depending on her the way Nana depends on me.

Sitting there with my computer open and my notes spread out on the table, though, I find inspiration and let it take me in whatever direction it needs me to go in. As much as I love organization, I don't plan my books. I see the story in my head and the way I get there, but the fun part is figuring out the smaller scenes and all the ways to make those interesting so that no scene feels like it could be removed from the rest of the story.

Before I know it, I've typed almost three thousand words—major progress from where I started. My heroine, Malorie, has just been run off the road by the killer's equally unstable cousin, and her head is bleeding. As much as I want to sit and finish the scene, I decide to leave it on a cliffhanger. There will be plenty of time for me to revisit this world later on.

On the way out, I order a couple cookies and begin my trek home, my thoughts floating like zero gravity. How do I get my protagonist out of this situation? Is she too far gone now? And if she is, how can I give her the strength to fight her way out?

I'd like to be like her. Determined. Persistent. An all-around bad ass. But nothing like that ever happens in my life. Nothing this exciting, or dangerous, or reckless. Maybe that's why I'm writing. Nana and Madeline would say that I could have all that with a man. I shake my head and smile to myself.

Maybe they're right. Maybe I just need to find the right man.

2

ROMAN

Each of us is born with a gift. A special talent. Some people act, some people dance, some people sing a fucking jingle.

Me, on the other hand ... I kill.

And tonight is another chance to show the world my gift.

Waiting is the worst part of this job. Memories are the only thing that help pass the time. Leaning against the exterior wall of this nightclub, the memory of my first kill comes back to me. Like most of my memories, it ends with blood.

It was late August, when the weather was finally starting to get colder and the city folk began trading T-shirts for flannels and jackets. My father took my brothers and me hunting for the first time. We'd spent a good few months learning how to shoot both guns and arrows, and he wanted to see how well we'd do after our lessons.

The crunch of leaves under my boots was so vivid that I can feel the texture of them to this day. The wind whipped our faces as we hiked from our truck through the hills until finally, we stumbled into a bit of clearing. At first, there wasn't much to see. A squirrel clung to a large oak tree. A collection of rocks growing moss on the sides. My father asked us if we saw anything. We said no.

"Then look harder."

That's when I saw the tiny brown rabbit pressed against the trunk of a tree, quietly nibbling food. My father gave me a look. As the oldest, I knew what it meant. I'd seen it plenty of times before. Narrowed eyes, lips pulled into a thin, straight line. I had to set the example.

Quietly, I pulled an arrow from my quiver and nocked it, pulling back the bowstring. I steadied myself and set my jaw, holding the position until I could feel the right moment to strike. The air in my chest stopped and I felt the world begin to disappear, every external distraction ceasing to exist. Then I let go.

The arrow sliced through the air in silence. Before my brothers Gedeon and Ivan could blink, the rabbit was dead, pinned to the tree.

I let out a breath and glanced at my father. The only indication that I'd done a good job was the short nod of his head, the most subtle of compliments. It was enough to satisfy me—for a moment. One rabbit alone wasn't enough, however. I wanted more. I wanted bigger, more dangerous.

We worked our way up from there. My brothers didn't have a knack for killing, nor did they like it the way I did. Raccoons. Deer. Elk. Even a bear once, with a perfect shot through its eye. My father seemed pleased with my skill. For years, we honed it, improving how quietly I moved, how long I waited before pulling the trigger, savoring the exhilarating feeling of a perfect strike.

Like all good things in my life, however, it didn't last. My father didn't last, either. It took the murder of my family to push me onto the pursuit of the most dangerous game of all: men.

My father had two brothers, Aleksandr and Andrei. Even as a child, I felt the tension. They never stopped by the house unless there was trouble and they needed their big brother to come and fix their messes. Everything with them seemed to be business exchanges, no warmth or familiarity. They always bothered me. I was right to be suspicious of them.

The night they proved that, I was in the hospital with stomach pains. Food poisoning of some kind, nothing too serious. When the nurse stepped in with an officer, I thought I'd done something wrong. But they weren't there to chastise me. They were there to tell me that my parents and younger brothers had been murdered.

They didn't say by whom, or why, or answer any of the other million questions I had. They just told me that I couldn't go home. Police were there investigating. My uncles were on their way to pick me up.

None of it made sense. I was a kid, and in my mind, this was all some weird medically-induced dream. Or rather, a nightmare. But that solemn look on the nurse's face is seared into my memory like a cattle brand. She looked down at me with pity. And I knew she was telling the truth.

For a long time, I never knew exactly what happened. My uncles comforted me and helped when they could, but at seventeen years old, I was nearly an adult. I could live on my own. For a while, I managed. I rebuilt. I took my shit-covered situation and made it work. That's how I always was. I got by.

But then I learned the truth. It wasn't a random act of violence that stole my family from me. It wasn't some fucked-up junkie looking for a score, or a home invader with the wrong address.

The innocent blood was on my uncles' hands.

The same uncles who'd picked me up from the hospital on the worst night of my life, who'd been taking care of me in the months and years since … they were the ones responsible. They were the motherfuckers who ruined everything for me.

So I made a decision, then and there: I would make them regret not killing me too.

A scream across the street from the nightclub yanks me out of my memories.

I see a skimpily dressed brunette giggling and running away from a man. He has his phone out recording her, cheering her on and encouraging her to say something for her social media account. For a moment, they're the most entertaining thing around outside of this scummy club.

"Knock it off!" she chirps.

"Make me," he growls playfully.

They end up making out against the brick wall.

It's sad. It's pathetic. And yet in some ways, I'm almost jealous.

They're so naïve, it's incredible. In the timeless wonderland of their social media newsfeed, every moment is captured forever like a bug trapped in amber. They'll never grow old. They'll never die. They'll be young until the end of time. Untouchable.

They haven't seen the shit I've seen. They know nothing of the underworld vibrating beneath their feet and before their eyes. Oblivious and carefree, this night will be one they remember fondly, or forget entirely. But there's one man who will never forget tonight—Mr. Joshua Hollis.

The man I've been sent to collect.

The back door to the club opens and a drunk man comes stumbling out, patting himself down until he locates his pack of cigarettes. He takes one out and lights it. I watch as the cloud of smoke begins to fade into the night.

Bingo.

I don't know what my client wants with this man, and that's none of my fucking business, either. I learned a long time ago that not knowing is better. These are targets. They're not people. Get too attached to them and it just makes delivering the body that much more difficult. Out of the corner of my eye, I see the couple still making out, giggling and moaning softly. I want to yell at them to fuck off, to go find some cheap hotel to fool around in, but I can't blow my cover. Besides, it's go time.

I approach Hollis and in a low voice, ask, "Mind if I bum a smoke?"

He blinks, cloudy from all the booze in his system, but nods and quickly lights another for me. I stopped smoking ten years ago, but I breathe it in and blow it out like I've been doing this for years.

"What're you doing out here?" he asks, glancing at me.

A wry smirk crosses my face. "Undercover."

"You a cop?"

"Why, you doing something illegal?"

Joshua snorts and shakes his head. "Not unless you consider stepping out on your wife illegal."

I raise a brow and look at him once more. I hadn't pegged him as the cheating type. But then again, I'm a hired killer. Not exactly in a position to pass moral judgment on my fellow man.

Instead, I say, "What she doesn't know won't hurt her, eh?"

"I'd do the right thing and leave her, but it's just the fact that my kid needs me, man. He needs someone in his life and I can't do the same thing my dad did. I wish there was a way this could all just work itself out. But I'm sick to death of her …"

He continues on about his family, how he accidentally knocked his wife up, and to avoid upsetting her religious parents, he married her as soon as they found out about the baby. I let him talk and pretend to listen, all the while keeping the two horny twenty-somethings in my line of sight. I can't make a move until they're gone, but they continue to linger. The guy is trying to charm his way into a back-alley fuck, but she's not having it. She just giggles, shaking her head at him before kissing him once more.

I'm growing antsy, and I rock from foot to foot. Joshua glances at me and lights a second cigarette. "You okay?"

"I'm fine." I stomp out the butt of my smoke and lean against the wall, willing myself to be patient. This is just like the rabbit in the woods. It has to be smooth. Breathe. Focus.

Finally, the two strangers across the alley make their way to the street. I can finally breathe again. Now, Joshua and I are alone. No more witnesses. He gestures at me, offering another cigarette, but I wave it off.

"One is good," I say.

"Suit yourself. You know, my wife says these things are gonna get me killed one day," he chuckles.

If only he knew.

He turns away to light up another and that's my opening. I place the rag in my pocket over his mouth and nose. His sudden gulp of air is stifled by the damp cloth covering his face. He tries to jerk away. I grab him and pull him closer, holding him still as I watch his hands flutter. The man has more fight in him than I predicted. Won't matter, though. The drugs on the cloth take everyone, sooner or later. In a few moments, his body slides limply to the ground.

Transporting bodies is always easier in the movies. In real life, it's a pain in the fucking ass. I crack my neck, then bend down and hoist Joshua up over my shoulder. With a quick glance behind me to make sure no one can see us, I stagger back to my car parked at the end of the alley. He lands in my trunk with a loud thud. Inside, I fasten his arms behind his back and his legs together, then slap a piece of duct tape over his mouth.

My car starts up silently. I pull out of the alley. I know these streets like the back of my hand, so maneuvering through all the back roads and shortcuts comes as naturally as hunting for me. I consider twisting the knob of the radio but decide against it. It might wake Joshua up, and the only thing more annoying than those two strangers making out would be listening to the man in my trunk squirm and try to escape.

I steer away from downtown, towards the warehouse district. My mind starts to drift back in time again.

The anger born that night in the hospital never left me. In the years since, I've drunk gallons of booze and spilled ten times that amount in blood. But it's like a stain on my soul. Hasn't made a goddamn bit of difference.

I thought killing the men responsible would start the healing process. I was so, so wrong.

Because the things I learned while I planned changed my life forever. The anger inside me grew like an ulcer, like a cancer. Until it took me over.

Aleksandr and Andrei were part of some low-level bratva, a brotherhood of Russian criminals for hire. Petty bullies, drug dealers, the kind of parasites who prey on good people. Just like they did to me.

Money was the reason. Fifty thousand dollars was all my mother, father, and brothers were worth to them. Even now, the thought makes my blood boil. It takes everything I have not to lose my temper all over again.

They could've chosen poison. A shot to the head. Something quick and painless. But that's not what they did. They were methodical, starting with my father. A shot to both knees left him defenseless. They dragged my mother to the bedroom and made her watch as they killed her boys. Aleksandr was the one who killed them. He laughed as my mother cried.

They showed my family no mercy.

So I gave them none in return.

My plan was simple. I posed as a potential client looking to hire them for a hit, but because of my high profile, I said I couldn't let them see my face. Rather than communicating through the internet, I donned a ski mask for all of our meetings. I wanted to look them in the eyes as I led them into my trap. It was the ultimate test of control, sitting in front of them and not losing my shit. Every bone in my body, every fiber of my being, was alive with rage. Images of them bloodied and torn to shreds raced through my mind, and more than once, I almost lost it. When I spotted my father's ring on Andrei's finger, I nearly cut it off from the first knuckle. Instead, I clenched my jaw and gave them the details.

They were to break into the home of a specific address. It would be an easy job. In and out. They seemed gleeful, eager to do whatever it was I needed. I gave them the money up-front, a measly $10,000, and watched as they celebrated.

After that, it was easy. All I had to do was show up at the house before they arrived and rig everything up. The moment they stepped into the bedroom, it began to fill with gas, and unable to breathe, the two of them collapsed in a heap on the floor.

Aleksandr was the first to break. After the fifth tooth I tore from his gums, he finally confessed what they had done. Andrei, to his credit, wasn't as big of a coward as his twin. He took every ounce of pain with something I might consider dignity. He cried and howled, but he didn't cave.

Not until I made him watch as I used my knife to draw a line across Aleksandr's throat. That's what broke him—seeing his other half, the brother he'd spent every moment since the womb with, die before him. Had I had any mercy, I would've given him a bit of relief, perhaps waited a few hours to let Aleksandr's death settle before continuing, but mercy was in short supply and my patience was running thin. They'd both suffered adequately, and it was time to put this all to rest.

Somehow, Andrei was able to grease up his handcuffs enough to pull his bloodied wrists free, and as I approached him to finish the job, he took off for the door, hobbling for his escape. It was pathetic watching such a broken creature give his last swan song. He fell to his knees, his hands too slick with blood to get the door open.

I approached him and pressed the gun to the back of his head.

"Nephew, please," he murmured, gurgling on his words. "Spare me."

"You didn't spare my family."

Those were the last words I spoke to my uncle before I painted the front door with his blood. His body twitched just twice before he stilled and the light faded from his eyes.

It was done.

None of it made things right again. I didn't feel whole. It didn't bring my family back from the dead. But I don't suppose that's what I was looking for. I knew deep down that their deaths wouldn't be the path to enlightenment. No, they were something else. The start of a new career.

I was good at killing. I'd been good at it my entire life. And with nothing and no one holding me back, I could throw myself into this career. So, that's what I did.

It started small. A couple thousand dollars to rough up a cheating husband. Some money to bash in a car or scare some people who needed to straighten up. Simple things that paid the bills. Enough to prove myself to those who hired people like me. Soon enough, I was assigned my first paid hit. In and out, no blood, no witnesses.

Then another. And another. So many I lost count.

Things haven't changed. I still do what needs to be done for the highest bidder. Right now, the man with the money is Mr. X. I don't know who he is and I don't give a fuck. I just take care of whatever he needs me to take care of.

Right now, that's the man in my trunk.

We make it to an abandoned warehouse near the docks a few miles away from the nightclub. The drive took a bit of time, but it was nice to soak in the silence. There won't be much of that once Hollis wakes up again.

There's a vehicle waiting for us. I park my car a few feet away from the unmarked black BMW. I can see the outline of two men inside. One in the front, one in the back. I step out, move to my trunk, and pop it open. Joshua seems to be waking up from his fog. His bleary eyes part as he looks up at me, wide with fear. The tape muffles his screams.

He tries thrashing around when I attempt to pull him from the car. My fist connects with the side of his head and the fight is gone, flicked off like a light switch. Now that he's not struggling anymore, I drag him out of the trunk and close it with my elbow. His feet scrape against the cement as we make our way towards the black car.

I give two taps on the rear window and watch as it slides down just a crack. Mr. X takes no chances with being recognized.

"This is your guy."

Mr. X nods. "Collect him," the man calls up to his driver. His hulking chauffeur steps out from the driver's seat and stalks towards me, scooping up our hostage like a baby. Joshua looks light as a feather in his arms.

Mr. X slides an envelope through the gap in the window. I take it and peer inside, thumbing through the money.

"It's all there," Mr. X assures me. "You may count it if you wish."

I know that tone. It's just on the verge of being insulted at my distrust. "I believe you."

"Good. Now, for your next assignment." Mr. X slides a piece of paper through the crack in the window. On it is a name and an address. "I need you to take care of him tomorrow. Can you manage?"

I fold the sheet of paper up and slip it into my pocket. "That won't be a problem." Without another word, the window rolls up. Conversation over.

I return to my vehicle and roll the windows down. It's not too chilly out tonight, and I need a bit of fresh air after the long drive. As I press on the accelerator and pull away from the parking lot, I hear two sounds in quick succession:

A loud pop, and a man's agonizing scream.

Mr. X and his driver didn't wait too long to begin the torture, it seems. I don't care to stick around to listen. To this day, I hate the sound of gunshots. In my mind's eye, I can still imagine my mother's screams. I squeeze my hands around the steering wheel even tighter.

It's been a long night. I need to get away from these thoughts for a while. I need to fucking sleep.

Tomorrow, another hit awaits.

3
LUCY

I don't like to be dramatic, but there's no hope in being a writer and I should honestly give up the dream right here and now. I could probably be getting so much more work done if I wasn't pretending to be a hot-shot author. I could be making money to help Nana, or covering for a friend at Rudy's who couldn't make it to work today. Anything would be more productive than sitting in this café with a blank screen staring me directly in the face.

I want to scream. It's like someone's stolen the words from me and locked them up, leaving me with only a bunch of shapes and squiggles on my keyboard. Everything seems foreign. I want to disappear.

Instead, I put my forehead on my folded arms and suppress a long, draining groan. It's dramatic—such a first-world problem—but I need to just take a break from this. Spend some time doing something else. I don't know where these blocks come from, but I still haven't mastered the art of breaking through them. I don't have a fancy ritual for unsticking myself from this wordless trap. I don't have any regular solutions to inspire myself.

All I know is that when I was younger, this didn't happen. I could spend hours in the living room, typing away all kinds of stories. None of them made sense, but dammit, I was writing something. At the very least, I had words on a page and not just the vast emptiness of white that I can practically feel staring back at me through the screen.

Rather than forcing myself to sit here and figure out a way to write myself out of a narrative hole, I close my laptop and put it back into my bag. There's no point in wasting time trying to force the words if they're not going to come.

I slip my phone from my pocket and dial Madeline's number, drumming my fingers on the wooden table as I wait for her to pick up.

"Hey," she says, chipper as always. I'm jealous of how much energy has, even after she's worked all day and dealt with less than favorable employees.

"Hey! I was wondering if there's any room for me there?"

"I thought you were taking the day off and getting some writing done!"

"Yeah, so did I," I laugh bitterly, rolling my eyes at myself. "I've got major writer's block and I'm tired of sitting here and staring at all my work. I'm afraid if I do that any longer, I'll realize how much I hate it and erase all of it."

"Oh please," she says. "I've read some of your work. You're a great writer. In fact, you made me like true crime books when that stuff used to scare the shit out of me."

There aren't many people that I've let read my unfinished work, but one day while I was at Rudy's, typing away, Madeline stood over my shoulder, her eyes skimming over my screen. At first, she thought that I was doing an essay about murder, but as she read more, she eventually realized that it was fiction. Ever since then, she's demanded that I keep her up-to-date and send her chapters of this new manuscript.

I want to be annoyed because I know that it's the writerly thing to do, hiding your work until it's finished, but I need that encouragement. Madeline supports me when all I want to do is delete every word I've ever written and punt my laptop into outer space.

"I'm glad you liked it," I say, biting back a bashful smile.

"Don't delete anything, okay? Just keep it and come back to it whenever you're feeling less stressed. I'm sure you're probably already stressed taking care of your grandma too, huh?"

I hadn't even thought about that. Whenever I find that I can't seem to put anything down on the page, it's usually when things in real life are harder. After Mom and Dad died, I didn't write for years. When I went through finals during my senior year of college, the last thing my mind could do was conjure up a good chapter or two. And now, with Nana's health becoming more of an issue, I've lost my way again.

"You might be onto something, actually," I murmur.

"I told you, I'm a lot smarter than I look." We both laugh at her bragging. "Anywho, Tina just left for the day, so if you want to come by and fill in for her, I think Rudy would be cool with that. I'll double-check after this call, though."

"That sounds perfect. Thanks, Maddie."

"No problem!"

I'm feeling just a little less dejected. There's an actual reason that I can't write. Too much is going on for me to focus on my protagonist and her dangerous situation. I swing my bag over my shoulder and head up to the front to order a coffee to go. I figure I'll walk to work since it's not too far, and on the way there, I can drink my favorite mocha to keep me warm.

"That'll be $5.48," the new barista says. He's cute, but I still prefer the one I normally see instead. Sometimes he gives me a discount, which I definitely appreciate.

"Sure," I reply. I pat my pockets for my wallet, and my stomach sinks when I feel nothing but my phone. When I check the other pocket, I find that one completely empty. The woman behind me lets out a noise of impatience, and when I give a panicked look to the barista, he keeps his expression blank, like he's unamused with me.

"Sorry, I just ..."

Anxiety starts to roll over me, and I search through my bag, placing down a few coins that I know won't add up to the price of my drink. I want to shrink into the bag and hide forever, but I'm frozen in place, frantically praying that somehow, I can come up with enough to buy this drink and escape this uncomfortable situation.

"Ma'am," the barista says, "You can step to the side if you need to look for more money."

The tone of his voice tells me that isn't just a suggestion. He needs me to move because I'm holding up the line. My face burns hot with humiliation. I nod, biting down on my bottom lip to keep from bursting into tears. The lady beside me impatiently steps forward, side-eying me on her way up.

I keep fumbling, coming up with hairpins and chapstick tubes, but no more money. When the lady in line gets her order, she brushes past me, knocking my bag from the table. It falls to the floor facedown, spilling all of the contents inside. Stuff ricochets in every direction. She looks down at my items and turns her nose up, walking away without even offering to help.

I can feel the eyes of everyone in the café on me. Not now, not today; this is all just too much. I need to get out—right this second.

I stuff everything back into my bag and pull it over my shoulder, not even checking to see if my laptop is okay after the fall. I just have to get away from here. The barista looks at me expectantly, and I'm all too aware of the burning stares from the other people in the café. Without a word, I turn and head for the door, pushing through and rounding the corner of the building.

Once I'm alone, I take a slow breath and hold back tears. I don't consider myself shy, but the way everyone in there looked at me, like I was too poor to afford a coffee ... I haven't wanted to disappear like that in a long time.

I don't like to think about money any more than I have to, but I don't know how much longer I can keep this up. With all of Nana's medical expenses piling up one after the next, I've had to make my checks spread even more than I used to. She gets disability, and that really does come in handy, but the bills keep growing more and more expensive every day.

I wish I could just take a vacation from life. Unplug, shut down, and just sleep forever. I don't want to work anymore. I don't want to write anymore. I don't want to go through the same nightmare about my parents over and over again. I just want to sleep.

But I know Mom and Dad wouldn't want that.

They'd tell me to keep my head up. Change is always coming, and things are always darkest before dawn. The sun is going to come up and I'll be able to see my way again.

Maybe.

After a few slow breaths, I feel my heartbeat return to normal, no longer on the verge of having a full-on panic attack. There are no prying eyes, no audience waiting to see my next blunder, wondering if, for my next trick, I'll drop my coffee or spill it on someone else. Today isn't my day, but I'm not going to let a few embarrassing moments ruin the rest of it for me.

My phone vibrates, and I see a text from Madeline. Rudy says it's cool if I come in and fill Tina's shift. *There we go,* I tell myself. *Something to look forward to.* Covering for Tina will give me a little more spending money, and the next time I see that barista, I can buy a lot of drinks and rub it in his face. I can afford a latte *and* a cappuccino, thank you very much.

But then there's a thunderous boom above my head, and I know immediately that today is proving not to be my day. The sky is cloudy and gray, and when I tilt my head up to look, something wet splashes down on my nose. Almost immediately, rain begins to pour down, and I shake my head.

"What did I do to offend you?" I growl at the universe. I grab my bag and put it over my head, hurrying through the alleys and trying to hug the wall. I knew I shouldn't have walked to the café. Now I need to head home and change. On the plus side, I can grab my car. There's no way in hell I'll be able to get to work in this kind of weather.

Maneuvering the alleyways is like a sixth sense to me. I've learned all the quickest shortcuts and ways around the city, mostly to save on gas and not spend so much time waiting. New York traffic is something terrifying, and that's coming from someone that writes about homicidal maniacs running around rural towns.

As I step around a sleeping man covering his face with a newspaper, I hear people arguing around the corner. I know that I should mind my business, but they're getting louder and my curiosity cat needs to know what's going on. As I approach, I walk with lighter steps, trying not to draw any unwanted attention my way.

My heart begins to race, and I clench the bag over my head tighter, my throat squeezing. Just as I reach the curve of the alley, there's a hand on my shoulder. I spin around to find a homeless man standing there, smiling a grin filled with blackened, rotting teeth. I swallow back a scream and clamp a hand over my mouth.

"Spare change?" he asks. The way his voice sounds, I don't think he's asking. He's demanding.

Rather than arguing, I hand him the change I'd planned on using for my coffee. "That's all I have."

"This is perfect. Thank you, miss." He buries his hand in his pocket and hurries off towards the opposite end of the alleyway.

When my nerves are steeled and I'm not feeling so uneasy, I head back to the corner. I don't have much time for this, so whatever their problem is, I need them to make room so I can walk through.

"Stop!" the smaller man cries, struggling in the grip of the other, taller man.

I poke my head around the corner and watch as the taller man tosses the other across the alley, slamming him into the brick wall. My heart falls to my stomach. I may love exploring true crime cases, but in real life, I've never been able to handle violence. Even pushing and shoving sets my teeth on edge.

Part of me considers intervening, but I stay planted where I am. If this man can throw a relatively big guy around like that, I'd be toast to him. The bigger man lifts his head, and I can see his face much better.

He has dark brown hair that falls in front of his eyes, sopping wet from the rain. His jawline is strong and masculine, and his nose is perfectly straight. If I were an artist, he's the kind of good-looking that I would want in my sketchbook. Though he's handsome, something about the way he holds himself seems rugged. Dangerous. His allure is almost palpable, and though he's beating a stranger up, I feel myself gravitating towards him.

"Please," the smaller man begs, his hands in the air.

Everything happens so quickly. Without even flinching, the man standing reaches into his jacket and pulls out something shiny and sleek. The other's eyes get so wide that I can see the whites. He parts his lips one last time, there's a sharp pop, and then he's slumped over.

It takes a moment for me to register the spray of blood on the wall behind him. When I do, a scream bubbles out of my throat with a mind of its own. My ears echo, ringing louder than they ever have, and for a moment, none of it makes sense. I don't understand. I can't be seeing this right now. It takes everything in me not to double over and vomit.

He's dead.

I just watched someone be murdered. That statement echoes in my head like voices down an empty hallway, over and over. I saw someone die right in front of me. Then the other fact settles down on my mind: his killer is standing right there. Slowly, he turns his head to look in my direction.

Everything in me goes cold. For the third time today, I want to disappear. Only this time, the stakes are much, much higher.

The handsome shooter's eyes meet mine, and I expect to see tangible anger. I just witnessed him shoot a man at point blank range. Instead, something completely unexpected radiates between us. I don't know what it is, and for the first time in my life, I don't know how to put it into words. I feel an unnerving sense of calm, like a deer frozen in the headlights. He's a speeding car, and yet I don't jump.

I look back at him, my mouth hanging open, shivering in the downpour.

And then just as quickly, that space between us shatters and everything inside me screams *run*.

I don't second-guess myself. I turn on my heels the moment I see him take a step in my direction. I make a beeline for the other end of the alley, the one I entered from, my heart racing a million miles a minute. As I sprint, I toss one look over my shoulders to see if he's still there.

He chases after me, shouting something incomprehensible in the ruckus of the rain, but I don't stop. If I do, I know without a doubt that I'll end up like the other man. I run hard enough to make my muscles scream. The street is right there. Almost there.

Then I trip.

A loose brick sends me tumbling forward. I slam my head against a dumpster, letting out a sharp cry of pain. My balance takes a hit and I stumble to the right, off-kilter. I try to stay upright, but my vision starts to darken at the edges and I collapse.

I hit the cement with a thud, soaking every inch of my clothes in the puddle I've landed in. A frigid chill shoots through me, but the world is wobbling. Darkness grows larger, now covering the edges of my vision.

Walking slowly, the stranger approaches. His gaze no longer looks dark. He seems almost … concerned. He squats before me. "You almost made it," he says matter-of-factly.

I try to form words but they all come out wrong.

Don't … please … no …

My brain won't connect to my mouth. Everything is shutting down. Just before I black out, I feel him slide two arms beneath my body and hoist me up. I try to fight, try to escape, but my body goes slack, and despite the screaming in my head, I fade into unconsciousness.

4

ROMAN

The scream that rips through the alleyway makes the hair on the back of my neck stand up. I spin around and make eye contact with a girl that can't be much older than twenty-five, though, drenched in the rain and her eyes wide with fear, she looks much younger.

I don't know how I managed to fuck this job up so badly. It's not like me. I don't make mistakes. Everything that I do is planned perfectly, with little margin for error. That's why I've been hired by so many people and why I make the kind of money I do.

What I didn't prepare for was my hit being tipped off that I was coming.

The job was supposed to be simple. Mr. X made it clear that he wanted this done fast, not his usual M.O. On any other given assignment, he'd take his time. He'd want me to make these men suffer, bleed them out if necessary, so long as I got the information that he required. But this was supposed to be clean, quick, and easy.

I trailed behind my target, Evan Cleary, for a few hours, waiting for him to step off into a secluded part of the city so I could strike. With how quickly X assigned this job and the time crunch that I was in, I had to forgo my usual stakeout. No days spent hiding in the shadows, watching a target and finding a pattern, some kind of schedule they operated on. I should've known from the start it was a bad idea.

Perfecting the art of blending in is something I've spent years doing, and on any other assignment, I would've gone undetected. That is, unless the target knows my face. As he crossed the street and glanced to his left, I made eye contact with Evan Cleary and watched as recognition settled over him. That same realization hit me.

I'd seen him before. It was an assignment years ago. Simple recon. Mr. X did business with a local strip club and wanted to figure out where his money was going. He'd been coming up short thousands, and whoever was behind the missing cash was going to pay in many ways.

I try to work alone, but X knew that I couldn't just waltz into the building and fit in with the others. I stuck out like a sore thumb compared to all the suits. The local crowd at the strip club was very tight-knit. At Glamour, everyone knew everyone's name, and at the time, no one knew me from a random stranger on the street. After I donned my best suit, a few of X's men, including Evan, walked me into the club and sat me down. With that crowd around me, no one questioned who I was. I was part of the group automatically, no questions asked.

The idea of depending on others while on a job made me itch, but I managed to contain my distaste long enough to fake interest in a few strippers. Nice girls, all of them, but I made it a point not to fuck around while on assignment. The last thing I needed was to get distracted by a Diamond or Trisha.

It was easy to figure out where the money was going. Sneaking upstairs, I could overhear a pair of men talking in hushed tones. Then there was the exchange of bundled cash between the two. I recognized the owner of the club, and the man he handed money off to must work for him, I decided. The owner instructed him to deposit the money in their bank account immediately.

Rather than just returning with the information, I decided to do Mr. X one better. I waited until it was closing time before striking, knocking the owner unconscious and stuffing him in the trunk of my car. Evan stumbled out, drunkenly asking if this was part of the assignment.

"Go home," I warned him. "Unless you want to join Tony here."

Evan gave me a sloppy smile, understanding that I had no qualms about putting him in there as well. He nodded and headed home, so wasted that I was sure he'd forget this night entirely. Mr. X appreciated the fact that I got the thief for him, but what he enjoyed more was the suitcase full of cash that I placed on the table the very next morning.

Holding Tony's assistant at gunpoint and making him withdraw all the money he'd been siphoning off X was the cherry on top. It was a clean, easy assignment, with no loose ends and no unnecessary violence. Or so I thought.

I fucked up in thinking that Evan would just forget. The moment he looked back at me on that street, it all obviously came rushing back to him. He knew what it meant to see me. He knew that bad things happen when I'm close by. So he ran, dodging honking cars.

"Fuck!" I cursed, chasing after him. I knew I should've worn a hat, or something that could cover my face. Even an umbrella would've made for good cover. He wasn't about to come quietly and shoved his way through the crowd, sending civilians tumbling into my path. The little fuck must've run track in high school.

But I'd never lost a target before. I wasn't about to start now.

Grinding my jaw, I picked up speed, until I cornered the rat in an alley.

He put up a good fight. Got a few good hits in and even slashed me with a knife. But he was fighting from fear. I was fighting from a lifetime of violence. All it took was an uppercut to knock the resistance out of him.

"Roman, please," he panted, one eye bloodied and swelling. I watched the rain wash the red away from his face. He was a desperate man. A kinder person than me might have sympathized with him. But his cries made me feel nothing.

Per orders, I made it quick. The pop of the gun was hidden behind a roar of thunder, but then there was the high-pitched scream of a woman. It cut through the noise like a crackle of lightning.

I turned to see her standing there, shivering, and soaked from head to toe. Blonde hair clung to her forehead, and despite the low light of the alley, I could see her bright eyes staring at me with a mixture of fear and something else. Was it curiosity? Terror? We stood still for what felt like an eternity. Before I could say anything, she turned and ran.

I followed behind her, determined not to let her get away. The last thing I needed on this already fucked-up job was an eyewitness. At least this chase was easier. I turned the corner just in time to see her trip and hit her head hard. She fell to the wet pavement. I holstered my gun and approached.

Now, standing over her, I see she looks much more innocent and frail. Beautiful, too. Like a butterfly caught in a spider's web. Part of me wants to leave her here, let her go back to her normal life.

But the professional in me knows I can't do that.

With how long we stared at each other, it would be easy for her to go to the police and file a report. Soon, I'd have a sketch of me all over town. No, I can't run that risk.

Looking down at her, I shake my head. "You almost made it," I murmur. Her eyes fall closed, and I watch her slip into unconsciousness. I hover over her and look up at the other end of the alley. Any minute now, someone could come along and see her lying in the rain. I don't know who this girl is, but I can tell that this isn't where she belongs.

I reach down and heft her up. She weighs nothing. Carrying her to the car I've parked a few feet away, I drop her off in the back seat, pausing to tie up her arms and legs. When I'm sure she's secured and won't be getting away, I head back to Evan. His corpse still lies facedown on the cement. The rain has thankfully washed most of the blood away so there won't be much of a clean-up, but I already know he's going to bleed when I put him in my trunk, which means I'll have to clean that out soon.

I shake my head and curse under my breath again. So messy, so unlike me. I need to get the fuck out of here before something else unexpected thrusts itself into this shit pile of a situation. Evan hits the trunk with a thud, and I slam the lid closed, taking a seat in the car and pausing to collect myself.

Mr. X doesn't have to know how quickly this all soured. As long as I keep the girl quiet and take care of Evan's body, as far as X knows, everything went according to plan. I didn't fuck up too badly. This is all still salvageable.

But there's still the loose end of the girl to tie up. For all the shit I'm paid to do, I don't kill women or children. I refuse to put them through anything close to what my mother and brothers felt. The only people I take out are men who deserve it, which Mr. X is fine with. He has plenty of other men to harm anyone else he deems worthy.

This would all be so much easier if I could make myself pull the trigger and take the blonde out as well. I damn near lost her anyway. If not the rain, she might've gotten away, and then I'd be royally fucked.

I pull onto the road. The rain hasn't let up any, so it's hard to see. At least the rain keeps people from peering inside my car too closely. The last thing I need is someone calling the police because I have a woman tied up in the back seat.

Now, where to go? Home is my first thought, but it's a bad idea. She's seen my face already. The last thing she needs is an address to go along with it.

Instead, I head to a small motel that I've stayed at before. It's a ratty thing, mostly used for men cheating on their wives and women trying to score drugs or a pretty penny for fucking. Nobody asks questions there, which is exactly what I need.

I halfway expect the girl to wake up and throw a fit, but to my surprise, she stays unconscious the entire ride. Transporting her is the difficult part. I pull up as close as I can and quickly stride through the lobby, paying for a room all the way at the back of the building, as far away from prying eyes as I can manage.

The man behind the desk doesn't ask questions. He must assume that I'm having some kind of illicit affair and want as much privacy as possible. When he hands over the keys, I give him a short nod and head back to the car, pulling it around and parking underneath a large oak tree.

Every time I think it's safe to throw her over my shoulders and head inside, someone steps out onto the balcony for a cigarette or to take a call. It takes nearly thirty minutes of waiting, but finally I have an opportunity to move. I pull a blanket out and toss it over her. It's not much, but from a distance, she looks like a rolled-up rug.

I hustle inside and set her down in the dingy bathroom, untying her hands and wrapping them around the base of the sink. As I reach for the rope I set on the toilet lid, I feel her stir. She blinks away the sleep and focuses on me.

"Get off me!" she screams suddenly, thrashing against my grip. She's stronger than I thought, and it takes a bit of effort to keep her pinned. "Let me go! Someone help me!" she howls.

"Stop," I growl, and for a moment, her fire dims a little. I don't want to hurt her, but I might have to if she doesn't cooperate.

But just as quickly, she's angry again, fighting with me as I reach for the rope once more. Growing sick of the struggle, I pull a rag from my pocket and stuff it in her mouth. This cuts off her screaming, but it doesn't help that she's still writhing beneath me, trying to twist free from my grasp. Quickly, I grab the rope and secure her wrists around behind the base of the sink.

Once that mess is taken care of, I stand up and look at her. She kicks at me, but she's just out of reach. For someone so small and demure-looking, she's vicious. Under other circumstances, I might find it endearing, but right now, this girl's a pain in my ass. First, she's eavesdropping and watching from the shadows, and now she's trying to tip off the whole motel that she's in here against her will.

"Look," I say, my voice echoing off the walls of this tiny bathroom.

She does as instructed, her wide blue eyes facing me.

"I don't want to do this to you, but if you don't stop, I'm going to leave you here with that rag in your mouth. Do you understand me?"

She nods slowly. For a moment, I question whether this is a good idea or not. I don't need her blowing this a second time tonight. Still, it doesn't sit right with me, seeing a woman tied up, blind rage running through her like some kind of wild animal. There's not much of a conscience left in me, but this weighs heavy on it.

Carefully, I reach forward and pull the rag from her mouth. "Fuck you," she spits. She opens her mouth wide to scream again, but before she can get it out, I stuff the rag back inside, silencing her.

"What did I just tell you?" I ask. "Now you have to stay like that until I get back."

Her eyes start to water, but I straighten up and look at myself in the mirror. There's a large bloodstain on my side that's growing larger, but I don't have time to worry about that right now. Instead, I zip up my jacket and grab the car keys, locking the door on the way out of the motel room. She'll be all right while I finish this assignment.

～

Down in the parking lot, I pull my phone from my pocket and dial Mr. X's number. The phone rings three times before he picks up. There's no response, just the sound of his heavy breathing.

"Evan is taken care of," I reply.

"Get rid of him. Then come to the warehouse." Then X hangs up the phone. A man of few words, as always. Not that I'm complaining. I don't imagine we'd have much to talk about aside from me telling him where all the bodies are buried.

I pull out of the parking lot and head to a swampy marsh out of the way. The drive takes about forty-five minutes, but there's no hurry anymore. The woman from the alley is safely secured at the hotel, Evan is dead, and, in just a few minutes, he won't be my problem anymore. The sooner that happens, the better.

I don't notice the pain in my side until I begin digging the hole for Evan, but I clench my jaw and work through the sting. This is the final task before I can collect my money and head back to the motel. I can tough this out and worry about fixing myself up later.

Evan's body hits the soft dirt with a dull thud when I drop him into the hole. I pause to look at him. Death smoothed out the scared-shitless wrinkles in his forehead. In fact, he almost looks peaceful. Lucky bastard.

I don't know what he did to piss Mr. X off, but in this line of business, I've learned not to question the men with money. I don't need to know why someone is on their shit list. All I have to know is where they are and what the price is. Gripping the shovel again, I toss the dirt onto him. His face disappears.

Against my better judgment, my mind wanders back to the woman and the way she looked at me in the alley. It wasn't just my imagination. I know that much for certain. Whatever happened between us, she felt it too. She felt that standstill sensation, the limbo where our eyes locked and for a moment, neither of us made a move.

She's beautiful. There's no point in denying that or pretending that I haven't noticed. I'm not fucking blind. I've always been attracted to women with her features, especially the smattering of freckles that covers her nose and cheeks.

She's feisty, too. Feistier than I expected. I like the fight in her, even if it made my next move harder.

She deserves better than the fate she's going to get. Evan here was scum from the start. He knew the life he chose, and he knew the risks that came with it. But the girl ... she just walked down the wrong alley at the wrong time.

But it's out of my hands now.

I return to my car and toss the shovel in the trunk. I have money waiting for me. After I receive my payment, I'll worry about figuring out what to do with the woman in the motel. Until then, I can compartmentalize and breathe easier. Evan is dead and I'll have my money soon.

That's a good enough distraction for now.

5

LUCY

My head is still pounding when the hazy fog of sleep finally disappears. I blink a few times, turning my head and immediately regretting it. The ache is worse than any bad hangover I had in college, and it almost makes me nauseous. I squeeze my eyes tight and take a slow breath, trying to talk myself through the pain. I would kill for an ibuprofen right now, but my oh-so-generous host doesn't strike me as someone that will be particularly keen on running errands for me.

How the hell did I even get in this position?

Today was supposed to be simple. All I had to do was write a bit, then head to Rudy's and fill in for my coworker. But then things took a left turn. Worse than that, actually.

I watched someone die today.

Just remembering that detail, the thick red glop painted on the wall, makes me want to puke again. One moment I could see the life in his eyes, and the next, it was gone, blown out through the back of his head. I want to kick myself. I should've been quiet. I should've stayed hidden, or run faster, or tried to hide. If I did, I wouldn't be here, tied up in the bathroom like a pig awaiting slaughter.

I don't know what he's going to do to me, but I've heard these kinds of horror stories before on all my favorite true crime podcasts. Women like me don't fare well when it comes to being kidnapped by murderous psychopaths. If I don't act fast, I could very easily become the next victim people are talking about.

The idea of being killed—or worse—lights a fire inside of me. I have to get out. I can't die like this. If I do, who's going to take care of Nana? Who's going to bring Konstantin to justice after what he did to my family? No, there's no way that this is going to be the end of me.

I look around the bathroom for something that might help me. We're in some kind of motel, I can tell that much. The little bottles of shampoo bear the logo, and the monogrammed towels are a dead giveaway as well. On the side of the bathtub, there's a small razor, and my heart beats quicker. I can get that and cut these ropes on my hands. I slide my legs out from under me and reach one foot out, desperately trying to reach the bathtub. My foot stops short just past the toilet, and I let out a cry of frustration, trying not to lose my cool entirely. Repositioning myself, I get further, but it's still not enough. When I feel like I'm about to tear my arms out of their sockets, I take a break, sitting up straight again.

That's not going to work. I can't reach it. *Think, Lucy. Think.*

Aside from the razor, there's not much else in the room that can help me. I could try and reach for the shampoo or conditioner to help slick my hands up enough to slide out of the rope, but with how tight the binding around my wrists is, that might be time wasted that I could be putting towards something else. Something that might actually help me escape.

Frustrated, I tug against the rope and stifle a yell, panic threatening to overtake me. The feeling of being trapped is like a wildfire and it spreads throughout me, every part of my mind on red alert. The only thing I can focus on is getting free.

Breathe, I tell myself. Talking it out works wonders, and that bubbling of anxiety slows down.

Lying outside of the doorway of the bathroom is my purse. I can just barely see my cell phone poking out of the top of it. Hope sparks again, and I take a deep breath. This is going to hurt. It looks closer than the razor, but still a bit out of my reach. I have no other choice, though. I have to do this. I have to get away. My eyes close, and I try to collect myself. I can do this.

When I'm calm, I slide down on my back and stretch my legs forward, patting around on the ground in search of the strap. My arms scream for mercy, but I can't stop. I have to reach further. I have to grab the bag. This is the only way that I'm going to get out of here alive. My captor could return at any moment, and every second I spend not calling the police is another second wasted.

When I finally feel the strap hook against my foot, I swell with excitement. I'm not finished yet. I still have a chance. I close my eyes and tug my foot back hard, yanking the bag closer to me. I slide it more and more in my direction, sitting up straight when it's finally close enough for me to poke around inside with my foot.

No ... I frantically move things around inside the bag. It was right there in my purse. I know it was. I saw it!

But the phone's not there.

I search through the bag in a flurry, tears welling in my eyes. I look up where the bag was and see that the phone has fallen out. It lies facedown, taunting me. I ease back down onto my back, repeating the same method as before, but this time, I can't reach it. Everything hurts. My head throbs even harder, my eyes sting, and the muscles in my arms burn as I try with everything I have to make myself longer. But it's not enough.

I'm going to die here.

∽

A quick kick to my leg wakes me up this time. I must've passed out. My head still hurts, but the throbbing hasn't gotten any worse, thankfully. I tilt my head back and see the stranger standing over me, a blank expression on his chiseled face.

"Wake up," he says simply.

He's quite the talker, I think bitterly. My eyes fall to what's in his hands. He has bags of chips, prepackaged sandwiches, and two bottles of water.

"Eat."

The last thing I want to do is have dinner with this nutcase. I imagine breaking free from these ropes and scratching his eyes out, shoving him out of the way so that I can make my escape. I couldn't take him in a fight one on one, but if I had the element of surprise, I could probably outrun him. His large frame is dense, like he's spent his whole life training, and I imagine he must move slower than me.

I sit up straight and grit my teeth. The names I could call him right now would probably land me in deeper shit than I'm already in, so instead, I bite my tongue and continue to stare at him with malice.

"Eat," he repeats, tossing the sandwich and chips in my lap. He reaches forward and tugs the gag from my mouth, letting me speak.

"Am I supposed to eat with my feet? You need to untie my hands."

His emotionless gaze remains on me for a long moment, and I start to wonder if my sarcasm has gotten me in trouble. I don't know this man. I don't know what he wants from me. He could be some kind of sex trafficker for all I know, and here I am, sassing him and mouthing off like my life isn't literally in his hands.

Rather than lashing out or striking me for my insolence, he simply takes a seat on the toilet and grabs the food from my lap, unwrapping the plastic surrounding the sandwich. He points it in my direction, and that's when I hear my stomach growl. The fighting spirit in me says that I'd rather starve than do what this bastard says, but the part of me that hasn't eaten since breakfast this morning is ravenous.

Tentatively, I lean forward and take a bite from the corner of the sandwich, never once taking my eyes off his. He looks back at me with the same intensity, the same hesitant curiosity, and I have to wonder what's going on in his mind. Is he going to rape me? Kill me? Sell me?

He brings the sandwich to my mouth again, and this time, I feel his warm finger brush against the corner of my lips. I swallow hard and look at him with wide eyes, unsure whether it was intentional or not. And even worse, I can't help but enjoy his touch.

It's so fucking stupid. The idea that I find a murderer attractive makes me want to recoil, but I can't deny that when I look at him, there's something that lights a fire between my legs. Maybe it's the pensive look he wears, his eyebrows knit together deep in thought, or the way his lips remained pressed in a hard line and his jaw clenches. The clouds swirling in those deep brown eyes.

Whatever it is, the entire experience is unreal. I know, logically, that he could easily switch his whole motive and take me out here and now. I'm supposed to be afraid of him, to cower in the corner and pray that the police find me somehow. And yet ... I'm not.

"Are you going to kill me?" I ask, my throat dry. Before answering, he uncaps a bottle of water and lets me take a drink from it. His answer doesn't come for a long time, long enough that I grow uncomfortable.

"No."

It's short and sweet, and it should make me feel relieved, but it doesn't. If he's not going to kill me, then what? "Are ... are you going to rape me?"

There's a flash of emotion in his eyes, like he can't believe that I would even consider that possibility. "No," he says, firmer. "I don't hurt women."

That calms me down a bit more—as calm as one can be tied to a bathroom sink. "Then what?" I insist. His dark eyes almost look black under the light of the bathroom. "If you're not going to hurt me, then why am I here? Please just let me go. I won't tell anyone. I promise. I didn't see anything. I just fell and hit my head, and some nice man brought me back to his motel so that I wasn't lying in the rain."

I try my hardest to make this easy for him. If he unties me, I'll keep my mouth shut about everything and pretend like none of this happened. He said he doesn't hurt women, and so far, he hasn't.

"I'm not letting you go," he says, biting into his sandwich. He slumps down against the back of the toilet and looks at the wall across from him, sighing. His chewing is methodical, slow and repetitive, and it's irrationally frustrating to me.

"Why can't I leave?"

"Where are you from?" he asks, changing the subject.

I debate whether I should tell him about my life. What if he's lying about not hurting women? What if, when I tell him about my friends at Rudy's and Nana, he makes them the next targets? I can't do that to them. I can't let him know that much.

So I lie. "I'm from here. My parents died a few years ago, so I'm on my own. I have a son. His name is Joey, and he'll be six next month. Right now, he's with his babysitter, who I'm sure is worried sick."

The man's hard gaze falls on me again, only this time, he's not lost in thought. "Bullshit," he says, shaking his head.

"I'm not bullshitting you," I protest.

"I know a liar when I see one. I've met plenty of them. Worked for plenty of them. And you're full of shit."

I don't know how he can tell, but being called out only makes me more irritated with him. So what if I'm lying? He's the one kidnapping a woman and holding her hostage in a motel room. He has no room to judge me. Especially if he's working with people that are liars.

"What are you, then? A paralegal?"

Surprisingly, the corner of his mouth lifts just slightly. Was that almost a smile? He looks at me again. God, those eyes are gorgeous.

"No, not a paralegal."

"Then what? You killed that man in the alley. Do you kill people for a living?"

The look the man gives me sends a shiver through my spine. He doesn't have to utter a single word for me to know that I've hit the nail on the head. He's a hired killer, someone that takes people out for others with a lot of money. My head spins.

This kind of thing only happens in books like the one I'm writing. I didn't think it was real, this kind of dark, seedy world. But everything about his expression tells me that he's not lying like I am. He's a hit man, plain and simple.

"So that man in the alley ... Was he a target?"

He hesitates, then nods.

"How much?"

He looks at me carefully. "I don't talk about that."

I swallow hard. It must've been a lot of money then. I can't imagine anyone putting hits out on people and not paying top dollar. "Okay," I say, nodding slowly. "How did you get started?"

"I don't talk about that, either."

I feel myself growing annoyed at how tight-lipped he's being, but it makes sense. I'm some random woman that witnessed him killing a man. He probably doesn't want to tell me every detail about his life and his finances. "Can you at least tell me your name?"

This question isn't immediately shot down. Like before, he takes a bite of his sandwich and chews thoroughly, his eyes on the wall ahead. "Roman."

"Roman," I repeat, leaning against the sink. "I'm Lucy."

"Lucy."

I know it shouldn't affect me, but the way he says it makes me feel warm inside, like he's stoked a fire that's just beginning to ignite. None of this makes sense to me, rationally. He's a killer, cold enough to shoot a man right between the eyes, yet he makes me feel hot. It shouldn't be happening, yet I can't deny that magnetic feeling between us.

"Are you going to make a scene if I untie you, Lucy?" he asks.

Hell fucking yes, I think. The first chance I get, I'm getting the hell out of Dodge and never looking back. "No," I tell him, shaking my head. "I promise I won't."

I hold my breath, waiting for him to decide whether he wants to untie me or not. We both know that if I attack him, he'll easily handle me. As it stands, I'm no threat to him physically. I could yell, but I look up at him, trying to mentally communicate that I won't scream if he lets me go. I could've done that the moment he took the gag from my mouth. But I didn't.

"Don't make me regret this," he says, flipping his blade out and reaching behind the sink to cut the ropes. When he's finished, I pull my hands close to my chest, rubbing my wrists.

"Thank you," I say softly, inspecting my hands. There are marks where the ropes once were, and I know there'll probably be burns there in the morning. All that tugging and pulling I did is coming back to bite me in the ass.

"I need to go to the bathroom," I say, and he nods. He collects the food and walks out, leaving me alone. When he's gone, I close and lock the door, looking at myself in the mirror. I look like I've been dragged through hell twice. My skin is blotchy and my eyes are red from crying. It's not a pretty sight, and I struggle not to physically turn away from my reflection. Instead, I take a moment to clean myself up. I wash my face with the soap on the counter. My skin isn't going to like it, but it makes me feel less dirty, like I wasn't lying unconscious, soaking wet in an alley just a few hours ago.

I use the restroom, and after I wash my hands, I start for the bathtub. The razor is no longer sitting there on the side of the tub like it was before. For a moment, I want to curse, but I have to give it to him. He's smarter than I thought. I'd planned on using that razor to make my escape, but he's one step ahead of me.

Trying not to look too disappointed, I leave the bathroom, stepping out into the main part of the motel room. Roman stands in the center of the room, his eyes glued to the television. The news is on, and the local anchorwoman is talking about some of the crimes that have happened in the past few days.

"You looking to see if I'm the only witness?" I ask. His silence is all the answer I need. It makes sense why he'd be hovering over the television like this. I assume that because this is his profession, he doesn't usually make such a big mess. He doesn't strike me as a sloppy man. He seems much more methodical; more controlled and constrained.

When the program ends, he clicks off the television and turns around to face me. Up close, he's even taller than I thought. He has a good foot and half on me.

Without a word, Roman grabs the hem of his bloodstained T-shirt and pulls it over his head. I almost gasp. He's absolutely shredded, thick with muscle that ripples along his arms and back. A vein wanders along his bicep and disappears into his chest, which is covered with a light sheen of dark hair. He looks like an athlete, a Greek statue. *Stop it,* I warn myself. *He's a killer, not an Abercrombie model. Quit fawning and focus on getting the hell out of here.*

I start to avert my eyes when I notice a gash along his side. The words catch in my throat and I stare at him. It looks pretty bad.

"How deep is that?" I ask.

Roman glances at the wound and shrugs. "Half an inch, maybe. It's not that bad."

I don't know what comes over me, but I instinctively reach out a hand and brush my fingers over the skin just above the cut. His body is warm, tight, and lean, and I feel his muscles tense up. His eyes meet mine again. "I can fix that," I whisper. "I take care of my grandmother."

Roman doesn't automatically pull away or scold me for touching him, which is a good sign. Any other man as dangerous as him might've done something to hurt me. I pull my hand back and start to say something, like apologizing for crossing the line, when his phone rings. He glances at the table, and almost reluctantly, he pulls away, grabbing the phone and heading out into the hall.

I watch him leave, chewing on my bottom lip. Now I have the chance. I hurry over to the table and pick up the knife he used to cut my ropes with. It's a simple switchblade, and I flick it open, creeping towards the door. Through the peephole, I see his back to me and his phone to his ear. There aren't many words that I'm able to pick up, but it sounds as if he's repeating information back to whoever is on the other end of the phone.

Instantly, I start coming up with scenarios. This whole thing has been a lie, a way for him to get my defenses down and trust him; that way when he comes back in here to kill me, I won't see it coming. No witnesses. That's what he wants. I'm the only person that saw, and when he comes back in the room, he'll make sure I'm the last. The secret will die with me.

I grip the handle of the knife even harder, my breathing growing shallower. I don't care how big he is. I don't care if he towers over me or if he could crush me with one hit. I'm not going to let him take me down without a fight. But my resolve crumbles the moment I hear him say one man's name.

"Abram Konstantin."

My jaw drops. For a moment, I'm sure I've misheard him. This can't be happening. This is not real life. I'm gonna wake up any second, right? Safe in my bed with a crazy dream to tell Nana about.

But seconds tick by and nothing changes. This is as real as it gets. I'm the prisoner of a hit man, and I just heard him say the name of the man who killed my parents.

What does he know about Abram? Is this man a client? Or could he possibly be the next hit?

Roman is a trained killer, and I'm in the business of stopping Konstantin from hurting more people the same way he hurt my parents. At the same time, Roman could be working with the man. What if Konstantin is behind this and he wants Roman to take me out so that nobody else will stop him?

These thoughts hit me a mile a minute, so hard that I almost don't see Roman end the call and slide the phone back into his pocket. I feel the room closing on me, demanding that I make a choice.

Do I stop Roman before he gets the chance to hurt me, or do I wait it out and see if he can help me? Kill him or question him?

I clench the knife tighter in my hand.

Then the doorknob twists and Roman walks back in.

6

ROMAN

I try to make my call as short as I can. It's a simple job, one that might take a bit longer than usual, but I don't mind it. Mr. X is paying more than twice what he would normally for this hit. Whoever this Konstantin man is, he's pissed X off pretty bad. It's a warning to anyone else not to cross him, I'm sure. Not that I need a warning. I know well enough what happens when he gets upset.

But there's another problem waiting for me to take care of before the Konstantin hit. A feisty blonde problem on the other side of the motel room door.

I slip my phone back into my pocket and twist the doorknob.

For a brief moment as the door swings open, something feels very, very wrong. There's a sense of tension lingering in the air. I learned long ago to trust my gut, and it just isn't right in here.

The door opens fully and I scan the room on high alert. But everything is where it should be. Lucy sits on the bed, bouncing her knees like she's anxious about something. For a heartbeat, I stay by the door, watching her stare at the television. She's switched it to something other than the news. From the censored beeps and high-pitched fighting, it must be some trashy reality show.

When she finally pulls her gaze towards me, she smiles faintly and asks, "Was that about your next job?"

It's unsettling how easily she can read me. I don't like it. What makes this job easy for me is that not many people get under my skin. Not many people can decipher what I'm feeling. But this girl? She's better at it than I'd like. Part of me wants to dump her off on the side of the road. When she aims those big blue eyes in my direction, it's like staring at a mind reader.

"Yes," I say. There's no point in lying. She doesn't know who I'm talking about. No harm in admitting that much.

"Oh."

The silence between us is too much, and I drop down on the bed, a few feet away from her. The motion causes my injured side to throb, but I clench my jaw and grimace through the pain. I'll worry about that later. Stitches are gonna be a bitch, but I'll manage.

Lucy's offer comes back to me. But I've never liked the idea of letting someone close enough to do damage to me. My entire career, I've made it a point to look after myself. No hospitals. No nurses. Involving those people only made things more complicated. All those questions, trying to figure out why I ended up on the table with stab wounds and someone else's blood on my shirt? No thanks, hard pass.

But for the first time, I almost considered it. Lucy said she took care of her grandmother, and that makes me wonder why. Is the old woman disabled? Is that what Lucy does for a living? I know that story about her having a son is bullshit, but I didn't doubt her when she mentioned her grandmother. The conviction in her voice was pure.

To be honest, most everything about her seems pure. Sure, the girl has a fighting spirit, but anyone with an iota of courage would do the same in this situation. What makes her different is that she didn't run. She had plenty of chances to call for help but didn't. She could've screamed. Attacked me. Jumped from the balcony and taken off running. All these escape routes, yet here she is, watching trash TV in this rundown hotel with me.

It's fucking insane. That's what it is.

I don't get this girl, but part of me wants to. That's what's making this harder for me. I could kill her and be done with her. I wouldn't have to worry about her snitching later on down the road. The only problem is, it feels like a sin. Like killing a dove. She's a tiny thing, probably doesn't weigh more than a hundred and ten pounds. It wouldn't take more than a few good hits to take her out.

But I don't hurt women. I don't kill women. That's what makes this shit complicated. The logical, emotionless side says to make it quick and painless. A pillow over her head tonight. A lethal dose of something I keep in my glove compartment. Even just a bullet between the eyes. All swift, but all brutal. And yet, when it comes to Lucy, just looking at her in the wrong way feels too cruel.

Goddammit.

She interrupts my thoughts when she turns around and says, "I'm tired."

I glance at the clock. It's almost eleven at night. It's been a long fucking day, but I've been in clean-up mode. I haven't even noticed how exhausted I am. "You can have the bed," I say, standing up.

"Are you sure? There's a lot of room," she offers.

Sharing a bed with her is too dangerous. If one brush of her fingertips could tempt me into letting down my guard, what would having her little frame beside me do? I don't even want to think about it.

"I'm sure. But I have to tie your feet to the bed."

She looks at me in shock. "What?"

"You heard me. You could still run, and if you do that, I'm going to have to break my rule about hurting women. If you're tied to the bed, you can't run, and I won't have to hurt you."

"Roman, please …"

The softness in her voice is like a mousetrap. "No. Either you sleep tied to the bed or tied to the bathroom sink. Take your pick."

Like a bratty child, she crosses her arms over her chest and looks at the bathroom. Deciding it's in her best efforts not to fight with me, she turns off the television. "Fine," she grunts. "I'll sleep on the bed."

I pull the blankets aside and grab a long piece of rope, waiting for her to get settled down before I wrap it around her ankle. She doesn't fight me. Instead, she watches silently. I consider tying it tight, but decide against that. Maybe it's the sadness on her face. Maybe I'm just feeling generous. Either way, I give her a bit of wiggle room this time. After I'm done, Lucy pulls the covers over herself and lies back.

I grab a pillow from the other side of the bed and lie on the floor beside her. When I pull the hood of my jacket over my eyes, the world goes dark.

~

Trying to fall asleep is easier said than done. Between the horns honking outside, the sound of our neighbors fucking, and Lucy's soft breathing, it's impossible. I try to ignore it all, but it's incessant. She's not asleep. I'm not asleep.

"Go to sleep."

The bed squeaks as she rolls over. "I can't."

"Try harder."

"It's kind of been a hard day for me," she says snippily. "I don't normally get kidnapped and tied to beds before I sleep."

Frustrated, I pull the hoodie over my face and look up at her. Her nose is scrunched and her eyebrows are turned down, unhappy. The fact that she looks cute even like this pisses me off. I want to tell her to stop. Stop looking like that. Stop confusing me.

"You shouldn't have been walking through the alleys then," I reply.

Anger flashes on her face. "Says the murderer!"

She's impossible. I try to sleep again, but I can't. In the bathroom, I fill up my bottle of water and take a long drink, trying to clear my head. I'll just have to wait her out. I'm clearly not going to be able to sleep before her, so there's no point in trying now. When I return to the bedroom, I start to lie down again. Then I notice my knife sitting on the nightstand.

It wouldn't be a problem if it were facedown. I always keep it that way. Some dumb, superstitious shit my dad told me years ago. When I left the hotel room, it was facedown. Now the brand name is visible, flipped the other way.

She must have touched it when I stepped out to take Mr. X's call.

Instantly, I'm livid. Here I was, thinking she was a good girl. That she didn't run away because she was pure, because there was something between us. What a crock of shit. All this time, she had my knife. Was she going to use it on me? Did she think she could overtake me?

"You touched my knife," I say in a low voice. It takes everything not to yell at her.

"What?"

"Don't play stupid. You touched my knife when I was outside in the hall. Were you going to kill me, Lucy?"

She rolls over again, turning those eyes towards me. The same as before, I can see her lie as it leaves her lips. "I don't know what you're talking about, Roman—"

I'm on top of her in a flash. I grab her throat and push her into the mattress. Her eyes bulge, practically out of her head. I've had enough of her lies for one night. I thought that I could trust her, but all along, she was feeding me nothing but bullshit. Her grandmother probably doesn't even exist. That must've been some kind of lie, too. A way to get me to let down my guard. Make me trust her. Not any fucking more.

I squeeze her throat harder than I should. "Don't fucking lie to me again," I warn her. "You lie again and I'll have to break my own rules, and when I do, I won't feel bad about it. Do you understand me?"

Her nod is quick and panicked. "Yes," she forces out. My grip loosens just enough to let her speak easier.

I take a moment to calm down before I ask my next question. "Did you touch my knife?"

"Yes."

"Were you going to use it on me?"

There's a moment of hesitation before she nods. "Yes."

My stomach sinks. I trusted her, after everything. She didn't scream. She didn't fight. It wasn't because she was cooperating. She was waiting for me to let my guard down so she could stab me. I'm a fucking idiot for thinking that she wouldn't. I've been trained to expect the worst from people. To never turn my back on someone. At any moment, they could strike. And Lucy's proved that point completely.

It takes all my strength not to squeeze her neck and punish her for her plans. But I can't just yet. I have to know why she would do this. When I ask, she swallows hard.

"I ... I overheard you on the phone out in the hall," she confesses. "I grabbed the knife and listened in on your call. I couldn't hear much, but I heard you mention a man. I recognized his name, and I decided that it was better not to hurt you."

"What name? Konstantin?"

She nods. "I know that man. More than I ever wanted to."

"How?" She looks away, and I can tell that she's debating whether she should tell me or not. I add more pressure to her throat and she snaps back into focus.

"He killed my parents. When I was a girl, my parents died in a house fire. The wiring inside wasn't up to code. The house caught on fire, and it burned them alive inside. I watched them wheel my parents out in body bags. And as a child, I thought people that did bad things paid the price for them."

Tears well in her eyes, and I watch as they run down her cheeks.

"But Konstantin didn't get what he deserved. Nobody pressed charges. Nobody made a big deal out of it. My parents got swept under the rug like they were nothing. And all these years, I've wanted to hurt him. I've wanted to tell him that what he did to my parents wasn't just unfortunate. It was neglect. His neglect is what killed them. He would've gotten away with it had I died in the fire, but I didn't. And now I have to make him pay."

The idea of this little thing taking on someone with ties to a Russian mob is almost funny. She could barely take on Konstantin, let alone all the men she'd have to get through to reach him. But I don't laugh in her face. I can see that she's hurt. I can see the anguish in her. It's like looking at a mirror.

The death of my family brought on the same emotions. For years, I didn't know what to do. All I had was the anger inside of me, a fire that wouldn't die down. I wanted to hurt everyone I could. I wanted to tear apart the people behind their deaths. And when I finally did, I felt that sense of peace. It was hollow, but it was peaceful knowing that the right people had paid for their crimes against my family.

The part of me that hasn't recovered from being orphaned wants to let her go. I want to encourage her to seek her revenge. Make the motherfucker pay. She has the passion I had, the drive to right Konstantin's wrongs.

But I'm not stupid. I know she'd never get far. She's innocent; fucked up by the world, but still holding onto her virtue. Riling her up and sending her in his direction is a surefire way to get her killed, and I can't let that happen. I won't let that happen. Even if she was planning on stabbing me and leaving me for dead.

"Please, Roman," she says. "I need this. You're the only person I know that can help me. You're a trained killer."

"What do you expect me to do?"

"Let me help you! I've spent so long researching Konstantin. I've grown up my whole life watching him. I probably know more about him than your boss does."

I want to argue, but she's probably right. Mr. X kept his call short and sweet. He gave me a name, a bit of background information, and that was it. It was clear that this man has been putting his nose where it doesn't belong, and it's my job to put a stop to that. Whatever Lucy knows might actually be useful.

Too bad there's no way in hell I'm letting her tag along.

"No," I say, shaking my head. "I'm not going to do that."

This situation with Lucy is already complicated enough. Spending any more time with her would only be a distraction, and that's the last fucking thing I need. I've already made a mess of one job thanks to her. Adding her to another would have the same results.

On top of that, I can already tell that being around her clouds my judgment. When I'm with Lucy, I let my guard down. I'm not always looking for danger. Nabbing the razor was good in hindsight, but she still managed to get ahold of my knife. It's sloppy. Being around her makes me sloppy, and that's not what X tolerates. In my line of work, one moment of sloppiness is enough to get you killed.

Her eyes are still aimed up at me. "Roman …" Her voice is on the verge of tears, but I keep my resolve. I'm not going to let her fuck up another job of mine, all for a moment of revenge.

There's also the fact that the way she says my name, so sad and soft and delicate, makes me hard as a fucking rock. She's putting a spell on me, and I can't tolerate that kind of distraction. I turn away and breathe, trying to reassert control over my body. It takes a few moments before I'm calm again.

When I don't give her an answer, she turns her head and I watch the tears run over her nose. Even in the dim light, I can see the freckles. Something tells me to reach out and wipe her eyes, but I don't. I won't. I can't.

Both of us fall silent. All I hear is her steady breathing. That's when I realize what I'm doing. Still straddling her. Still pinning her to the bed. I try not to let my mind get away from me, but the thoughts are hard to stop. I imagine what it would feel like to straddle her for real. To part her legs and slip inside. If the touch of her fingers fucked with me that much, what would being inside of her do to me?

When I feel my cock stir to life again, I clear my throat and climb off. Better safe than confusing myself anymore. She looks defeated, pouting like a child. She'll get used to it. In the morning, I'll drop her off.

It's not the smartest idea, but I can't keep her around any longer. I've already fucked up showing her my face and telling her my name. Letting her go could be just as idiotic, but I need to be rid of her. Only then can I get my head back in the game. I have a new assignment that I need to worry about, and taking care of Lucy is not part of the job description.

∽

For the rest of the night, Lucy doesn't say a word to me. She rolls over and pulls the covers up high. I wait quietly, until finally I hear her breathing begin to slow. Her body relaxes, and finally she falls asleep.

Exhausted, I pull my hood over my eyes for what I hope is the last time. This is all too fucking much. Thankfully, after a few minutes of listening to Lucy, I finally fall asleep too.

But my dreams are a confusing mess.

7

LUCY

I dream about Roman.

It's the only dream I have, but it's vivid. He's on top of me again, that passion still burning in his eyes, but something about it is different. He's not furious that I considered knifing him when he least expected it. Instead, he looks at me with a different kind of intensity, something I've only experienced once before. He could hurt me, but instead, his hands loosen their grip on my wrists and begin sliding down my sides.

I stiffen for a moment, my breath catching in my throat. It's wrong to admit, but the sensation of his touch is delicious. He's a loaded gun, capable of causing harm to anyone around, but in this moment, the safety is on.

For now.

His hands continue the journey lower, but when they reach the hem of my shirt, he slides them higher, rough fingertips against my soft skin. The combination forces goose bumps in their wake, tiny trails that he leaves up and down my body.

One hand returns to my throat, but instead of squeezing hard, threatening me, it feels like a gentle reminder. He's the one in control. I'm the one tied to the bed, vulnerable to his every whim and desire. He could just as easily hurt me as bring me pleasure, and that flip of the coin is what makes me grow wetter.

In the moment, I want him more than I've wanted anything before. I want to feel his calloused hands all over me, claiming me, giving into his desires. The look on his face tells me he's struggling, torn between whether he wants to give in or pull away. I see the wrinkles in his forehead and the indecisiveness in his eyes, and I know.

I don't want him to stop. I can't let him stop.

"Please," I whisper, my voice barely loud enough for me to hear it. "I need you, Roman."

It's as if a dam has broken. He leans forward and presses his lips to mine. Overcome, I taste the mint on his tongue and smell the soap on his skin and any fight left in me disappears entirely. I'm not angry that he kidnapped me. I'm not scared that we're in this hotel room. I don't even consider the fact that he knows who Abram Konstantin is.

All I'm conscious of is this desire buried deep inside me that's finally beginning to wake up from its slumber. I let it flow through me, brushing my tongue against Roman's, whimpering at the rough stubble on his chin. He fits against me so perfectly, his towering, looming frame dwarfing my own. When he breaks the kiss and attacks my neck with nipping, teasing bites, I choke on a cry of pleasure. I'm writhing against him, raising my hips to close the gap between us.

I feel the bulge in his pants and I'm on fire again, consumed by a need I haven't felt in months, if not years. I need this more than anything. More than I need to hurt Konstantin. More than I need to take care of Nana. Right now, the one thing on my mind is being closer to Roman. Feeling his weight press down on me, and when he eventually undoes the fly of his pants, feeling him fill me.

When he pulls away to look at me, I feel my heart beat faster than before. His lips glisten, wet from our kiss, and if my hands were free, I'd pull him down and kiss him again. Rather than saying anything, Roman slips a hand between us and I hear the unmistakable sound of his zipper. The look shining in his eyes tells me exactly what's coming next.

Pounding.

There's a pounding at the door that ruins my dream. I sit up in one quick movement, my head spinning. It's not the kind of knocking that housekeeping uses. It's a forceful knock, authoritative. I turn to the floor where Roman went to sleep and find him looking between me and the door.

"Open up," the booming voice on the other side of the door orders. "This is the police."

For a moment, I feel my heart leap. This is what I've wanted for the past twelve hours. I don't know what's going on, but if I wanted to, I could scream and make all of my problems disappear. The officer outside would save me from Roman.

I've been saved.

But a second later, I realize that I can't go.

Running away would stamp out any chance I have of finding where Konstantin is. Roman couldn't help me stop him. If I turn Roman over to the authorities, it just means that my opportunity to make Konstantin feel what I felt is gone once more. I may never get another chance like this. When I look back at Roman again, he's staring at me, practically daring me to say a word.

"Untie me," I say.

"What?"

"*Now*," I hiss.

If I were him, I wouldn't trust me either. He doesn't know my intentions or what I plan on doing, and in the kind of business he works in, trust doesn't seem to be given so generously. Still, I need him to do exactly that. I frantically gesture to my feet, pleading with him. Reluctantly, he undoes the ties. I rub my ankles for a second, then hop up from the bed and shimmy out of my pants.

Roman gives me a curious look, but I ignore him.

When I reach the door, I twist it open just a crack and look up at the officer behind the door. Poking out around him, I see the small beady eyes of a man in his late fifties. He clears his throat.

"Sorry to disturb you, miss, but there was a missing persons report filed for a Lucy Walker. I'm the manager. I wanted to make sure that everything is okay."

The officer nods in agreement, tilting to the side to look behind me. I keep the door closed just enough so that Roman is hidden. "I'm Lucy Walker," I say, feigning confusion. "And I'm certainly not missing." My laugh sounds forced, but the two men don't question it.

"It says here that your grandmother and coworker came into the station. They hadn't heard from you in twenty-four hours. You were last seen walking into an alley, and security footage across the street witnessed one man leaving in a car. He later checked into this hotel," the officer reports.

Despite everything, I'm touched that Nana and Madeline came looking for me. If I really was in danger, those two would've saved my skin. Instead, I'm just being tied to beds and bathroom sinks by hitmen. Nothing dangerous about that at all.

"Gosh, my nana is such a worrywart," I giggle. "I take shortcuts through the alleys on my way back from the coffee shop I visit. I ran into an old friend who told me about the shortcuts in the first place, and … one thing led to another."

I shift my weight to one side to let them see the outline of my hip, clad only in panties, at the same time that I let my thought trail off, hoping that they're able to pick up where I'm going. It takes them a moment, but when they make the connection of why I'm staying in a shady motel, they're both instantly embarrassed. Both men smile bashfully and look down at their feet.

"Ah," the officer says, scribbling something down with a pen he pulls from his pocket. "I'm sorry for the misunderstanding, ma'am."

"Don't be," I say, shaking my head. "It was honestly my mistake. I just got a little wrapped up and forgot to let my nana know where I was." I give my biggest flirty smile again.

"To be young and in love," the manager says awkwardly.

I grin and shrug, trying my damnedest to keep calm. I feel transparent and obvious, but as far as I can tell, the men seem satisfied with my answers. The manager nods again and starts to walk off.

But just as the officer makes to follow him, he glances at my wrist where I have my hand against the doorframe. I follow his gaze and swallow hard. The bruising on my wrists is even more evident now that time has passed.

He looks at me with a piercing gaze. In a much lower voice, he says, "Ma'am, if you're in any trouble, nod once."

This is my chance. I could nod and this would all be over. I'd be safely away from Roman and back to my normal life by the end of the day. No more hit man, no more bondage, no more fearing for my life.

But no more chance to kill Konstantin, either.

I make my choice. "What?" I give a little laugh and look at my hand again. "Oh, this? Well, I've always loved *Fifty Shades of Gray* ..."

The tension in the officer's body relaxes and he takes his hand off his gun. Another shy smile. "My mistake. Sorry for interrupting you again, by the way. Please give your friend and family a call and let them know where you are, okay?"

"Will do, officer. And I apologize for having everyone so worried!"

"You have a good day, miss," he says. Together, the two of them head back down the hall, talking in low voices. I close the door and press my forehead to the cheap wood. It takes a moment to get my breathing back to normal.

When I turn around, Roman is standing in the same place I last saw him, lips pressed together tightly. He looks at me with an expression I haven't seen before. Brows slightly raised, eyes softer than before. Maybe I'm being presumptuous, but he seems almost ... impressed?

"What?" I ask, trying to bite back the rising pride I feel coming on. Maybe I did lie to police and throw them off Roman's trail, so what?

"Why did you do that?"

The way he asks it, I think back to the night before. He seems just as unsure about me, wondering why I didn't take the opportunity I had to stab him when he came back in the room. He sees me as a hostage, someone desperate enough to do anything to get away. Maybe I was at the beginning, but hearing him say that man's name, the one who took everything from me, changed my perspective.

We're in this together now.

"Because you can't help me if you're in prison."

"Help you with what?"

I give him a look. He knows what I'm talking about. "I want to make Konstantin pay, and I don't have the same set of skills that you do. I don't know how to kill people, or transport bodies, or torture someone to get information out of them. I don't know the first thing about that. What I do know is that something brought us together. Something put me in that alley at the same time as you. Something that wants me to end Abram Konstantin."

Wordless as always, he simply stares at me. I'm suddenly aware that he's shirtless, and I try to keep my eyes from traveling over his body. I do notice that he's stitched himself up, though. Part of me is disappointed. That was another opportunity to touch his hard body. My nipples tighten at the thought, and I'm suddenly acutely aware that I'm not wearing any pants right now, either. I walk over to where I ditched them and shimmy my legs back into the fabric.

"You don't trust me, Roman. I get that. I don't entirely trust you either. You probably think I'll turn you in at any moment, but you wanna know the best way to stop me from doing that? Let me become your accomplice."

He laughs bitterly, like I'm some kind of child.

"You may not have anything to lose, but I do," I insist. I don't know the first thing about his family or his friends, but the way Roman talks makes me think that he doesn't have many. Or any. He's a lone wolf, looking out for number one above all else. "I have a grandmother that needs me. I have friends. I have things I want to do in life. And they're never going to get done until I do this. I *need* this, and that also means that I need you."

My stomach twists at the last three words, and echoes of my dream drift back into my mind. The way he touched me. The way his lips felt against my tender neck. I needed him then, too.

"This is a bad fucking plan," he grunts, shaking his head.

"Why? Because you work alone?"

"Exactly," he says, taking a seat on the bed.

"You don't have to work alone anymore."

He looks at me with contempt. "It's on purpose. I work alone because I like being alone."

His comment stings, but I try not to let it get to me too badly. He's not outright shooting down my plan, so I still have a chance. "Do you know what it feels like to have your family stolen from you?" I ask. Despite the anger vibrating in every vein running through my body, I feel the ache of loneliness coming on. "Do you know what it feels like to bury your own parents, Roman? I was just a little girl when Konstantin took them from me. He ruined my fucking life. Can you possibly imagine how that feels like?"

He doesn't look at me, and it makes me want to shake him. He's still stuck in his ways, and by showing him how upset I am, I've ruined things for myself. Men like him, ones that take lives and play God, don't comprehend empathy.

"Fine."

It's one word, but it knocks the wind out of me. "What?"

"We'll do it." I start to thank him, when he cuts me off. "No more talking about it now. Go shower and get dressed. We'll talk about it while we eat."

A bit dizzy, I give him a silent nod and hurry to the bathroom to wash up. While the water heats up, I stare at my reflection. There are still tears in my eyes, but for the first time in months, they're not bitter.

I'm almost there.

∼

Roman looks out of his element at the diner a few blocks away from the motel. He shifts in his seat uncomfortably, glancing around whenever there's a clang of pans or scooting noise of chairs. But more than that, he looks uncomfortable simply being around me.

I try not to let it offend me. After all, he just agreed to let me help with his hit on Konstantin. It'd be ungrateful to throw a fit. Still, after the dream I had last night, it's a bit of slap in the face to see him so uneasy in my presence.

To distract myself, I cut into a pancake and swirl it around in syrup.

That sandwich last night barely put a dent in my hunger, and I ended up tied to the bed before I could even finish. It's almost embarrassing how quickly I eat. Almost.

"You were kind of vague about what this assignment is," I note.

"There's not much to discuss. I'm supposed to kill Abram Konstantin. He's got ties to the mob. He works in real estate. He also has a history of shady dealings and lawsuits that keep getting shoved under the rug."

That's an understatement. Konstantin's gotten away with murder, and not just with my family. In high school, he became an obsession of mine. I kept alerts on my cell phone, always waiting to find out something new about him. After getting away scot-free with murdering my parents, Konstantin had plenty of other run-ins with the law. Faulty concrete foundations that sent children falling to their death in the basement. Poor wiring that electrocuted many pets. He even managed to avoid a sexual assault scandal with one of the women living in his apartment buildings. And that's just the stuff that made the news. City message boards sometimes hinted at much darker stuff. Guns, drugs, weapons, women being bought and sold. Nothing that could ever be proven, but the whispers I found were too persistent to be completely fabricated.

His reign of terror is well-documented.

"I'm glad he's on your list," I mutter.

Roman looks up from his plate of bacon at me. "Do you really mean that?"

"Seriously?" I ask. "That bastard is the reason I grew up without parents. Nobody in this town held him accountable, and look what happened afterwards. So many others were hurt. And him? He got off without more than a slap on the wrist. Knowing that someone is finally taking care of him is the best news I've heard all year."

"Okay," he says, conceding. "So what can you do? On the way here, you were talking about guns, right? You ever shoot one?"

I blush and occupy myself with eating. During the ride to the diner, I did end up getting a bit overzealous, going into detail about everything I knew about a line of business similar to Roman's. The information came out of me without a filter. I told him I knew plenty of ways to kill people and make it look like an accident. How to work a gun. How long it takes to strangle someone, contrary to what television and movies portray. He listened without interruption, but in hindsight, it was probably amateurish to be so excited.

If only he knew that it was all based on a lifetime of reading true crime novels.

"No," I admit, finally meeting his gaze. "I haven't used a gun. But I write crime fiction. I have to know these kinds of things."

"You never told me about that."

"You put a gag in my mouth the first time we met," I remind him.

That smirk returns, just for an instant, before disappearing again. "You were too busy screaming to mention what you did in your spare time."

"Regardless," I say, biting back a smile, "I've always loved the research. Learning about cases, finding out how the police discovered the truth. It's enthralling, to say the least. And then I met you."

The words come out more wistfully than I mean, and I quickly stutter out, "I mean, you ... y'know, take care of people. And you get away with it. I'm fascinated. I want to know how you do it. How you got so good at it. How did you train for this?"

Roman's face hardens, and I can practically see him receding back into his shell. That momentary warm, the brief glimpse of his smile, is fading before my eyes. "I'm going to tell you right now, Lucy: I'm not talking about my past. I don't care if you want to know for your books. Stop asking me."

There's no room for negotiation with him. It's probably best not to push him. He's already given me an inch, and here I am trying to take a yard. "Sorry," I murmur, stabbing at my scrambled eggs. The air in the room is heavy, and I try my hardest to circle back to his assignment.

"Can you tell me about Mr. X? What's he like? Is he a James Bond villain?"

"I don't know much about him," he admits. "I met him through a previous client. He pays twice as well. I don't ask questions for paychecks that large."

"Smart," I say.

"He's Russian. I know that much. If I had to guess, I'd say this assignment is about getting rid of the competition. Konstantin being part of the Bratva means he's more than likely stepping on X's toes. He doesn't like people getting in his way. He's had me kill people over smaller crimes."

This is so surreal to hear about. "I'm on Mr. X's side with this one."

He practically scoffs. "You wouldn't be saying that if you knew the things he does."

"Let's hope I never do then," I say, trying not to shudder at the thought. Just the description of the mysterious man unsettles me. "How long do you think it will take to handle Konstantin?"

"Not long. Standard hit. In and out."

"I wish I could be there."

This gives Roman pause. "Seeing this kind of shit changes you, Lucy. You don't want to see what happens to people when they die."

"I already have, in the alley. I didn't know that man, but I saw him go.

That's too merciful for Konstantin. He deserves a slow death. For all the people that he's hurt in his life. All the bodies that are in the ground because of him."

I don't realize how hard I'm gripping my fork until my hand aches. Roman's eyes fall to my hand, and I loosen up, putting it down on the table.

"You hate him," he says simply.

"More than anyone else in this world."

"Then I'll make it painful for him."

What kind of person would I be to admit that I'm touched by the offer? 'Make it painful'... Have I lost all sense of humanity? Have I become as cold and emotionless as the man sitting across from me? The thought of being so stoic sends a chill through my spine, but I can't deny that this is what I've wanted for so long. I thought I wanted justice, but that's not it at all. Justice would be locking Abram Konstantin in prison for the rest of his life, and the thought of that isn't enough.

I don't want justice. I want something more.

"You should go outside and call your grandmother. Let her know that you'll be busy for the next few days." He slides his phone across the table. I pick it up and begin sliding out of the seat. Before I can get very far, he puts his hand on top of mine. His palm nearly covers my entire hand, and I feel the heat of his fingers wrap around my wrist.

His eyes stab straight into mine. I can't read the emotion behind them. He doesn't blink or say anything for a long moment. "I'm trusting you, Lucy."

I know what he's saying. *Don't pull another stunt like the knife back in the motel room.* He doesn't know me, but he's trusting me enough not to let him down again. I don't know why, but I nod, suddenly filled with the desire to please him. I don't want to screw this up. I don't have any plans on calling someone else or reading his messages.

Something tells me he doesn't say that often. Knowing that, I try not to smile too wide. "I won't. I'll be back."

I grab the phone and pull away, telling myself that I shouldn't want to stay there, his hand on mine. When I step outside, I walk around the corner of the building so I have a bit of privacy. When I dial Nana's number, she answers on the second ring.

"Hello?"

"Nana, it's me."

"Oh my gosh, Lucy! I've been so worried about you. Where have you been? Please tell me you're all right!"

Hearing her concern almost makes me cry. The thought of worrying her to the point of visiting the police station with Madeline makes me feel guiltier than anything else has in a long time. "I didn't mean to worry you, Nana," I say. "I met up with an old friend and we decided to reconnect."

"Is it a man?"

And just like that, I'm laughing again. Of course. The mere mention of me meeting a man is enough to make her forget that I've been missing for twenty-four hours. "Maybe," I say bashfully.

"What's he like?" she asks.

"He ... a mystery. But so far, he's been nice to me. It's good getting to know him ... again."

"Well, I for one am so happy that you're starting to date again. I'm sure your boss won't be happy that you blew off work for this, but ..."

"That's what I wanted to talk to you about," I say. "This new guy offered me a job, a writing gig, and I really want to do it. I know Rudy is going to be mad, but I think I should follow through with this. This'll be my first big project."

I need an excuse for why I won't be home for the foreseeable future, otherwise I'll be in another situation with the people that love me sending the police to come and find me. "Sweetheart, what is your heart telling you to do?"

I choose my words carefully. "It says that I'm exactly where I need to be. That I should take this job because it's the only opportunity I'll have to do this."

"Then that's what you should do," she says. One thing I've always loved about Nana is how easily her opinions come. She follows her heart a lot of the time, trusting her gut over everyone else, and all her life, she's been right to do so.

"Okay," I say, leaning against the wall. "I promise I'll call you back and keep you updated on everything, okay?"

"All right, sweetheart. You be safe, and you two have fun. I love you."

"I love you too, Nana."

When I end the call, I place the phone to my heart and take a deep breath. It hurts having to keep her in the dark, but I know if she ever found out what I was planning to do with Roman, she'd try and talk me out of it. I know that she wants justice, but she's moved on from what happened to Mom and Dad. I haven't.

And now I finally have the chance to do something. I'm not just sitting around, waiting for someone to finally make Konstantin take responsibility. With Roman, I have the chance to play an active role in getting revenge. It may hurt being away from Nana and Madeline for so long, but that's a price I'm willing to pay.

I won't let anything stop me from doing this.

8

ROMAN

There's a voice in the back of my head telling me how stupid this is. How fucked everything is going to be. Lucy is a distraction, especially when she looks at me like she did when I told her that I'd let her help. If Mr. X finds out about this, he'll probably send someone after me the way he's sent me after people that upset him.

I can already hear him now. Telling me what a fucking idiot I am. How unprofessional this is. That he should've killed me when he had the chance a long time ago. I put my head in my hands and take a deep breath, trying not to lose it.

Everything in me says that this is wrong, yet here I am. Sitting in this rundown diner with a girl I tied to the bathroom sink, like we're on some kind of date. That is one thing I swore off permanently, one thing I need to keep reminding myself of.

No attachments.

I don't make bonds. I don't make friends. I don't fall in love. I learned from childhood that love is dangerous. It keeps you off your game. It makes you feel secure, and then when it's taken from you, you're fucked. I won't let Lucy be another lesson I learn the hard way.

But saying that is one thing. Executing it is another.

I'm not blind. She's attractive, the exact kind of woman I would normally go for. She's small, easy enough to lift off the bed and throw around. Easy enough to have my way with. And pinning her to the bed last night made me realize exactly that. I could practically hear her thoughts. Those wide blue eyes staring up at me hid a dark side, and if I weren't me and it wasn't such a shitty idea, I just might have wanted to see that side of her.

But this is strictly business. I didn't agree to let Lucy work with me because I want to fuck her. If I wanted to do that, I could've just said so. I agreed to let her on this assignment with me because it's been years since I've seen that kind of blind rage and hatred for another living person.

The last time I recognized it was when it was looking back at me in the mirror.

I know what she's feeling. I know how self-destructive this shit is. It can tear a person apart from the inside if they learn to channel it. Lucy's channeling it into hurting my next target, and I've never been one to pass up the chance for revenge. That's the sick part about me. There aren't many things I feel nowadays, but that fire that I saw burning in Lucy's eyes?

I could feel it on her skin.

So, I'll let her help. Maybe she has information about Konstantin that Mr. X doesn't. She said she's been researching him since she was young, watching him the same way I do when it comes to assignments. That kind of information can be useful, so long as she knows that after this, we'll never see each other again.

After this assignment, she'll go back to writing her books and I'll disappear, cleaning up Mr. X's business in the shadows where I belong. Anything more than that is how a guy gets killed, and in this business, I'm the only one that gets to do the killing.

Lucy's taking a while to get back, so I survey the room, scanning. You never know when something can happen, and I need to be aware of my surroundings at all times. I take note of the three exits. The front door, the side door, and almost certainly a back exit in the kitchen that leads to the trash cans. The diner is relatively empty. There's a couple in the back corner, maybe in their sixties, whispering and laughing over eggs and bacon. Two men sit at the bar, a few seats apart, while one reads the newspaper. Two waitresses, a cook, and a man wiping down the empty tables and picking up trash.

The news plays in the background, but I focus on my coffee, finishing off the cup of bitter black liquid. A moment later, there's a waitress at the table. She wears a plastic smile and bats her lashes as she offers to fill my cup again.

"What happened to your girlfriend?" she asks. She reaches for the mug and fills it to the top for a second time.

"Not my girlfriend," I grunt, looking out the window. For a moment, I worry that she left me here. It's an irrational flash of panic, I know. I tell myself to calm down. She's still out there. She's just taking a while on the phone.

"Sorry," the waitress giggles. "I just assumed you guys were together. Do you have a girlfriend?"

I look back at the woman with a blank expression. Is she really trying this shit right now? I'm sure if she knew what Lucy and I are planning on doing, she'd run screaming. That, or she'd call the police. From just this small interaction, I can already tell she's not built the same way Lucy is. She's probably never experienced heartbreak a day in her life. What I wouldn't give to be that vapid.

"I don't have a girlfriend."

She puts her hand on her hip and tilts her head, chewing her gum as she says, "Now, I just find that so hard to believe. A handsome guy like you, all alone without a woman to keep him company at night?"

"Terrible, isn't?" I mutter sarcastically. If only she knew that I had someone in my bed last night, and she was tied up with me on top of her.

"Well, if you're ever looking to fix that problem, my name is Amber." She leans forward and scribbles her name and number down on a napkin, sliding it toward me. "Give me a call and I'll come running."

I fold the napkin and put it in my pocket. "I'm sure you will."

With a wink and switch of her hips, Amber sashays off to help the next customer. It's almost amusing how wrong she's read me. Even if I were looking for a quick fuck with no strings attached, she wouldn't be high on my priority list.

When she's gone, I sit back in my chair and shake my head. This whole thing is ridiculous. I need to stop kidding myself. I'm sitting here in a goddamn diner, getting hit on by overly confident waitresses, waiting for the girl I kidnapped to come back with my cell phone.

And just like that, I change my mind. This has to stop now. Lucy can't come with me. I need to retreat, reassess, reassert control. And I need to leave her behind.

Right then, Lucy walks back in with a smile on her face. She takes a seat and returns my phone, folding her hands on the table. "Okay," she says, smiling. "What now?"

"Nothing. I've changed my mind. You're not helping me."

In an instant, that smile drops. Her face falls, and she looks at me with a blank expression. "What?"

"You heard me."

"But ..."

"I changed my mind. This isn't something you need to be doing. You should go back to your normal life and pretend none of this happened." The more I speak, the more upset she gets. Her shock turns to anger, and she glares at me like a child.

"You're such an asshole," she says through gritted teeth. "You're an asshole and a liar!"

The people sitting in the booth across the room look over at us. I can feel their judgmental stares without even turning to see them. I lower my voice and lean forward so that only Lucy can hear me. "Stop it."

"No!" she cries. "You told me I could help you, and now you want to go back on your word. I could've run away so many times, but I stayed because I wanted to prove that you could trust me. This whole time, I should've been the one wondering about whether or not I could trust *you*!" She stands up from the table, knocking a glass over. It shatters to the floor loudly.

The air in the diner shifts, and I can feel everyone staring at us now.

I push myself up too, trying my hardest to control my temper. Goddamn her for doing this right now. Does she know how dangerous this is to talk about in public? Does she know that anyone could overhear and we'd both be in jail by the end of the day?

"Lower your voice," I warn her.

Lucy glances around self-consciously, and then does what I say. "You're a douchebag and a liar, Roman. You're a fucking *liar*."

"I'm not involving an amateur in this shit. I'm going to take you home and drop you off and you can go back to living your life exactly how you were living before you ever met me." Saying it feels wrong, but I know it's right. This has to end before I make any other stupid mistakes. Not killing her was the first. Thinking I could trust her with something important was the second. There won't be a third. Fuck no.

Telling her this only makes her angrier, but I'm tired of this.

"Liar! Fucking liar!" she hisses again. I can hear the sizzle of food in the kitchen, the creak of the eaves on the roof. Everyone is pretending not to listen, but I know full well that they haven't missed a word. I feel an overwhelming itch to escape. I was born for the shadows, not the spotlight. And certainly not for the patrons in this shithole diner to gawk at.

I grab Lucy's arm and tug her to the bathroom. She yelps and tries to drag her heels, but I don't give a damn right now. Once we're inside, I lock the door, spin her around, and shove her up against a wall, hard.

"Are you fucking crazy?" I demand. My face is inches from hers. "Do you know who could've overheard that conversation?"

"I don't care," she spits. "You told me you would help me hurt Konstantin. You told me I could work with you after I told you how bad I need this, and then you turn around and say I'm not doing this with you anymore? That's such bullshit!"

There's anger in her voice, but also something else. It's vulnerable, a kind of hurt that she probably doesn't want me to see. I can't help but feel for her. Even when she's mad, she still looks innocent. It's enough to cloud my judgment about the whole thing.

She shoves me, making me stumble back. For a moment, I'm in shock. With how little she is, I never would've expected all that strength. "You're a liar, Roman. Fuck you." When I reach for her, she shoves me again. There are tears in her eyes.

Fuck.

I am a liar. And I am a piece of shit for doing this to her. I can only imagine how upset I would've been had I not given Aleksandr and Andrei what they deserved. I grab Lucy by both arms and start to pull her to my chest when she slaps me across the face. My next move happens in a blur. I spin her around and push her into the sink, bending her over it.

I see her reflection in the mirror, eyes wide with fear. When I lean in and press my lips to her ear, she shivers. "Get it the fuck together," I warn her.

Her eyes harden. "Or what?" She pushes back against me, and last night comes back to me. I could feel her pulse against my palm as I held her down. I watched her chest heave up and down as she caught her breath. In that moment, I wanted to do more than just interrogate her.

"You know what," I reply. I push my hips forward, against her this time.

"I don't believe you."

She knows what she's doing. She knows how she's making me feel. I'm sure she can feel the hardening of my cock against her ass, pressing into her insistently.

"Prove it," she says again. She's playing with fire and doesn't even know it. She will soon. To wipe that smirk off her face, I reach around and unbutton her jeans. The look on her face tells me she wants to fight me, but thankfully she doesn't. I yank the fabric down her thighs, exposing her smooth, round ass and the tiny pair of blue panties she has on.

Before I even consider touching myself, I run my hands over her smooth skin. Goose bumps follow wherever I touch. Lucy doesn't even expect the swat until I give it to her. She jumps and yelps, covering her mouth with her hand. The second spanking is harder, and it leaves a red mark on her cheek.

When my cock aches hard enough to be a distraction, I finally undo my pants and free myself as well. Teasing, I drag the tip of my dick over the thin fabric, feeling her heat. I can feel her wet excitement already, and it makes me leak even more.

"Are you going to show me or what?" she says. Her voice is low and husky, daring me. Pushing me. Tempting me.

Fuck.

"Remember you asked for this," I warn her. A second later, I jerk her panties to the side and bury myself deep inside of her.

Sliding inside of her feels like heaven. She's hot and warm and wet, and with her legs together like this, even tighter than I expected. She lets out a soft moan when I fill her, her eyes falling closed. I steady myself before I begin to move. Let her get adjusted to my size. Let her become used to the stretch of me. When I'm sure she's ready, I pull my hips back and thrust forward without warning.

"Fuck!" she cries, knocking against the sink as I move back and forth. I clamp a hand over her mouth, silencing her.

"Quiet," I say in her ear, flicking the lobe with my tongue. "They'll hear you." I angle my next thrust, sliding deeper inside of her, faster than before. She whimpers against my palm, and I'm tempted to slide two fingers inside her mouth. I want to feel both holes, see how wet she can get for me, but I can't. Now's not the place for that.

I fuck her quickly, the sound of our bodies connecting echoing in the room. She groans in unison with me, one hand sliding down between her legs to circle around her clit. Just when she's worked up a steady pace, I swat her hand away and take over for her.

Lucy gives me a pleading look in the bathroom mirror, using her eyes to beg for something. Anything. Any kind of attention that will relieve the pressure she's feeling. I wouldn't normally be this generous, not after she slapped me and told me that she wasn't going to behave, but I give in. I roll her tiny clit between my fingers, slow circles, grinding my hips at the same time.

Her pussy walls suffocate my length, squeezing mercilessly. The feeling sends shivers down my spine, and I bite back a groan of my own. Just when I think I've found my pace, it's Lucy's turn to surprise me. She rolls her hips back to meet mine, proving that she's not going to let me have all the control.

"Fuck," I growl, widening my stance and bending her over the sink more. I thrust into her faster than before, each time eliciting a satisfying noise of pleasure from her. I fit perfectly inside, and she takes me as best she can, crying out when I slide nearly out and then right back in.

"That's a good girl," I murmur, leaning over her. My fingers on her clit are wet with her juices and slide around her with just enough pressure. "Does that feel good?" I ask.

She nods enthusiastically, pushing her hips back faster. I feel the warmth in the pit of my stomach start to rise, and I know that I only have a few more moments inside of her before I reach my peak. I push her head down and thread my fingers through her hair, ramming her, chasing that feeling. My hand slips away from her mouth and she nearly screams.

"I'm so close," she pants, thrusting against me. "I'm almost there. Please don't stop, Roman."

I don't have any plans to.

It doesn't take much to send her over the edge. I speed my fingers up, adding more pressure, and drag my teeth along the curve of her shoulder. Her eyes meet mine in the mirror just as I bite down.

"Yes," she whimpers, and I feel her whole body stiffen as she comes undone. The walls of her pussy contract around me, convulsing violently as her own orgasm tears through her. It's enough to take me tumbling down with her.

A deep, throaty growl escapes, and I pump her with shot after shot, my hips snapping forward roughly, practically slamming her into the sink.

When I've finally emptied myself, I fold over her, burying my nose in the back of her head. She smells like motel shampoo and the heat of what we've just done. I don't know what comes over me, but I'm tempted to kiss her. Spin her around and plant my lips on her, exploring her mouth as well.

I keep my composure, but fuck if it isn't hard.

I can imagine myself against her, tongues dancing together greedily. She'd fight me at first before letting go and enjoying it. And when I'd pull away, she'd pull me back for more, because underneath this good girl is something even more delicious. Something more exciting than the innocence she has for the world and the life I lead.

Slowly, almost reluctantly, I slip out of her and tuck myself back into my boxer briefs. She does the same, pulling her panties up and then her pants. She pauses to fix her hair in the mirror, then turns around to glare at me. It's amusing to see her pretending to still be pissed at me given how much she begged for me just moments ago. That sound isn't leaving my head anytime soon.

Once we're dressed, I start for the door. Then I hear something.

There's a loud bang outside, followed by a scream. Lucy bristles, and I feel myself tense up. I hold up a hand, wordlessly telling her to stop. Lucy nods.

I turn the knob slowly and open the door just a crack. When I poke my head out, I can hear more yelling and screaming. There's another loud thud, then the sound of glass shattering. A husky voice shouts at the customers in the diner.

"Get on the floor! Now!" the yelling man orders, pointing his gun at the older woman in the back of the restaurant. "Get your ass on the floor right fucking now." Terrified, she lies down flat on the tile, shaking like a leaf in the wind.

"What's going on?" Lucy whispers.

"I don't know. It looks like a robbery."

At least, that's what I think it is until I hear another man somewhere in the restaurant say. "Where is he? Where's Roman?"

My blood runs cold. Hearing my name activates something in me. They call it fight or flight, but that phrase implies there's another option besides violence. To me, there isn't. There's only fight—only killing these two men. I don't know who they are or what they want, but they're clearly after me.

Let them come. It'll be the last thing they ever do.

"Here." I reach under my jacket and unholster my second gun, placing it in her hands. "This is the safety. This is how you click it off. When you shoot, steady yourself, and prepare for the kickback."

Lucy's eyes go wide with fear. "Wait, what? You can't go out there, Roman!"

"Those people will get hurt. Whoever these guys are, they want to see me. So let them see."

Her lips purse like she's about to argue some more, but I cover her mouth and look into her eyes. "If they come at you, you don't hesitate. Do you understand me? You don't hesitate or give them a chance to get any closer. You pull that trigger."

Lucy nods and tightens her grip on the handle of the gun. I feel relief seeing that. "Good girl," I say. "I'll be back."

Stepping out into the hall, I hold my gun out in front of me and inch closer into the main room of the diner. Everyone in the building lies flat on their stomachs while the masked men question them. One grabs the waitress, Amber, and pulls her up to her knees by her hair. She screams and fights, but his grip is relentless.

"Where did he go?" he shouts, silencing her cries.

Amber, nearly in tears, says, "H-he went into the b-bathroom."

I can't fault her for telling, but I wish she hadn't. Stepping into the view of the bar, I point my gun and squint one eye, firing twice. The man holding Amber stumbles backwards, two circles oozing blood from his chest. Amber screams and collapses, rolling into a ball.

"Fuck!" the man shouts, clutching his chest. When he raises his gun to shoot, I fire again, this time hitting him in the heart. His arm falls limp at his side and his head droops. A moment later, he's dead.

The other man in the room turns to his partner, shouting his name. "Rick!" When he sees that he's dead, he grabs the old lady from the ground and pulls her to her feet, holding her close. A human shield. The fucking coward.

The first shot he fires my way is off, but the second is closer. Too close for comfort. I dive behind the bar and press my back to it, catching my breath. The room is filled with screams and shouts, but I block it out, listening for the other masked man. I glance to my left and see a shiny napkin dispenser. In the reflection, the man is approaching, gun drawn.

Moving quickly, I throw myself to the other end of the bar and pop my head out, gun drawn. He leans over the counter where I was, ready to shoot, and that gives the woman in his arms enough time to squirm away. She runs to her husband, and I point my gun at the assailant, firing once. He collapses in a slump, the hole in his head leaking onto the counter.

The customers have all cowered into the corners, holding each other, watching. Amber looks at me with terror on her face. That confidence from before is gone. Distracted, I almost miss a third man running from the kitchen down the hall. Towards the bathroom.

Lucy is still in there.

He's a few steps ahead of me and I'm terrified that I won't be able to close the gap. I spring forward after him, rounding the corner just as the man crosses through the open door and comes face-to-face with Lucy. I hear her scream, and my world narrows to just that noise.

If he touches her, I'm going to make him suffer.

But I don't get that chance. She screams again, he lunges forward, and a moment later, there's another loud pop. The man stops in his tracks, knees buckling. He holds onto the wall as he slides down to his knees. Lucy's face is peppered with speckles of blood, and she drops the gun, stunned. She did it. She fucking shot him. I'm stunned and impressed and relieved and on high alert, all at once. A million thoughts race through my head at the same time like a swarm of bees.

"Lucy," I say, but it's like she can't hear me. She stares back at the man, watching as he clutches his bleeding chest. He gasps infrequently, mouth opening and closing aimlessly. She doesn't look at me when I call her name again.

She's in shock. I don't have time to comfort her right now, not with this man bleeding out at my feet. Instead of dealing with her, I grab the man Lucy shot and tear his mask off. He doesn't look familiar. I have no idea who he is, but he clearly knew me. Time to find out why.

Without hesitation, I press my gun against the oozing hole in his chest. He cries out in pain and struggles to pull away. "You're going to die here on this floor," I tell him, leaning in close. "Either you make this easy on yourself and tell me what you know, or I let you bleed out and suffer longer."

He squints and looks up at me, disdain on his face. "Fuck you," he spits. His blood lands on my shirt.

Taking a slow, controlled breath, I push the barrel of my gun against him harder, causing him to whimper again in agony. "I'm not going to offer you mercy again. Who sent you?"

He doesn't reply immediately. I twist the gun deeper. He groans and finally says, "I don't know his name. Some rich motherfucker that wanted you gone. Didn't say why. Just that you'd be with a blonde girl. He paid us twice what anyone else would have. Said that if we couldn't get you, someone else would. For a price that high, anyone would be willing to take a shot at you."

I look to the side, cursing. This is just what I need right now. More distraction. More problems on my plate. Whoever this person is, he knows about Lucy, too. I wonder if Konstantin got the drop on Mr. X's hit and sent out his guys to stop me before I could execute the job. If that's the case, we need to get the hell out of here, immediately. More men could be coming to finish what these bastards started. I stand up and put my gun in the holster, grabbing the one Lucy dropped, too.

"Let's go," I say to her.

She looks through me, somewhere far away. I can see the panic has her in its claws. When I try to move her, she doesn't even react. Frustrated, I lift her off the ground and throw her over my shoulder. She doesn't resist in the slightest. I turn to exit the bathroom. The man's voice stops me. It's a low, sick laugh.

"What happened to mercy?" he rasps.

I pivot back around slowly to face him. It's obvious that he won't last much longer. Not even paramedics could stop the bleeding from his chest and stomach. But his eyes are hopeful. He wants me to put him out of his misery. I could do that. But I won't.

"I don't show mercy to anyone who lays a hand on me or my woman." I draw my gun and fire once into his foot. His screams echo against the tile as I leave.

We make our way out to the car. I settle Lucy into the passenger seat. In the distance, police sirens go off. They'll be here any minute.

"Buckle up," I order her. To my surprise, she listens. When we're both ready, I pull out and whip the car around, peeling off in the opposite direction. We have to get out of town. If there are people coming after me and Lucy, I need to get off the grid for a little while. Disappear. And I know the perfect place. Somewhere Lucy will be safe.

But for how long?

9

ROMAN

"Lucy."

She doesn't look at me. All she does is stare straight ahead, shuddering occasionally. Her lack of response is unsettling.

"Lucy, look at me, goddamn it." The sharpness in my voice makes her head snap towards me, and I see that little girl inside of her. The one I met in the alley yesterday afternoon. She's scared, in shock, and trying to process what she did. I can't imagine how hard this is for her. But we don't have time for this right now.

"You need to pull yourself together," I tell her. "I can't have you freaking out right now."

It seems to go in one ear and out the other. For a moment, she says nothing. She only stares at me blankly. Then her face slowly contorts into a pained expression. Her eyes water and she folds in on herself. She wraps her arms around herself, rocking back and forth.

"I killed him," she whispers, over and over again. "I killed him. I killed him."

I reach a hand out, trying to comfort her, but it doesn't seem to help. I don't have time to pull over, so I squeeze her shoulder. It's supposed to be reassuring, but all Lucy does is repeat the same sentence over and over again.

"He was going to kill you, Lucy. You did what you had to do."

Suddenly, she pops up, eyes wild. "I'm not you, Roman," she exclaims, tears streaming down her face. "I can't just kill people and pretend like it's nothing! That man was a person! He had a family and friends, and I killed him!"

Before I can get in another word, she doubles over and begins sobbing again.

I knew she wasn't ready for this. I thought, stupidly, that she could handle this life. That look in her eyes when she told me about Abram Konstantin made it seem like she could handle anything. She was unassuming, and that was what made her passion better. Nobody would expect that rage from such a little woman.

But now that she's like this, I can tell she was never ready. She had the drive, but not the iron stomach. Not the steel nerve it takes to actually take someone's life. She hasn't built up a resistance to it yet. She's not disconnected like me.

I should've stopped him.

Had I been a few seconds faster, I would've been the one to shoot him and Lucy would only be dealing with the fact that another man died before her eyes. I could've spared her from this. I could've stopped this panic attack from hitting her so hard. And if she'd gotten hurt? If she hadn't been able to pull the trigger; if that man had gotten his hands on her? I don't know what I would've done, but it wouldn't have been pretty.

"The blood," she whispers, shaking her head. "The blood. He bled out. It's my fault. It's my fault he's dead." Her ramblings devolve into simple phrases. She says them over and over, like a broken record. I've never seen someone lose it this badly. I know I shouldn't care—

she's my prisoner, after all—but it's like a knife in my gut seeing her get this bad.

"Lucy, look at me." My voice, surprising even me, softens. "Please."

She sits up and wipes her nose. "What?" Her voice is barely above a whisper.

"That motherfucker isn't worth all this. He isn't. He was some low-level thug. Some rich asshole's little bitch. Someone that was going to hurt more people if you hadn't stopped him."

She looks at me with confusion. "How are you any different, Roman?"

Her response stuns me.

I know she's going through this trauma, but that question is a slap in my face. It takes me a minute to find my voice. "Because I don't murder just anybody. I would never come after you, or any woman. I would never involve so many people. I'd never use an old lady as a fucking human shield!"

My knuckles tighten around the wheel at the memory. That bastard could've gotten that elderly woman killed, if I'd had no morals about shooting hostages. If I were someone else, she might be dead right along with him right now. An innocent old lady, bleeding out in a diner, alone and scared.

"He did that?" she asks.

"He pulled her off the ground and used her to take the bullets for him. He was just like the one that attacked you. A spineless fuck that had no issues killing anyone he had to. I'm nothing like that." I say the last sentence through gritted teeth, my jaw clenched hard enough to make it hurt.

Her eyebrows soften and she nods. "I'm sorry. I didn't mean—"

"It's fine," I say, shaking my head. "It's fine. I just need you to calm down. Don't lose your mind over some piece of shit. You stopped him before he could hurt other people. It doesn't feel like it, but you did a good thing."

She scoffs and wipes her face. "A good thing. There's nothing good about murder."

She's headstrong, and I know she probably won't question herself or her own beliefs without being prompted. So, I say, "You sure? Even if it's to stop someone from doing something horrible to others?"

Her eyes cut towards me and she's glaring. I know my question got to her and she doesn't want to answer it. Instead, she presses her lips together and shudders. I can see another wave of panic coming, so I quickly say, "I thought the same thing as you. I thought all killing was bad. Black and white, no room for gray."

She sucks in a deep breath and looks at me. "What changed?"

"I ..." There aren't many times when I find myself at a loss for words, but right now is one of them. I swallow hard. "My family was killed."

Her eyes go wide. "Oh my God. I'm so sorry, Roman."

"They were killed in brutal ways, too. Terrorized before they died. And when I found out that it wasn't a random break-in, that my uncles did it, I ... I lost my mind. I didn't know what to do. I had so many emotions. I was angry. More than anything, that's what I felt. Anger. When the shock wore off, I knew that there were exceptions to be made for every rule. Killing included."

She looks at me like I've told her the most horrifying story in the world. "You mean, you ..."

"I killed them, yes." I've never admitted this to anyone, but it feels right. I want her to see the kind of person that revenge creates. If she knows what I went through and who I became because of it, maybe then she can decide if she really wants to help me with this. It's not an easy road, and I came out worse for it, but that's life. This is what I chose. It's up to Lucy if she'll choose this as well.

"That's horrible, Roman. I'm—I don't know what to say."

"You don't have to say anything. You just need to know that revenge isn't always easy. You lose a part of yourself when you dedicate so much of your time to one terrible thing. To one terrible purpose. Watching your enemy. Learning them. And after you kill them, you're still left with that grief. It doesn't make it any easier to deal with. The only thing that changes is that the sorry sack of shit that you took care of isn't in the picture anymore."

She nods and hugs herself again, a lock of blonde hair slipping from behind her ear and framing her face. Like this, she looks so much younger. So much more innocent. It's not fair, all of the shit that's happened to her. She shouldn't have to be making these kinds of decisions. But that's life.

It takes the most innocent people and fucks them up.

That's how the world goes.

The rest of the ride is quiet. Lucy's panic attacks become less frequent until she's left leaning against the window and watching the streets pass by. The house I'm headed to is a bit out of the way, but it's safe there. Nobody knows that I own it. Unassuming, low-key, and distant. It's the safest place I can think of.

We pull into the neighborhood twenty minutes later. I decide to park in the garage; that way, no one gets a good look at us. I have blood on my shirt. I don't need any of the neighbors asking what's going on. I've had enough trouble for one day.

Inside, I pull off my shirt and change into a fresh one, tossing the bloodied one in the garbage. Lucy sits in the living room, her eyes on the blank television. "You okay?" I ask.

"No," she says simply. "But I'm doing better. I guess."

"It's hard," I say, sitting next to her. "But that shock will go away."

She looks at me with glassy eyes. "I'm afraid that when it does, I'll lose my humanity."

Almost reluctantly, I pull her into my arms. She fits perfectly against me. "You're not going to lose your humanity, Lucy. You're not emotionless. That's what makes you a good person. What would worry me more is if you felt nothing. If you shot that man and kept going like it was nothing."

"Like you did?" She looks up at me with those wide eyes and I can't deny her. She's right.

"Yeah," I mutter, looking away. "Like me."

"Sorry," she says. "That was bitchy of me."

"No, it was right. You were right. You do this enough and it takes a piece of you and you never, ever get it back."

"I just need a break," she says, sighing deeply. "These past few days have been so much. First in the alley, then in the motel, and now the diner. It's all so much. I just wish I could have a second to catch my breath before the next gunshot goes off."

I smile slightly and brush a hand through her hair. "As long as we're here, you'll be safe. You can relax."

"Yeah, that's what I thought last time, too."

"I mean that," I insist. "This is where I come when I really want to be alone. When I need to escape the rough situations out there. When I'm sick of fucking talking to Mr. X. I disappear here for a few days and get my head back on right."

Lucy nods and relaxes against me. "I guess everyone needs a place to unwind. This is a pretty good one to pick." She yawns, deep and loud, and closes her eyes. Eventually, neither of us speak. I listen to the sounds of her breath growing deeper and deeper. Finally, she's asleep. I debate whether or not I should move her up to the bed. It'll be much more comfortable, but she seems happy here.

Eventually, I lift her up from the couch, scooping her into my arms. She stirs, but stays asleep. When I make it upstairs, I put her on the king-sized bed and watch as she sinks into the mattress, comfortable. Much more comfortable than she was against me.

Something about the way she sleeps is beautiful. The worry lines in her face soften out and she looks like she's never had a bad thought in her head. She's smaller, daintier, and it makes me want to be gentle just being around her.

An unusual feeling stirs in the pit of my stomach, followed by dread. I know what that emotion is. It's been years since I've let it in. Years since I've let anything close to it pop up. The last thing I need is feelings for Lucy to cloud my judgment, but I can't ignore them and pretend that they're not there.

Lucy is fucking incredible.

She's not afraid to defend herself. She's stood up to me more than any other woman would ever dare. And the way she felt in the bathroom of the diner, her body vibrating as she came, was something I don't think I'll ever get out of my mind. She's more than the nosy woman in the alley when I first met her. She's something else entirely, something that I want to claim as my own.

But I can't.

Fuck, I can't.

I can't entertain those kinds of thoughts. Having feelings is what leads to disappointment and heartache. And more than that, it leads to distraction. Letting her help me is already a big enough distraction on its own. I don't need to be confusing my lustful emotions with something deeper.

It was just the sex. That's it. That's the reason I'm doubting myself and questioning my feelings. The sex was enough to confuse me, but in a few hours, I'll have a level head again.

Instead of worrying about what I'm feeling for Lucy, I need to come up with an exit strategy. She knows and I know that after this assignment with Konstantin, that's it. There's nothing that can happen for us. My line of work is too dangerous, and she has to get back to her life at the diner she works at. She has a grandmother to take care of. I can't babysit her or work her into all my assignments.

But how?

How do I get her back to her normal life without making problems for everyone? I've dug myself into a hole, I know that much. The smartest thing would've been to leave her in the alleyway, but we're long past that being a solution.

There are too many loose ends to come up with a plan of action, and I try not to make a noise of frustration. Lucy is still peacefully asleep, and after the past twenty-four hours she's had, some sleep might do her good. I have things to take care of, anyway.

I need to research Konstantin and learn more about him. Who is he, what is his schedule, and if I have time, just how badly has he pissed off Mr. X?

It takes all my strength to slide out of bed. If it were up to me, I'd sit there watching Lucy sleep for hours. I'd watch the rise and fall of her perfect chest or listen to the mumbling she does when she's deep in sleep. But I have work to do.

I leave the door open just a crack and head downstairs for my laptop. There are things that need to be researched, and quickly. The faster I finish this assignment, the faster I get Lucy out of my life and back to her grandmother. Old lady must miss her.

I take a seat at my computer and begin looking Abram Konstantin up, but as I continue my search, I find an article about the fire Lucy told me about. There are pictures of her on the front lawn, crying. I never thought I'd care about someone else's pain again, but seeing her sobbing, just a little girl, makes my heart squeeze.

Jesus.

I'm starting to think I have it bad for this woman. I don't need the extra drama, yet here I am, complicating things even more. Whatever's wrong with me, I need to get it together, too, just like I told her to do. If I don't, I'm sure everything will go off the rails, and more people could get hurt. For the first time in what feels like years, I don't want that. Rather than kill, I want to protect.

I want to protect Lucy.

10

LUCY

When I wake up, I halfway expect to find myself in my own bed at Nana's. Everything that's happened has all been some sort of screwed-up dream where I did things I would never do in real life. I wasn't kidnapped. I wasn't given a gun and instructed to shoot a man. I didn't watch him die in front of me. It was only a bizarre fever dream.

But when I rub the sleep from my eyes and roll over, I realize that this isn't my bed. I don't know where I am. I sit up suddenly, my heart pounding. I'm alone. Did something happen to Roman?

Saying his name reminds me of the night before. Listening to the story of him and his family. Before, he struck me as a lone wolf, but I'm starting to see him as something else. He didn't wake up one morning and decide that a life of crime was something he wanted to do for money or fun.

Before all of this, he was just a boy, with a family that loved him and that he loved back. His life was simple, like mine. I'm not sure what changed for him and turned him into this, but a big part of me mourns for what he must've been before we ever met. The little boy that had his childhood stolen from him.

It's strange to think that I'm empathizing with someone like Roman. What he does is wrong. Good people don't kill others, and they certainly don't do it for money. They don't work with shady underground crime lords who have ominous names like "Mr. X."

But ever since yesterday, I'm beginning to wonder what being a good person means anymore. Am I a good person? I want to say yes. I want to say that me coming home to take care of Nana was a good thing. Me always being willing to fill in for coworkers without question is a good thing. All the times I've ever donated, helped when I didn't need to, or given someone a hand are all good things.

But I've also done bad things. Shooting that man in the diner was a bad thing, even if Roman says that I saved lives. It doesn't feel like it. It feels like I'm no better than those three men. And now I'm supposed to move on and forget it never happened? I'm supposed to continue living while the knowledge of what I did weighs down on me? Impossible.

There's a little voice in the back of my head that asks, *"How else are you going to take down Konstantin?"*

I can't be soft if I want to make him pay. I can't be worried about morality when it comes to taking him out. Me being good won't help me save another life. Shooting one of the attackers in the diner didn't feel like saving lives, but shooting Abram Konstantin? Shooting him and watching him die sounds like a mercy killing to me.

How can I say that?

How can I say that watching someone die would be good? Have I really become so cold in only a few days? Have I become the monster that I imagined Roman to be when I first encountered him in the alley?

Back and forth and back and forth my thoughts go. I can't settle on one or the other, and I can't stop the chaos of endless thinking. I see Konstantin and Nana and Roman and my parents, all pointing in different directions and shouting at me with voices that don't make any sense. It feels like my head is going to split open.

My breathing grows shallow and I bring my knees to my chest, another panic attack on the horizon. I can feel it creeping, sneaking up on me like a creature from my nightmares. I squeeze my eyes and try to breathe slowly, concentrating on something else—anything else.

The time Dad took me swimming. I'd been terrified of the water ever since I stayed up too late and watched *Jaws*, and after that film, I never wanted to swim again. Dad loved the pool, and after a lot of convincing, I finally gave in and went with him. He didn't throw me in the water. We eased into it, first with our toes, then our feet, and then eventually our entire bodies.

I can still hear him telling me to keep breathing. To focus on steady breaths and not the anxiety threatening to drown me. Picture all the good times I'd had in the water. Birthday parties, late-night swims, all of it. It took a long time for me to finally swim again, but when it happened, it was beautiful.

I wasn't afraid anymore. I wasn't afraid of swimming, or sharks, or anything. Ever since then, I've used that technique. Taking whatever scary situation I'm in and remembering the good things. It takes a minute before I'm able to stop panicking, but soon the thoughts come back.

Listening to Roman telling me about his family was nice.

Feeling him on top of me in the motel room and inside of me in the bathroom.

Watching him throw himself into the face of danger to protect the people in the diner.

These are what bring me back, and soon, I feel the anxiety ease away, slipping back under the bed like the boogeyman. Calmer now, I take a deep breath and open my eyes. The house we're in is silent, save for a bit of noise coming from downstairs. After I pop into the bathroom to look over my face and fix my hair, I tiptoe down the staircase and peek around the corner, following the soft noise.

To my surprise, I find Roman in the kitchen, shirtless, singing to himself as he cooks. I bite back a laugh so he doesn't notice me and lean against the wall, watching him as he works. I can't tell what he's making, but whatever it is, it smells delicious. Roman's voice isn't the best, but the fact that he's off-key makes him almost ... endearing. It's a strange feeling, saying that about someone who's killed three people since we started talking.

What finally makes me break and laugh out loud is Roman doing a little dance to go along with his singing. The second I giggle, he stops singing and spins around. I've never seen a grown man blush before, but whatever Roman is doing now comes pretty damn close to that.

"What are you doing?" he demands, his eyes hard.

"Just watching you perform. Don't stop on my behalf," I say, waving a hand. "Keep going!"

"No," he mutters. He turns his back and goes back to cooking, this time not singing anything at all.

I let out a sigh and cross the room until I'm right behind him. "I liked your singing."

"No you didn't."

"I did!"

He glances at me, trying to discern whether I'm being honest or pulling his leg. "I'm not any good at it. I just like doing it whenever I cook."

I know what he means. I'm a terrible singer as well, but whenever I'm in the shower, you can't tell me that I'm not Mariah Carey or Celine

Dion. I'll belt it out to my heart's content, ignoring the fact that I sound like a dying cat with a cattle prod up its ass. It's embarrassing, but I think that's what makes it fun. The fact that I don't care that I don't sound good is empowering in a way.

"Do you cook often?" I ask. I take a seat on the counter beside him, watching as he stirs peppers and onions together in a small skillet. The smell is to die for. On the burner in the back, bacon fries loudly.

"I usually don't have time to cook anything. Breakfast is my favorite, but I sleep through it most days," he says.

"The good thing about breakfast is that when you have it for dinner, it tastes even better. Pancakes are so much better after dark."

"You're right," he says, looking up at me and smiling.

I'm not prepared for it, because the way my heart squeezes makes me feel like I'm in a silly rom-com. I shouldn't be feeling this way about someone like Roman. I may have done a few bad things, but this is his life. His life, his main source of income, revolves around killing people, and not just people that have done bad things, like hurt others or endangered people. He kills anyone that his shadowy boss tells him to.

This is like some book that I'd write. There'd be a heroine that knows herself and what her morals are, only to question them when she falls for a dangerous criminal. The only difference is that in those stories, there are happy endings. Something tells me that the way our story ends isn't as happy and carefree as one I'd write.

We can't possibly make this work.

Not that I have any feelings for him or anything.

Thoughts of yesterday morning come flooding back to me. The way he held me against his chest as he pounded away, rough and brutal. I've never considered myself someone that enjoys sex that way, but with him, it made sense. He couldn't be sweet and tender, not in a scenario like that. Not after I slapped him and yelled at him. And I'm glad he wasn't kind. I'm glad he didn't sugarcoat his advances towards me. There was something undeniably sexier about him telling me what would happen and me pressing his buttons anyway.

Swallowing hard, I look at the eggs he's scrambling in a small glass bowl. "My mom used to love her eggs super runny. I never liked that."

"No?"

"Nope. I always ate them when she made them, but I hated it. I like them firmer. One time, I was sick of her cooking, and tried to make breakfast for myself. I had to be seven, maybe eight. I thought I knew everything about cooking." I can barely start to retell the memory without laughing softly. "I woke up super early and decided that day was my culinary debut. I had all the ingredients laid out and everything. The only problem was that I didn't know how to work the dials for the burners. I buttered the pan and turned it on, letting it melt the butter while I ran off to go watch cartoons.

"The problem was, I turned on the wrong burner, and the washcloth that we used to clean the counters was sitting on the back burner. By the time I came back after a commercial break, the whole rag was up in flames."

Roman's eyes widen, and a smile forms on his face. "Are you serious?"

"Dead serious!" I exclaim. "I almost started crying, but I had to think on my feet. I grabbed the rag and hurried to the sink, soaking it to put out the flames. When I was finished, I wiped my forehead like I got away with it, but my mom was standing behind me the entire time, watching me make a fool of myself." I shake my head and laugh some more.

Mom was *pissed*. She never let me forget it, and even now, as I retell the story to Roman, I can remember the angry lines forming in her forehead. She'd told me time and time again not to mess around in the kitchen, but I didn't listen. I was young and hardheaded, and I had something to prove to her. It's a wonder the house didn't burn down then and there. No, that would come a few years down the road.

After we stop laughing, Roman looks at me and says, "You've never been good at following the rules, have you?"

"Maybe not," I say, shrugging. "But following the rules is boring. It's more fun to learn the rules and then learn how to break them without getting in trouble."

Roman sighs and glances up at me. "You sound like my brothers."

"What were they like?" I ask.

"Gedeon was a smartass," he says, mixing up the eggs. I watch as he seasons them, leaving them chunky and fluffy, just how I like them. "He always ran his mouth. Always got us all in trouble. And Ivan followed him like a shadow. If Gedeon did something, Ivan wanted to do it too. He was that way for me as well, but he really attached himself to Gedeon."

I smile fondly. I can see that dynamic perfectly. They must have been younger than him. It makes sense, Roman as the oldest. The leader. The role model.

"One time, Gedeon decided that he wanted to be some sort of survivalist. He'd been watching TV shows about it, and decided that forest life was for him. Our mother told him that he wasn't allowed to do something like that, but he didn't agree. He packed up his bags in the middle of the night, and he and Ivan ran away from home."

I cover my mouth. "Oh my God. Your parents must have been terrified!"

Roman nods. "My mother was frantic. She thought someone had broken into the house and kidnapped them or something. Eventually, we found them a mile away, living in a tent they'd set up by the river behind our house. Dad was fuming. Now that I look back, it was kind of funny to imagine them running away and living off the land for a night, but in the moment, we were sure a bear had gotten them or something."

I can't believe that I ever thought what I did was dangerous. I was just cooking inside the house, meanwhile Roman's brothers were turning into Bear Grylls, roughing it out in the middle of nowhere. My story doesn't hold a candle to his.

"Were you a good kid?" I ask.

Roman doesn't say anything for a long while. He takes all the food off the burners and begins plating it, dividing everything into two. Behind us, the toaster pops and four pieces of bread come out, perfectly cooked.

"I wasn't a bad kid," he says. "I don't think I was good, but I didn't cause trouble. I stayed to myself. I kept out of trouble."

Roman as a child is a funny thing to imagine. For some reason, I just picture him as the same person he is today, all hard eyes, strong jawline, and muscle. The only difference is, he's fourteen or so.

"Is what happened with your parents … what made you decide to do this for a living?"

I can tell that question isn't something he expected, because his whole body tenses up and his lips flatten into a paper-thin line. I swallow hard, realizing that I've crossed a line I didn't quite know existed. I mean, I knew his descent into darkness was a touchy subject, but I thought maybe he would be more willing to talk about it now that we were sharing stories.

I just want to know how he got from well-behaved and mild-mannered child to cold-blooded, emotionless killer. That kind of drastic change in personality doesn't come without an interesting backstory.

"You don't have to tell me if you don't want to," I say. After the laughs we've shared this morning, I don't want to ruin this. I don't want to make things awkward after everything we've been through. He's just starting to open up and not look at me like I'm the biggest mistake he's ever made. Pushing him further than he's willing to go would jeopardize all the steps forward we've taken.

"I'd rather not," he says.

"Okay," I nod. "We'll talk about something else."

I rack my brain for a new topic, something that doesn't make the air in the room feel so stuffy and suffocating. I consider bringing up shows I've been watching, but I don't think Roman will be able to relate to that. If our night in the motel was any clue, it seems he only watches the news, and that's just to check and see if his murders were noticed by the police. But maybe that's it. Maybe business is the language he prefers to speak.

"We should talk about how you're going to let me be a part of this now," I say, bringing my plate to the table and sitting down across from him. Roman picks at his food, eyeing me suspiciously.

"That's what I'm doing?"

"That's what you're doing," I say. I take a bite from my bacon and chew, staring him down. I dare him to tell me that he's not going to help me now. "I shot someone, and we left him to die. I'm in this now. I heard what they said. They knew that I was with you. They knew what I looked like. Had you never taken me to the motel, I wouldn't be in this mess."

Roman shakes his head. "Had you never gone down that alley, you would've never seen me complete an assignment."

"Had you not been killing people for money, I wouldn't have seen anything walking down that alley," I retort, raising an eyebrow at him. I have people on my ass now because of what his job is. Those people weren't there to kill me; they were there for him. I just happened to be with him, and now I'm caught up in the same chaos.

"Roman, you got me into this mess. No matter how we try to spin it or make it like it was my fault, I'm not the hit man. I'm not the one that goes around killing people. That's you. And I almost died yesterday, so I think the least you can do is let me help you take out Konstantin. That's all I'm asking. We can pretend we don't know each other when it's all said and done, but at the end of the day, I want to help."

Roman eats silently, mulling things over in his mind. What I wouldn't give for just a moment inside it, picking apart his thoughts and seeing him weigh all the options. Does he consider me a liability? Maybe I'm not fully recovered from what happened yesterday, but the fact still remains that I didn't need him to come and save me. I took care of that masked man on my own, without any help. He may have put the gun in my hand, but I pulled the trigger. And if the next time I do it, as long as I'm aiming at Abram Konstantin, I think this mess will all have been worth it.

"Fine," he says, glaring at me. "You can help me. But that doesn't mean we're partners. When I tell you something, you listen to me. When I tell you something is too dangerous, or that you need to stay out of the way, you listen to me. Okay?"

I don't necessarily like the terms of this agreement, but I'm really in no position to renegotiate. He's the one with the power. He's the one that gets to decide what we do now that whoever wants him dead also probably wants me out of the picture too.

"That's fair," I say. "But I also want you to listen to me sometimes. I'm not some annoying sidekick. I know things about Konstantin that even Mr. X wouldn't be able to figure out. I've been waiting for this moment my whole life. This means so much to me, and—"

Roman cuts me off. "I know. I know what it means."

Of course he knows. He went through this same thing with his family. He went through the pain of losing them and the all-encompassing rage of knowing that the people that did it got away with no consequences. Not even so much as a scratch on them. He knows the sleepless nights, the bone-rattling anger, and the bottomless despair. If anyone in the world would understand what I'm going through, it's Roman.

That must be why he's letting me work with him. Maybe he pities me because of what happened to Mom and Dad. He figures he's kicking me a bone, giving me something to do that will make me feel like I'm contributing. Even if he is, I don't care. It's something. It's something better than crying every other night, feeling helpless to the evil in the world.

I have agency. Finally, I have some say in what's happening to me and around me. I'm not a damsel in distress, sitting helplessly while the evil men of the world get away with anything they please. It took a lot to get here—if I'm being honest, I'll probably need therapy after this—but it's been worth it. Knowing that soon, Konstantin will pay? It's worth every last moment since I've met Roman.

"Enough murder talk," he says, giving me a look. I don't want to argue with him. "Finish eating your food. I slaved over the stove for this."

Following instructions, I scoop up a forkful of eggs, peppers, and onions and take a big bite. After I swallow, I smile at him. "You know, if you ever get tired of shooting and strangling people, you might have a successful career in cooking. You're not too shabby at it."

"Probably tastes better than a burnt dishrag, too."

My mouth falls open, and I laugh incredulously. "Did you just ..."

"I did." He smirks as well, then takes a sip of his black coffee.

"After Konstantin," I say, grabbing my butter knife and lightheartedly pointing it at him, "you're next on my hit list."

∽

After dinner, Roman and I quickly wash the dishes and head upstairs for the night. On the way to the stairs, he grabs me and lifts me off the ground, wrapping my legs around his waist. I let out a small laugh but don't fight him on it.

"What are you doing?" I ask, running a hand over his cheek.

"I'm thanking you for helping with dinner," he replies. He steals a slow kiss from me, and I return the favor, breaking it only to pepper more along his jawline. He lets out a low humming noise, then begins walking upstairs.

"Be careful," I laugh. "You're gonna drop me."

"I'm not going to drop you," he groans.

"I'm just saying!"

We make it up to the bed in one piece, and he finally does drop me, this time on my back. I start to roll away when he climbs on top, pinning me to the mattress. I could squirm and fight him, but right now, underneath him is exactly where I want to be.

There's something about him that always surprises me, and this time, it's how he takes his time undressing me. Before, when we were in the bathroom at the diner, he was quick and needy, practically tearing our clothes off so he could get inside of me. Tonight, he's careful with what he does. He's in no hurry to peel my pants from my legs or tug my shirt over my head. And when I'm lying in only my underwear, he leans in and presses gentle kisses to my skin.

His hands find my bra, and he removes it easily, dropping it on the floor next to the rest of my clothes. "You're fucking beautiful," he tells me.

I want to blush or argue with him, but I can't find the energy to be humble. I just want to be with him, absorbing everything he has to say to me. His firm, calloused hands feel perfect against my body, and I feel myself practically gravitate towards him when he slides it down my stomach and between my legs.

Two fingers slip inside of me, and I let out a soft moan. "Ah," I whisper.

He locks eyes with me, a smile on his face. "Tell me how that feels."

"It feels ... it feels good," I manage to say. I haven't had a lot of sex in my life, but something about Roman's touch feels special. He feels like what I imagine the men in all the romance novels Nana reads must feel like. Strong. Dominant. And yet, soft ... when he wants to be.

Roman's fingers begin to move faster, sliding deeper inside of my pussy, stretching me out wider. Another deep moan vibrates from my throat and I feel my back arch.

"That's it," he encourages, spreading my legs wider. "I'm gonna make you come for me."

I open my eyes and meet his. He stares at me intensely, and when he presses his thumb to my clit, tapping it, I shudder beneath him. For a long time, neither of us say anything. I just stare into his eyes as he touches the most sensitive parts of me, working me like he's known my body his entire life.

He must be able to sense when I'm close, because he presses his lips to mine again, hungry like we didn't just have dinner. His tongue dancing with mine combined with how skilled he is with his fingers, it's no wonder I feel that rising swell of pleasure growing too strong to handle. I can't contain it anymore.

Clutching his upper arm for dear life, I feel myself come undone, my orgasm spilling over. A silent scream passes my lips and I stiffen entirely, shuddering at his touch.

"There you go," he growls. "That's a good girl."

I feel hot all over, and I fall back on the bed, panting desperately for air. While I catch my breath, Roman kisses my neck and explores my body with his free hand. He cups my breasts firmly, teasing the nipples until they harden, then sucks them into his mouth. Post-orgasm, it feels even more incredible than it normally might.

Just as I start to come down from my climax, Roman removes his fingers, licks them clean, and begins undoing the fly on his jeans. I watch with my breath held as he pulls himself free. His cock is quite large, and normally, I'd be skeptical whether I'd be able to take it, but I already know. He managed to fit just perfectly in the diner.

He lines himself up and presses the head in slowly. He's much bigger than his fingers, and I let out a steady breath as he fills me. His movements are precise, building up a decent pace. Feeling a bit cheeky, I run my fingers through his hair before catching a handful.

"How's that feel?" I ask.

Roman chuckles and leans in close to my ear. "Like fucking heaven," he says. His warm breath on my skin sends chills through my body.

It doesn't take long for Roman to increase his speed, thrusting faster and faster. I bite back another cry of pleasure and take him for all he can give. My hand falls to my clit, where I begin to rub circles, teasing myself. After my first orgasm, I'm already sensitive, but with Roman inside of me, everything is heightened.

I writhe beneath him, grinding back, meeting him in the middle. That seems to be good for him because he lets out a deep rumble of a moan. I've only heard it once before, but it's already my new favorite sound.

"Yes," I whisper, groaning as he buries himself inside me completely. "Don't stop."

And he doesn't. He moves forward and back, knocking the headboard of the bed against the wall, over and over, unrelenting and without mercy. I take him as best I can, and just when I think I might lose it all, he leans in and bites my shoulder again. The heat overtakes me and I come again, clenching around him as my body explodes with ecstasy.

His orgasm hits at the same time because he pulls me close to him and snaps his hips forward without a break. I feel him fill me, and as strange as these two days have been, I wouldn't want this any other way. It's better than the dream I had at the motel. It's better than any fantasy I could craft on my own.

The real thing is so much better.

∼

Roman eventually slides out and sits on the side of the bed, hunched over. When I have the energy to move, I push up on my knees and crawl towards him, draping myself over his shoulder. I fit perfectly over him, like we were made that way. Like I belong exactly in this position with him.

"What's wrong?" I ask.

He turns his head to look at me, and where I expect a scowl or sour look, I find the smallest smile. "Nothing's wrong," he says. "I just haven't had sex that good in a while."

I crack a smile and say, "That's because you didn't know me."

"This sass ... I like it."

I press a kiss to his warm bare shoulder. "I like it too. But you know what I'd like even more?"

"What's that?"

"Sleep." I usher him into bed and underneath the covers. Once he's settled, I turn the lamps off and crawl under the covers with him. It's a unique feeling, lying in bed with Roman. He's a killer. He's done horrible things. But when I'm with him, he only makes me feel good. I don't exactly understand it, but right now, I don't need to.

I just like having him around.

11

ROMAN

Two weeks fly by in an instant. Normally, my days seem long and dull, empty, while I wait for another assignment from Mr. X. Something else to fill my time. Something for me to do to avoid sitting in silence. But with Lucy, things are different.

She wanted to learn how to fight.

After the shooting at the diner, she was shaken up, but she wasn't defeated. Rather than going into a shell, she figured it was better to protect herself. Killing didn't always have to be the only form of self-defense. It took me a while to come up with a few nonlethal techniques to teach her, but eventually I wrote up a sparring plan.

The first thing I taught her was punches. The proper way to hold her hand, punching through the target and not just *at* it, and how to perfect her form so that she didn't hurt herself. She's a fast learner. She picked it up easily, and soon we moved up to grapples and holds that she could escape from.

This took a little bit of practice. At first, she ended up getting so frustrated with me that she started to get teary-eyed. I had to give her pep talks, reassure her that she could do it, and then eventually she was able to work up the strength to escape my grip. The first time she did, she jumped up and down like a kid. It was adorable, I have to admit.

I have to remind myself that this isn't some relationship I'm in.

Lucy isn't my girl. She's someone I'm working with and she's been pretty damn helpful since we came to this house. She knows more than I ever expected, and because of her, I've been able to do plenty of research on him and figure out his schedule.

Something brought us together. It's annoying to admit, but I might actually need her to help me pull this assignment off.

"Earth to Roman," she says, punching me in the gut. The glove on her hand keeps it from hurting, but I blink and shake myself out of my thoughts.

"Sorry," I mutter, holding up the pads.

She punches them back and forth with surprising force. Something tells me that she's picturing Konstantin. When she sees those targets, she sees his face. I did the same thing. Every punch I threw when I spent months training, I imagined my uncles. I imagined the crunching of their noses, the howls of pain, and the blood. I wanted to see so much of it. I channeled my hatred for them into every punch I gave my heavy bag.

She sets her jaw and goes back and forth, left and right, over and over. She's worked up a sweat, but even still, she looks beautiful. Finally, she drops her hands and undoes the blue gloves. She drops them to the floor, and I pull off the pads on my hands.

I watch as she grabs a bottle of water from the patio, drinking it down in three large gulps. The sun beats down on us in the backyard, but I barely notice the heat. Seeing her improve is the only thing I focus on. When she's done, she walks back to me, a smile on her face.

"What?" I ask.

"I want to practice some holds."

"Okay." I grab her and jerk her forward, pulling her to my chest. I squeeze my arms around her, holding her the same way I would if I were trying to keep her from getting away. Lucy wiggles and squirms until she stomps on my foot and I loosen my grip. She now has some room to move around. Quick on her feet, she manages to slip out from my grip and grab me instead.

In a flash, Lucy knocks me flat on my ass. I'm too stunned to say anything, and in that time, she pushes me flat on my back and climbs on top of me. Her chest heaves as she pins me to the grass, and a satisfied smile appears on her face. It's impressive how far she's come in such a short time. Just three weeks ago, she probably had no clue how to do even half of this.

"Got you," she says confidently.

"You did," I reply. I reach up and grab her hips, tugging her down on me. This close, she can probably feel my growing erection against her thigh.

"What's my prize? Since I got you and all?"

"What do you want?"

Lucy taps her chin and looks around, considering her options. "I want to boss you around for a little while," she says finally.

"Oh yeah? Maybe."

"No 'maybes,'" she says, shaking her head. "Kiss me. Now."

Giving up control isn't my sort of thing, but with Lucy, I might reconsider. I pull her down towards me and press my lips to her. She lets out a tender moan and slides her arm under the back of my head, holding me just as close. Our kiss deepens and I brush my tongue over hers. She's impatient, eager to go further, and I love every second of it.

I slide a hand down to her ass and cup her. When I squeeze, she moans again, rolling her hips down against me. My cock stirs to life. That feeling seems to come up a lot whenever I'm around Lucy. If I had it my way, there'd be a lot more of this and less talk about my assignment with Konstantin.

I don't know what she's doing to me. Any other assignment, I would've handled it by now. But when I spend time with Lucy, I almost want to call this off. Throw in the towel and find another line of work. It doesn't make sense, and that frustrates me.

Lucy deserves the kind of guy that won't disappear for weeks at a time to kill someone. She deserves someone that can give her what she wants, like a family and a suburban home with a white picket fence. I'm not that kind of guy. I can't change that truth. All I can do is ignore it.

Which is exactly what I'm doing as I kiss her harder, hungrier, drowning out the doubts in my mind. There's no point in worrying about the future. Right now is good enough for me. Judging by the noises she makes, it's good enough for Lucy as well.

She slides her hands under my shirt and up my chest, and as I start to pull the shirt off, my phone rings. Lucy immediately rolls off me.

"It'll be quick," I say, sitting up. I grab my phone a few feet away and head inside the house where it's a little more private. I lean against the island in the kitchen and answer it. "What?"

A gruff voice on the other end of the line says, "I have it."

"Do you need me to come by and pick everything up?"

"Yeah."

"All right," I say, grabbing the keys from the counter. "I'll be there in twenty minutes." When I hang up, Lucy clears her throat.

"Who was that?" she asks. She leans against the doorframe, arms crossed over her chest and head tilted curiously. It's not the right time to be thinking about it, but she looks adorable in her workout gear. Her sports bra and leggings combo work for her.

"The supplies are here," I say, stuffing my wallet in my pocket.

"You gonna be long?"

"Probably not. I'm just picking it up and heading right back. Think you can hold down the fort?"

A smile crosses her face. "I think I can manage. Hurry back."

I kiss her on the cheek and head out to the garage. The trip won't take long, but I'm annoyed that it's interrupting time with Lucy. We were just about to have some fun before my contact, Andrew, blue balled me. He's lucky I need the paralytic for Konstantin, otherwise he would've gone straight to voicemail.

∽

When I arrive, the exchange goes quickly. I hand him his money, he walks me into the back of his house and grabs the bag of supplies that I need, then hands it off to me. In and out, very few words exchanged. That's the good thing about Andrew. He doesn't waste time trying to catch up. He's as focused on his money as I am on taking out Konstantin. Because of that, he makes for a good supplier whenever I need drugs that I can't get my hands on.

I turn the car around and head back to the house. There's a sinking feeling in my stomach that makes me wonder if Lucy will still be there. I don't know why, but I keep expecting her to disappear. Maybe she'll have a change of heart and decide that this life isn't for her. Maybe she'll realize that the business she's getting involved in isn't something you can really just back out of. Not when you're in my position.

That thought is always in the back of my head.

It's fucking annoying, always wondering if I'll wake up one day and find her gone. I don't like depending on her not to hurt me like that. And what isn't helping is how much time we've spent together. There are moments when I wonder what this is between us. Are we just temporary coworkers, or is there something deeper going on between us?

Last night I had a dream that we got away from all this.

We lived together in some farmhouse way outside of the city. She spent all her time working on her books. I was in the fields, tending to all our animals. We had a peaceful life. The thought of me giving up this life to become a fucking farmer is hilarious to me, but I can't lie and say I didn't like the simplicity.

I liked the fact that there were no shady men looming over me, sending me on missions to take out people they don't like. There was no killing, no drugging, no disposing of bodies. When I finished tending to the animals, I went back to the house and Lucy and I had sex. She whispered in my ear that she wanted to start a family with me.

Then I woke up.

Part of me was relieved, but another part was pissed. I wouldn't ever say it out loud, but I wonder. What would happen if that dream became a reality? Would it satisfy me the way working for Mr. X does? Could we really make a simple life like that work out?

I grit my teeth and tighten my grip on the steering wheel. I don't have time to wonder about these things. We're close to getting Konstantin. I can feel it. With all the information that Lucy's told me, I have his entire schedule mapped out. Now it's just a matter of picking the perfect time to inject him and get him in the car.

I pull into the garage and climb out of the car twenty minutes later. The house is silent. For a minute, I'm sure she did leave. Then I find her sitting in the living room, knees drawn to her chest, writing on a legal pad. I don't keep technology around the house, outside of my phone, but she insisted I get her some way to write.

There's something beautiful about the way she looks right now. She's lost in whatever world she's created. She doesn't look concerned about Konstantin or her grandmother or anything. She looks happy. That sinking feeling comes back to me, only this time, it's different.

The more time I spend around her, the closer I feel, and that can't happen. If it does, that means it'll hurt more when we eventually part ways. My rules are in place for a reason, and I can't go breaking them. Keep it simple. Lucy helps me with Konstantin, I kill him, and we never speak to each other again.

The hard part is convincing my body of this plan. Seeing her in her element stirs something inside of me that's more than just arousal. I'm not giving it a name. I'm not letting it be valid. Swallowing down that feeling, I step into the living room. She looks up at me and puts down her paper and pencil.

"That took longer than you said," she remarks, standing up. She's changed out of her workout gear and is now in a pair of shorts and a tank top.

"Sorry," I shrug.

She glares at me, then smiles. "Lucky for you, I had a stroke of genius."

"Did you now?"

"Yup!"

Lucy goes into great detail about a plot point that she worked her way through. After struggling with it for days, she finally figured out how to get out of the hole she'd written herself into. She won't let me read any of her work, but from the sound of it, it's probably something I'd be interested in reading. Sex, murder, and a dark underworld in a city most people think is lighthearted and scandal-free. Right up my alley.

I try to listen, but I don't exactly know everything she's talking about. Still, it's nice just listening to her go on and on. When she gets this excited, the last thing I want to do is cut her off. I like the way she talks. I like how animated she gets, talking with her hands, her eyes growing wider and wider. Finally, when she finishes her story, she hops up from the couch.

"You still owe me my prize." Lucy steps up to me and gives me a push, towards the backyard.

"You want it out there?" I ask.

"That's where we started. I want to finish it there."

I don't argue with her. Instead, I pull her close to me and kiss her hard. We move backwards at the same time, stepping into the grass. Without warning, Lucy does the same maneuver as before and sends me sprawling on my back. That's twice in one day, I note. She's getting too good at this. I need to keep my guard up around her.

She stands above me, slowly unbuttoning her shorts and pulling them off. She steps out of them, and I get a glimpse of her body. She's not wearing anything underneath. When she climbs on top of me, she doesn't stop to sit in my lap. Instead, she moves higher until she's right on my face.

I don't need any further instructions. I grab her hips and tug her down, tasting her. Lucy lets out a moan as I flick my tongue over the folds of her skin. My movements are slow at first. I want to tease her. Make her practically beg me to grant her some relief. Rather than diving right in, I kiss at her inner thighs, nipping with my teeth every now and then. I run my nose against her, inhaling the delicious scent of her body.

"Yes," she purrs, rolling her hips with me.

Finally, I lap at her hungrily, working my tongue against her pussy with skill. Her eyes squeeze tight and she bites down on her bottom lip, riding me faster. I let a hand slide up her thighs and over to her clit, where I rub circles. Her head falls back, mouth wide open, her long blonde hair brushing against her lower back.

My cock aches in my pants, but I don't even consider taking care of it. Right now, this is what I want. I want her to come undone. I want her to lose her goddamn mind with my tongue between her legs. I don't plan on stopping until she's trembling, putty in my hands.

"Fuck, Roman," she whimpers, reaching for my free hand. She laces her fingers through mine and squeezes tight. I smirk with satisfaction, but I never pull away to speak. I bury my tongue inside of her, deep, tasting every last inch I can. Lucy's hips move in a flurry and she grinds against me like it's the last thing she might ever do.

"I—I'm close," she manages to get out.

I slip my hand free from hers and grab her breast, twisting her nipple firmly. It hardens almost instantly, and following that, she begins a continuous moan. She slides against my face without stopping, and when I feel her thighs quiver and tighten around my head, I know she's there. She comes hard, crying out in pleasure. I soak up every sound, cruel with the way my tongue strokes her clit.

She finally rolls onto her back, tired, but I'm only just getting started. There are no breaks with me. I've wanted her every single night since we've been here, and I'm going to take her. Without missing a beat, I unzip my pants and free myself from the confines. I stroke my cock a few times, working myself in my palm.

I press the tip against Lucy's entrance, feeling the impossible heat send shivers down my spine. With one slow, long push, I bury myself inside of her pussy, up to the hilt of my erection. Her eyes flutter shut, and she takes in a sharp breath, releasing it as a moan between her teeth. There's something unspeakably sexy about seeing this transformation. Lucy from the living room, writing on that legal pad, is now this sex kitten practically mewling for me in the backyard.

I work up a steady pace at first, pulling my hips back and then thrusting forward, filling her again. Her body grows more and more relaxed. She stares up at me with a devilish look in her eye, something that looks so out of place and also right where it belongs with her.

She's gonna be the fucking death of me, I swear.

I take hold of her hips and begin jerking her towards me as I push forward, fucking her faster than before. A deep, animalistic groan rumbles in my throat, and I let it free, burying my face in the crook of her neck. There, I can feel her pulse, taste as it beats a thousand times a minute. Lucy wraps her legs around my waist, and soon I have little room to move.

I make do with it, my thrusts becoming shorter and quicker. Our bodies connect again and again. I feel her walls constricting around me and it sends chills through me. Fuck, everything she does has that effect on me.

I'm going to lose my goddamn mind with this woman, and I don't even care. She makes the idea of being distracted sound like the only thing in the world that I want.

With short, sudden bursts of energy, I pound into her, eliciting quicker noises from her throat. She turns her head and kisses me, and that's when I feel the heat building in my stomach. Her tongue glides over mine, and it's just the two of us. She's the only thing that matters.

I come harder than I have in months. I fill her in a frenzy, grinding against her, burying every last inch I can inside of her. Her hold on me doesn't loosen once. She keeps me firmly against her, helping me ride that wave.

I don't want to pull out of her.

I want to lie here in the grass until I'm hard and ready for another round.

Lucy makes me want to do the dumbest shit, but I can't find it in me to complain. When I go soft and slip free, I roll onto my back and pull her into my arms. This is so fucked. *I'm* so fucked. Every time this happens, I realize that I'm sinking deeper and deeper into this trap.

This is why I should've never gone this far with her. This is why I have these rules. I start to scold myself when she tilts her head and looks up at me. There's a warm flush of pink on her cheeks, and her smile is radiant. She looks fucking beautiful.

The killer instinct I've developed is wary. Anything so beautiful that's attracted to me must be dangerous. Anything that makes me consider giving up everything should repel me. Instead, she makes me want more. She's addictive, like my new favorite drug. I need to get a fucking grip.

"What's wrong?" she asks.

For one delusional moment, I consider telling her all of this.

If I'm honest, maybe it'll scare her away. She'll see that I'm not the kind of guy she belongs with. Anyone that considers her a trap should turn her off completely. But the idea of her being hurt by saying that doesn't sit right with me. It makes me feel guilty for even considering it.

Guilt is an emotion I thought I killed after taking out Aleksandr and Andrei. If I'm feeling it now, maybe I'm not as emotionless as I thought. Maybe I need to really cut deep and end things while there's still time.

Lucy looks up at me expectantly, waiting for an answer.

"Nothing is wrong," I reply, running a hand over her face. It's a lie, but she deserves to be spared. She's already been through hell because of me. This is one mercy I can give her for now.

12

ROMAN

Things with Lucy have become so domesticated. It's a foreign concept for me. My whole life, I grew up on my own. Nobody to look after me, nobody to just *be* there. Aside from just seeing my family every day, this was the one thing I missed the most. I missed knowing that if I ever needed something, I'd have someone willing to help.

Lucy has become that person.

In the mornings, she wakes up earlier than me. There's a pot of coffee on, and breakfast is on the table. I never have to think about what I'm going to eat because she has it covered. We've worked up that kind of rhythm, and it's surprisingly nice getting used to it. I try hard to hate it, to put myself off it so I don't become accustomed, but I can't.

After breakfast, she writes, and I work out. This is our routine. It's dependable. I don't wonder where she is or if she's safe because I know that she is.

But the part I like the most about these few weeks spent with her at the safe house is dinner.

We cook together. Lucy tells me all about how her grandmother used to be an amazing cook and that she learned everything from the woman. She's too old to take care of herself now, so Lucy had to pick up the recipe book and keep the wheels turning. Here at the safe house, she's brought some of the best recipes with her.

Tonight, we make honey-baked salmon, baked green beans, and a side salad with a sesame seed dressing. I don't say anything, but I'm kind of embarrassed that I've never had anything this nice. Before Lucy, I ate to stay alive. I didn't find anything particularly special about dinner. A slab of steak and something green, all seasoned lightly, was enough to get me through the evening. But now that she's introduced me to newer ingredients and flavors, I might be hooked.

"That's probably gonna be super spicy," she notes, glancing at the crushed red pepper I sprinkle on my salmon filet.

"I like spicy," I smirk.

"Fair enough. Don't let me yuck your yum." Once we're finished seasoning everything, she puts it in the oven and gets started on mixing the drinks. Since we've been here three weeks, she decided that she wanted to do something special and make cocktails for us. Same as my food, I usually drink liquor straight. I don't need any frilly things to make it tolerable. I'm not drinking for flavor, after all.

But again, I relent, letting her have her way. It seems to be something that makes her happy, and I'm happy to provide. She's good at this anyway. As she flits around the kitchen preparing the drinks, I sit back in my chair and nurse my glass of water. It's a big mistake, but I know that I could get used to this.

Unfortunately, after tomorrow, there won't be this anymore.

"I'm thinking we'll get started at dawn," I say. She continues to mix a pitcher of juice and alcohol when she turns to look at me.

"What do you mean?"

"I looked over everything, and tomorrow morning, we'll head out to get Konstantin."

A look of anticipation crosses her face. Her eyes light up excitedly. "Really?"

"Really."

I went over everything we'd need, and we have it. All the supplies are packed up and ready to go, I know exactly where Konstantin will be tomorrow, and soon, this will all be over. It's a blessing and a curse. Spending another day here only to never see Lucy again sounds unbearable, but I know it's for the best.

My biggest mistake was not pawning her off weeks ago. If I had, I could've saved her plenty of heartbreak after this is all over. Konstantin would be dead and I'd be back at the warehouse, taking another assignment from Mr. X. She'd be off somewhere working on her book and taking care of her grandmother. Our lives would be normal. Being able to get back to my normal self is why it's a blessing.

It's a curse because I know that Lucy has wormed her way into my heart. It almost makes me sick to say this, because it goes against everything I told myself to do. Never catch feelings for someone. Never develop a bond. Having bonds makes you weaker. It makes it easier for enemies to take advantage of your weakness. And in this line of business, the people you care about are always in danger.

I'm a fucking fool for letting it go this far, so now I have to fix it.

I can already see how mad she'll be when I tell her that we can't do this anymore. That defiant look will take over her face, and she'll probably curse me out the same way she did at the diner. I'll deserve it, too. I fucked up by letting her get close to me only to push her away at the end. It's a lesson I'll keep in mind the next time I ever decide not to work solo on an assignment like this.

"You don't know how long I've waited for this, Roman," she sighs, placing ice cubes into the pitcher. "Can I be there when you do it?"

"Of course," I say. "But I don't want you doing anything until I grab him. I don't need you in danger. When I get him tied up at the location, you can be there to watch."

Is it sick to say that it will be a bonding moment for us? I know how desperate she is to see Abram Konstantin pay for what he did to her family, and I want to help her find that momentary peace. If I had someone to help me get my uncles, it would've gone much smoother.

"Good," she says, smiling softly. Even when she's thinking about murder, the woman is adorable. I don't know how she does it. I don't want her to stop, either.

While we eat, she tells me more about her book and all the progress she's made. She's just wrapping up act two, and the heroine of the story is facing her toughest battle yet. I don't have a clue what she's talking about, but I'm almost tempted to grab one of the legal pads and read over it. She spends hours at a time writing on those things. Her creativity is something else that I enjoy about her.

Where most people struggle to see the bigger picture, Lucy has no trouble with it. When she writes, she looks outside of just what's happening right then. She tells me all the time that she can't start a book until she knows the ending. She needs to know the end before she knows the beginning. That's another thing I like about her. She's a planner, just like me.

∽

After dinner, Lucy and I wash dishes and she heads out to work on her self-defense techniques. I'm tempted to watch, but I need time to get away. I have to clear my head. I tell her I'm going for a drive.

In the car, I turn on the radio, hoping to drown out my thoughts. This is too much. She can feel it and I can feel it. I'm starting to care for this girl in more ways than just sexual. I've gone soft. The old me would've kicked my ass for even thinking about spending more than a night with someone like Lucy, but here I am.

I'm a dumbass.

On the ride back, I go over the plan again. Wait outside Konstantin's office building. Stick him with the needle. Transport him to the car. Get him to the safe house. Finish him off there. It's simple and easy. Nobody will see more than they should, and I won't have another situation like Lucy. No witnesses this time. I don't know what my next assignment after this will be, but I hope it's something less complicated. Something where I don't consider giving up my job. Not that Mr. X would even let me do something like that.

Ever since I met him, he made it very clear that he was interested in my talents, and he didn't have any problem doing whatever it took to make sure I worked for him.

Somehow, he knew about Andrei and Aleksandr. He knew what they'd done. He knew what I'd done. I don't know how or why he had that information, just that he did, and he used it to make me do whatever he wanted. He let me know of this in a church confessional years ago.

The meeting was set up by a mutual contact. I'd done a few assignments for Lana, the sole heiress of her father's multimillion-dollar company, and when she was done having me clean up the mess of investors that wanted to pull their funding because she was a woman, she set me up with Mr. X.

I thought it was tacky at first.

Meeting at a church to discuss murder. Seriously? But she insisted this was where he wanted to meet. When I got there, it made sense. He liked his privacy, and in the confessional, I only got a glimpse of his profile. The fewer people that could recognize and ID him, the better. I could respect that.

What I couldn't respect was his decision to blackmail me. He told me up front that he knew what I'd done to my uncles. He wasn't judgmental or holier-than-thou. He didn't have any room for that. He was simply putting his cards on the table. The authorities wouldn't be in agreement with what I did. They'd have me arrested and put me in prison.

He offered me a way out. At least, that's what he called it.

Really, he strong-armed me into becoming his personal hit man. He used me whenever he needed someone taken care of. At first, it was petty things. Beating up a few men, making something look like a random mugging, low-level crime shit. But things progressively got worse. Soon I was killing people that pissed him off. People that got in his way.

The money was good at first. After all, I'd developed a persona. Outside of the rules I'd set for myself, there wasn't much I wouldn't do. People knew my name and knew my work. Mr. X offered something more than notoriety: limitless cash. Working for him, I was quickly able to line my pockets with more than I could ever spend. The flashy life wasn't my style, so I put it towards more practical purposes.

The safe house is one of many that I own thanks to the money he's given me.

For a long time, I got used to it. I liked having dependable, steady work. I liked that he didn't bother me once he told me who my next target was. He wasn't a helicopter boss like so many of my other clients. Even Lana bugged me on assignments, trying to make me work faster. Not Mr. X. He knew that I would get the job done.

I had no other choice but to do just that.

But as of late, things have gotten more demanding. He wants his work done faster, cleaned up quicker, and I rarely have a break. Part of me wonders what would happen if I told him that I was done doing his bidding. Would he let me go without a fight? Or would he whip out the blackmail he used so long ago? That's not a risk I want to run.

Especially not with Lucy in the picture.

I don't want her to ever meet Mr. X. I trust him more than any of my previous clients, but in this business, trust is a hot commodity. You can't put your faith in anyone for too long. For the right amount of money, people will betray each other and look the other way as their henchmen beat someone to death. It's dog-eat-dog. It's rough, and I know that as tough as she may seem, Lucy isn't built for this.

Tomorrow, she'll never have to worry about this world again.

∼

When I get home, Lucy has showered and is sitting in bed, flipping through a book. I consider just sliding in with her and going to bed, but I need to get ready for tomorrow. I need to shower now so I'm ready to go before the sun comes up.

I take my time, washing up and letting the scalding water soothe my aching muscles. Training with Lucy has taken a toll on me, but I enjoy it. I like seeing her become more confident in her abilities. I want her to go through life knowing she can handle herself. She doesn't need me to come to her rescue or make her feel safe. She can do that on her own, by herself.

After the shower, I dry off and stare at my reflection in the mirror. I don't exactly recognize this old bastard anymore. Last month, my stare was dead, hollow. I could burn holes through anyone. But now, I can practically see the light in there. Lucy. She's the one shining part of my life.

For just a few more hours.

I turn away from the mirror and turn the lights off. In bed, I slide up close to Lucy. She puts her bookmark in the novel she's reading and slips down next to me. Her arm drapes over my chest and she looks up at me.

"Can I ask you a question?" she wonders.

"Go for it."

"If you weren't doing the work you do now, what would you be doing with your life?"

It's a tough question. I almost can't imagine a life without this. Without the pain and struggle that I went through because of my uncles. I don't know if I'd even like the man I might be if circumstances were different. But for Lucy's sake, I don't get into all of that. Instead, I say,

"I'd like to do something less stressful, that's for sure."

She cracks a smile and brushes a strand of blonde hair behind her ear. "Like what?"

"I don't know," I shrug. "Maybe something with security. Something where I'm not trying to get into restricted areas but instead trying to keep people out. Something where I can protect people."

I've never realized what makes that fantasy life sound so enticing, but I think I've cracked the code. If I worked for security, I wouldn't be harming anyone. I'd be protecting them, same as I did for Lucy. Same as I wish I could've done for my family. It's a natural instinct in me. It's the reason I don't hurt women or children. Everything in my bones says to keep them safe, out of harm's way.

"I can never predict what you're going to say next," she says, shaking her head.

"What does that mean?"

"I just thought you'd want to do something dangerous, like be a police officer or something. Maybe even a firefighter. But here you are, wanting the calm, safe job. Not that there's anything wrong with it," she says.

"What about you? What would you do?"

There's a long silence between us, but I don't fill it with wasted talk. I let her think, watching the thoughts swirl in her head. She gets this pursed up look about her lips, and her eyes narrow.

Finally, she says, "I'd like to be a teacher."

"Wow," I say. "Why a teacher? You have a special thing for not getting paid what you deserve?"

Lucy cracks a smile and shoves my shoulder. "No, smartass. I just ... My mom was a teacher. She said that it was the best work in the world. She taught younger kids with special needs, and I remember her coming home, always eager to tell me all the progress she'd made with her students. When she worked there, she knew her place in the world."

I try to envision Lucy as a schoolteacher and I can totally see it. She has that gentle side to her where she could easily teach children how to be kind to each other and not bite.

"Would you want to teach younger kids, too?" I ask.

"Maybe. I get attached easily, though, and since I love kids, it might be hard not to be sad whenever they have to go to a new class at the end of the year." She smiles fondly at the thought.

"Why not have kids of your own? That way you don't have to get attached to those."

She scrunches her face up. "I couldn't be a mother right now."

"Why not?"

"Well," she shrugs. "For starters, I have Nana. I'm supposed to take care of her, and a kid would only complicate that. Plus, there's the whole problem with having a kid. I'd need someone there for me as well. Someone to help take care of the baby with me."

She looks at me in a way that says she's talking about me, and I swallow hard. Fuck no. We can't be having this conversation tonight. We can't be doing this. I've let it go far enough with thoughts of our future together, but adding kids to the equation? That's where I draw the line.

I pull her close and steal a kiss from her. It's the only thing I can think to do to stop her from talking anymore. She doesn't seem to mind the gesture.

For a long time, we lie like that, just kissing, working our tongues together. There's no rush to go further. I let the pleasure of being with Lucy take over, simply enjoying her touch on me.

When our kiss breaks, she cuddles up next to me again, breathless. "Sorry about making things weird. I just … I've always wanted a family."

That hits me in the heart harder than it should. Of course she'd want to start a family of her own. She'd want something she never had growing up. She'd want to give her kids everything she dreamed of when she was a little girl.

"Don't apologize," I say seriously. "We're all allowed to have fantasies. We're allowed to daydream."

"I guess," she says. A bashful smile tugs at her lips. "You know, you're one of the few guys I've met that didn't run screaming when I brought that up."

"Did you happen to tell all those other guys your backstory?" I ask, eyebrow quirked up.

"No," she admits. "But I usually don't have time to. They're out the door in five-point-six seconds after I mention anything long-term."

"That's how guys are," I say.

"Is that how you are?"

I swallow hard, debating if I want to admit this. Her sincere eyes stay aimed at me. Fuck it. I'll tell her.

"I've never thought about having a relationship like that. In my mind, I'll end up alone. I can't put anyone in jeopardy. Not in this line of work."

She props herself up on one arm and looks at me closely. "So you've never just thought about what it would be like to have a family and not be doing what you do for work?"

"No," I say. She doesn't know about Mr. X. She doesn't know that because of the information he has, I'll always be his employee. The only way to get out of a contract like that is if he dies, and the bastard seems healthy enough to keep kicking for years to come.

"You should," she says, smiling.

"Why?"

"Maybe it's the writer in me, but whenever I think about the future, it makes me feel hopeful. It gives me a goal to achieve. It gives me something to look forward to every morning."

I lean in for another quick kiss, which she allows. "Right now, you're that for me."

"You're just saying that."

"Not at all," I reply. "You surprised me, Lucy. I like that you're always full of surprises."

When her grin becomes too much for her to bear, she climbs on top of me and places her hands on my pecs. She runs her finger over the gash on my side that's all but healed up now. She then slides her hands back up, teasing my nipples.

"I have another surprise for you," she says.

Playing along, I ask, "What is it?"

That signature devilish Lucy look appears again, and she inches down my body. "They say good authors always show rather than tell."

"Then show me," I say.

With a wicked smile, Lucy kisses down my stomach before disappearing under the covers. A moment later, her surprise arrives, and we spend the rest of the night enjoying it to the fullest.

13

LUCY

"Mommy, wait!"

No matter how many times I call out to her, she won't stop running. I pump my arms to keep up with her, but somehow, as fast as I run, she always stays just out of reach. From the corner of my eyes, I see Dad appear, and he speeds up so that he matches her pace. At eight years old, I don't have long enough legs to ever reach them.

"Daddy!"

My cries fall on ears that must be too far away to hear me. That has to be it. Why else would they ignore me?

We run for what feels like forever. I stop to catch my breath, tears stinging my eyes. None of this makes sense. Why can't they listen to me? Why won't they just stop? When I look up, I see that they have. Only, they stand perfectly still, their backs turned to me. I straighten up, a chill running through me.

It's like they're waiting for me. It's like they know that I've stopped running too.

"Please," I shout. "I'll stop him, I promise!"

I can hear the sound of him somewhere in the distance. That deep, mature laugh that only a man of a certain personality can have. Like the world bows at his feet. Like there's nothing and no one that could ever hold him accountable for what he's done.

Mom is the first to move. She turns around, her eyes far away. Her mouth is moving, but I can't hear her. Dad does the same thing, with more anguish on his face. They reach for me, and for a moment, I'm certain I hear them call my name.

"Lucy!"

I start to run for them, and that's when the flames engulf them. The scream that tears through me hurts my throat, and I fall to the floor on my knees, sobbing. It's like my heart has been ripped out and ice has filled the cavity in my chest, sending frigid shivers through my body. I bury my face in my hands, trying to collect myself. Trying to get it together.

Nothing helps.

When I look up again, I'm on my front lawn. The fire is still burning, raging worse than anything I've ever seen. The windows have all blown out from the heat. The grass around the house is singed black. Firefighters do their best, but it's almost too much to put out.

When they do, they wheel out two bodies in bags.

Mom and Dad.

Knowing exactly who's in those bags makes me want to die. At eight, I want to die. I don't want to be in a world without them. I don't want to exist knowing that the people that made it possible are no longer around.

I wish I could take everything back.

I wish I could rewind time and not leave the house to spend time with my best friend. We planned this day for weeks, but with our parents' crazy schedules, we had to put it off again and again. Finally, everything lined up. This was the only time I could make it to her house.

Nana picked me up after we were done hanging out, and on the ride home, she told me how much Mom and Dad missed me. Mom had called her, saying that she was worried. This was the first playdate where I was at someone else's house. She felt like I was growing up too fast, like she was losing me.

If only she knew what would come a few hours after that phone call.

If only I'd been home. I wouldn't hurt like this. I wouldn't be sobbing in the front lawn, orphaned by a fire nobody could've ever seen coming.

A shadow looms over me, and it takes everything I have to turn around and face whatever it is that's making it. I expect a fireman to tell me that I have to get off the property. That Nana is waiting for me, begging me to come back.

But it's not a fireman.

It's him. Abram Konstantin.

With his slicked-back dark hair and that ever-present, self-aggrandizing smirk dancing on his paper-thin lips. He scratches at his short beard, looking down at me like a petulant child throwing a temper tantrum over a toy I want.

I know that I hate him as sure as I know the sky is blue and the grass around me is green. I hate him with every possible atom that I'm made of. I hate him so passionately that I feel nothing at all. Just empty hollowness. A dark corridor where my heart once was.

He leans in close and I can smell the cigar on his breath. "Poor thing," he murmurs, looking me over. "Don't cry."

I wipe my eyes and push myself off the ground.

"That's a good girl." His words are kind, but I know they lack any warmth. He's mocking me. He's toying with me, because he knows that this "accident" won't affect him. He'll get off without even so much as a warning. He'll be fine. He'll continue to live while my parents are burned beyond recognition.

It's not fair. Even that young, I know it's not fair. But more than that, I know that I have to stop him. I stop crying, and I look at him like I could kill him. Like I want to hold his neck between my hands until he stops twitching and finally dies.

He sees it too. His mocking expression slowly turns vicious. Like a mind reader, he knows what I'm fantasizing about. He says nothing else. Instead, he whips his hand forward and lunges toward me.

∼

I wake with a start, a hand on my neck. I halfway expect to feel bruises like I've been grabbed, but I know that it was just a dream. Konstantin isn't here. He can't hurt me anymore. Still, it takes a few minutes for my heartrate to catch up with my brain. I lie in bed, trying to regain my composure, my chest heaving as my breathing slows down.

A voice in the dark asks, "Are you okay?"

I turn to see Roman looking at me carefully. For some reason, I'm surprised that he's still in bed with me. I've worked up this silly idea in my head that whenever I go to bed, Roman slips out from under the covers and spends all night planning and plotting and working out. And then, right before I wake up, he climbs back into bed and pretends to be sleeping.

Anything other than that feels foreign. Someone like Roman spending the night with me, sound asleep? It seems too nice to be real.

"Just a bad dream," I reply.

He reaches forward and brushes a hand over my cheek, his fingers stroking my chin. "Do you want to talk about it?"

I struggle with whether or not I do. On one hand, it feels personal. This isn't the first time I've had a dream like this. It doesn't happen often, but when it first started, I remember being inconsolable. I remember waking up in sweats, tears streaming down my face. It took an hour to calm down the first time it happened. Since then, I've gotten used to it. I left that day without any visible scars, but I'm sure my brain is screwed up. I'll probably always have these dreams.

My only hope is that they start to lessen once Konstantin is dead. I'd like to think that the only reason they still pop up is because I'm worried he's out there causing more people this kind of trauma. If I knew he was dead and couldn't hurt anyone else, I think I might be able to rest a bit easier.

"It was a bad dream. About him."

"About who?" Then it hits Roman. "Shit. I'm sorry. I'm here if you want to talk more about it."

This is a side of him I never get to see. When we first met, he didn't want to hear my side of things. He had no clue about Konstantin's actions or what he'd done to my family. And to be frank, I'm sure he didn't care that much either. But spending time with him in this safe house, I'm starting to see him less as the killer devoid of any emotion and more as a victim himself.

Had he never experienced what happened to his parents, he might be different. He might be the security guy that he told me he'd want to be if he weren't in this business. He might actually have a family. He might have the life so many men dream of.

But that was all taken away from him because of what his uncles did. Because of what his uncles almost got away with.

The idea that I might turn out like Roman scares me, not because I'm afraid of him, but because I can't imagine myself being able to pull back as well as he does. He's reserved and alone most of the time. I can't do that. I still have Nana and Madeline and all my friends at Rudy's. I can't just disappear without a trace. I could never do that to any of them.

"We don't have to," Roman says quietly.

"It's not that I don't want to, it's just …"

"It's what?"

"I'm scared, Roman." I struggle to find the words that I want to use. "I'm scared about tomorrow. What if I like watching him die? What if I like seeing him suffer too much? What if I've lost my humanity, like those guys at the diner?"

He stares at me for a long time, just combing his hand through my hair. The action is soothing, but the silence makes me feel anxious. Finally, he says, "You will never be like those men."

"How do you know?"

"Because I won't let you."

I laugh quietly. "You already taught me all the moves I'd need to get away from you. There's no stopping me now."

Roman cracks a smile. "You know what I mean."

I think I do. After our conversation last night, I'm starting to see him as someone that would rather protect people than hurt them. He doesn't want anyone to end up like him. Or I should say, the person he's been for so long, because I don't think he's unable to be saved. I know there's a person in there that just wants to know peace. In a perfect world, I might be able to help him rediscover that man and bring him to the surface once again.

But our future isn't written in stone. I don't even know what's going to happen after tomorrow. Will he keep in contact with me, or is this the last night I'll ever share with him? That thought hurts me more than I ever thought it would. I curl against his larger frame and press my forehead to his chest, breathing in the masculine smell of his body.

He wraps an arm around my lower back and holds me close.

There are times when I wish our circumstances were different. We wouldn't be meeting because I witnessed something I shouldn't have. Instead, we'd have a coffee-shop romance. We'd bump into each other somewhere, decide to grab a cup of coffee, and our story would start from there.

I know that would make everything much less complicated. I could tell Nana who he is without having to lie to her about his career. I could bring him around my friends. We could go on double dates with Madeline. Everything would be different.

But then I remember that if I didn't know about what he did for a living, I wouldn't understand so much about him. I wouldn't get his quirks or understand why he acts the way he does. Try as I might to imagine a world without knowing his dark history and the unspeakable things he's done, I don't see us working out if I didn't know the honest truth about the person that he is.

"You should get some sleep," he says, his words muffled as he talks against my tangle of hair.

"I know."

"We have to be up early tomorrow."

The reminder makes my stomach flutter with anticipation. This is what I've wanted since I was a child. This is the day I've dreamed of, when I can finally make Konstantin pay for everything that he did to me and the countless other people that he's left traumatized in his wake. He's finally going to be stopped.

So why do I feel so nervous?

Is it because I'm not sure where this will leave me and Roman? Possibly. I've never been good with not knowing how things are going to play out. That's why I try to outline as much as I can before I start writing. I don't like drawing blanks. I don't like being out of control of a certain situation, and with Roman, I have no idea what's going to happen ten minutes from now, let alone days.

But I also wonder, what will I be if I'm not vibrating with rage towards Konstantin? I know that he surely hasn't thought about me since the day he was found not guilty of negligence. To him, I must've just been a blip on his map, something to be forgotten about once he beat the charges. But to me? Abram Konstantin is my whole life.

He's the reason I got into true crime. He's the reason I have such a morbid fascination with people that can kill and feel nothing. Every book I checked out from the library that dealt with serial killers and the monsters of society was because of him. Every podcast I scared myself listening to was because of what this man did to my family.

What if I don't know how to be my own person once he's out of the picture? I've practically dedicated my entire life to this man, and once he's out of the picture, I have no clue who or what I'll be. Will everything in my world stop mattering? Will this book I'm writing remain unwritten?

There are too many questions racing through my mind to fall asleep, and Roman does so before I do. Not that I mind. My favorite part of sharing a bed with him is how soft he seems when he's asleep. I tilt my head back and look at his face, now smoothed out and resting. Lightly, I trace the line of his jaw with my fingertips, then brush them over his lips.

Tonight could very well be the last time I ever see him. I want to permanently burn his image into my memory, just in case.

Finally, after I take a slow breath and force myself to stop thinking the world is going to end, I feel my eyelids grow heavy and the thoughts of tomorrow fade away. In a matter of minutes, sleep comes for me, and I embrace it with open arms.

In the morning, I let out a long yawn and reach with my left hand to rub the sleep from my eyes. I get a few inches before my hand is yanked short. Confused, I blink away my dreams and turn to look to my left. What I see doesn't make any sense.

There's a rope around my wrist, tying me to one of the posts on the bed. My other hand is tied the same way, on the opposite post. My feet have been tied as well.

Panic bubbles in my stomach, and I tug at the ropes, fruitlessly trying to loosen them. "Roman!" I scream.

My mind begins to race with all kinds of scenarios. Someone found us and has already killed Roman downstairs. They tied me up, and now they're going to come back and do things to me that I wouldn't wish on my worst enemy. My heart begins to race, and frantically, I jerk my limbs back and forth, hopelessly.

"Roman! Help!"

He appears in the doorway of the bedroom, a somber look on his face. For a minute, I'm relieved that my worst nightmares haven't come true. He's okay. He's not dead.

But then it hits me: he did this.

"You ass," I say, laughing nervously. "Come untie me. This isn't a funny joke."

He looks to the side, clearing his throat. He won't look at me. "No."

"What? Stop being a jerk. Untie me."

"I'm not going to do that," he says, finally looking at me again. The tone of his voice is determined.

"Why not? I have to get ready. It's almost time to grab Konstantin."

"You're not coming with me."

That statement is like a punch to my gut. I feel the wind knocked out of me, and I turn my head to the left, trying to pretend that I didn't just hear him correctly. No, there's no way he would lie to me and lead me on like this. He wouldn't tell me that I could help him, take me to his safe house, and then just leave me here. No, that's not possible.

"This isn't funny," I whisper.

"I'm not joking."

Exploding with anger, I shout, "You fucking asshole, untie me!" I tug at the ropes again, harder, angrier this time. "Goddammit!"

"Stop struggling. You'll only hurt yourself." He slides his hands into his pockets and meets my gaze. "I'll call the police when I'm far enough away. I'll let them know that you're here. They'll come and untie you."

"Don't you fucking dare," I say. "Don't you leave me here."

"Lucy—"

"You never cared about me. You never cared about helping me stop Konstantin. You just wanted to use me. Is that what all this was?" I demand. "Did you just bring me here so I could be your little fuckbuddy until you had to kill him?" I'm crying, screaming, seeing Roman through the red glare of rage and a curtain of tears. This isn't fair, this isn't fair, this isn't fair.

The thought of him using me this way makes my heart break, but I'm too pissed to acknowledge that ache at the moment. Right now, I want to throw him across the room and scream in his face. I want to take all those moves he taught me and ... and ... I don't know. I just know that I'm practically shaking with anger.

"It was never like that."

"Then what was it? Because you told me I could help you. You told me you would give this to me. After everything that bastard did to me and my family, you told me you'd let me see him pay for it."

"And he will," Roman says simply. "But not with you around."

"I wish I'd never met you," I say, tears in my eyes. I try to cover my face by turning into my shoulder, but it's no use.

"Don't say that," he replies. It's the first time I've ever heard him talk to me in any kind of way that sounds vulnerable.

"You're the worst thing that's ever happened to me," I continue. "Nobody ever gave me hope that I could stop him until you came around. You made me think justice really did exist. But then you did this. So fuck you, Roman. Run away like you always do. Tell yourself you're a good person because you don't hurt women. But you and I both know that's a lie."

"It's not."

"You'd never physically hurt a woman," I say, sneering. "But you have no problem making a woman think she actually has a chance. You don't hesitate to fuck a woman knowing you're going to betray her the very next day. No, you don't hit women, Roman, but I think right now, I'd much rather you hit me than do this."

There's a bitter silence hanging in the air, and I want to fill it with the raging scream that's clawing its way up my throat. Venomous, that's what it is. It's poison, and I want to get it out of my system, but somehow, I manage to keep my composure.

For a brief moment, it seems like he's going to change his mind. He'll laugh it off and untie me and we'll go finish the job he swore we'd do. He opens his mouth to speak.

"The police will be here soon."

Without another word, Roman turns and leaves.

Even when he's gone, I don't give up hope just yet. There's a part of me that expects him to go back on this decision. He'll come walking through that door again, only this time, he'll untie me. He'll pull me close and tell me that he's sorry for thinking he could ever do this. And maybe, after he's done groveling, I'll forgive him.

But he doesn't come back.

I hear the sound of the garage door opening, and then a moment later, it closes. After that, silence. There's nothing but the birds chirping and a distant lawn mower humming. Only then, when I realize that he's gone for good, do I let myself fall apart.

The tears come again—hot, fast, and endless.

14

ROMAN

I'm a fucking monster.

I know that. I feel the truth of it deep in my bones. I shouldn't care—I've spent my whole life learning how not to care—and yet, I care more than I ever could have anticipated.

Backing out of the garage, I know I should feel relieved that I don't have to deal with Lucy anymore. I don't have to worry about her safety. I don't have to wonder if she'll turn on me at any moment. I'm free from that responsibility.

I should be happy. I should be jumping for fucking joy.

Instead, I feel like shit.

There hasn't been a single person in almost twenty years that could make me feel the way Lucy did, insulting me like that. I've been called every name under the sun. All that bounced off me. It was nothing, because I didn't care about the people calling me those names. But Lucy telling me she wished she'd never met me?

It gutted me.

It was almost enough for me to untie her. I almost apologized, considered begging for her to not hold it against me. But then I remembered what she said the night before. It was a reminder that even after shooting the man at the diner, she's still not built like me. She's innocent. She's *good*. Every good thing around me dies, so I have to leave her behind.

I grip the steering wheel tightly in my hands, trying not to think about her. She's probably tugging as hard as she can, desperate to get out of those ties. Tying her to the bed felt like I was stabbing her in the back. She looked so peaceful in sleep, not worrying about the shitty world we live in. She looked happy.

And I have to spare her happiness. I have to do this on my own. Involving Lucy in any of my assignments would only ruin her purity. She has so many people depending on her, unlike me. Me? I can disappear for years if I want. Nobody is waiting on me to get home. Nobody cares about me. But Lucy has her grandmother and her friends. She has a life outside of this evil, and the only way I can protect her is by keeping her as far away from Konstantin as I can.

That motherfucker is my responsibility now.

I can't stop thinking about what he did to Lucy's family, and the families that were also destroyed by his negligence. It makes me see red. It makes me want to grab his head between my hands and squeeze it until it pops. He's hurt people worse than I ever could, because he's hurt them while pretending to be a good guy the entire time. He wears the mask of a harmless older man, but deep down, he's as fucked as the rest of us. Maybe even worse.

I'm going to take pleasure in making him suffer.

I don't normally. In most cases, I keep it standard, clean. Pull the trigger, clean up the mess, keep it moving. But Abram Konstantin doesn't deserve a quick death. He doesn't deserve an emotionless kill. What he deserves is something tortuous, something that makes him remember all the people he's fucked over in his miserable life. And I'm more than willing to give him exactly that.

But first, I have to take care of the Lucy situation.

I pull a small phone from my pocket and debate whether or not I should call just yet. I know Lucy, and I know she'd be embarrassed if they found her with puffy eyes and a snotty nose. I also know that I'm not too far from the neighborhood yet, and I don't need anyone pulling me over and connecting me to that house.

I spent all morning cleaning. I got rid of every bit of evidence that tied me to the place. I've spent nearly my entire life disappearing, leaving no trace behind, so it was muscle memory. All the police will find is Lucy tied to the bed and the story she gives them about who I am. They'll spend months trying to find someone just named Roman, but I'll be gone by then. Assume another identity, become a different person.

It's easy.

It just feels wrong.

It tugs at my heart, imagining Lucy looking for me. I don't want her to. I want her to go back to the life she had before she ever met me. Before I ever threatened the perfect, normal world she inhabited. I want her to meet someone and have children with him and have the family she lost before growing up. I want her to grow old and be happy, and I can't give that to her.

That still doesn't make up for the bitterness rolling through my veins. This is why I don't do relationships. Bonds. I don't form connections because they're so easily threatened, and they hurt too much when they've been broken. Friendships, lovers, and anything more are a luxury I don't afford. I don't need them.

A part of me argues that I need Lucy. When I'm with her, I imagine a world where I'm not under Mr. X's thumb. I imagine a world where we're together. In my fantasy, I wake up with her in my arms every morning, and I end every night beside her. She's the first thing I see. The last thought on my mind. She makes me feel like I'm worth something more than a few hundred thousand dollars to whoever wants to cough up the cash.

It's a fantasy, though.

It's a trap.

That's how people make the mistake of falling in love. They let the potential of what could be cloud their judgment, and when they least expect it, everything falls apart. More people will come for Lucy and me the way they did at the diner. More people will die. The less I can involve her in all of that, the better.

This is the way it has to be. I just wish I could've done it without hurting her as much as I did.

After driving for twenty minutes, I pull my phone out again and dial the police. It rings twice, then a woman picks up.

"911, what's your emergency?"

"There's a woman tied to the bed at 9284 South Lilac Drive."

"I'm sorry?"

"She's tied to the bed. She's screaming for help. Please come get her."

The operator starts to ask me to stay on the line, but I end the call after repeating the address. I roll the window down and toss the phone out. In the rear mirror, I see it clatter and break against the concrete.

There.

Now she'll be free. Free for good this time.

After that's taken care of, I decide to head to Lucy's place. The drive is short, and I fill the uncomfortable silence with loud rock music, trying my best to drown out the guilt in the back of my head. I need the distraction, and it helps. When I pull up outside of Lucy's house, I turn the volume down and park a few yards away.

As I'd hoped, there's a car sitting across the street from the house. It's nondescript, easy to miss, and exactly what I'm looking for. I approach the passenger's side and climb in. The man sitting inside looks surprised, but he calms down when he recognizes me.

"Hey," he says, wiping the sleep from his eyes.

"Sleeping on the job?"

"No, I just ... It's been a long morning."

I snort. "You're telling me." I glance back at the house, narrowing my eyes. "Anything happen lately?"

"Nah. The old lady doesn't do much all day. Am I supposed to be looking for something interesting?"

I shake my head. "No. You're just keeping watch."

Dustin is a contact I made a few years ago. He's worked in security before, and is now a cop, so he was the perfect person to hit up a few weeks ago. I knew Lucy would be with me much longer than she told her grandmother, and I didn't want the old lady being home alone in case someone went after her the same way they did with us at the diner.

Dustin was more than happy to take the job when he saw how much I was paying. He let me know that he'd be available most nights, which seemed like a good idea for me. Between hospital visits and running smaller errands, the woman wasn't home during the day much. Having someone watch after her at night put me at ease just a little more.

"Where's the girl?" Dustin asks, glancing at me.

"Where I left her."

He laughs nervously. "What, did you kill her or something?"

I cut my eyes to him, and his laughter stops. He knows about my rules. He knows that's out of the question. I don't even care for jokes about it.

Lucy's words come back to me. She told me she'd rather I hit her than abandon her. That turned my stomach.

"Is she okay? I really don't want to have to tell this old lady that her granddaughter's in danger or something."

I give him another look. "I'd be the one to do that. Besides, she's fine. She's just … pissed at me. That's all."

"That seems to be how it is with you and women. You come back here acting all stoic and shit, and they're mad at you, calling you all kinds of douchebag and prick." He chuckles, shaking his head. Maybe it was a mistake sharing a few personal stories with him years ago. I don't think we're friends, but Dustin and I are as close as two acquaintances can be.

"I'm going for a walk," I say, unlocking the door.

"C'mon, man, you just got here. Stay a while, keep me company. It's lonely watching old women wander around their houses and stare at soap operas reruns all day."

"All the money I'm paying you is more than enough company," I grunt. I climb out and slam the door behind me. I cross the street and head back to my car when I see the front door of Lucy's house open and a small woman appear. She has a large container rolling behind her, and she struggles to get it out of the door.

I've never seen the woman before, but the resemblance is uncanny. She has the same piercing blue eyes, and I imagine that, before it grayed, her hair was the same sunny blonde shade as her granddaughter's. I'm not close enough to see whether she has freckles too, but something tells me that she does.

For a moment, I consider letting her do this on her own. I don't like to be in contact with too many people. The fewer people who can recognize my face, the better. But I feel guilty about what I did to Lucy. This is a way to make up for at least a little of the bad karma I've generated.

"Let me help you with that," I say, hurrying up the steps and taking over for her. She seems surprised that I'm offering but doesn't object.

"That's so kind of you," she says in a honey-sweet voice.

"It's nothing, really. You were struggling."

I drag the recycling bin down to the curb with the trash can, and a thought crosses my mind. Did she also bring that down here by herself? I almost have it in me to wring Dustin's neck. I'm sure he saw her dragging this thing down and did nothing to help. This is what I get for working with cops.

When I finish with the bin, I dust my hands off and look up at her. Just as I thought. She has the exact same freckles as Lucy. Genetics are crazy.

"I've lived here my whole life," she says, "but I've never had anyone offer to take these out for me. My granddaughter usually does it, but I haven't heard from her in a while."

That guilt returns. "I'm sorry to hear about that."

"Oh, don't be," she says, smiling mischievously at me. "She told me she met a nice man that wanted to spend time with her, so I'm not in any rush to have her back. I'm glad she's finally branching out. This is the first man she's ever shown interest in."

My gut twists, and I look away. "Is he?"

"Mhm, yes," she nods. "I just hope I get to see her settle down with a nice man before I go. She's been through so much. She deserves someone that will take care of her and give her the world."

Fuck.

I really need to go. This wasn't supposed to happen. I wasn't supposed to be standing here with Lucy's grandmother, realizing how shitty I've been to her granddaughter. This is what I get for trying to help.

"You must be busy, pardon me," she giggles. She steps forward and gives me a tight hug, surprising me. When she pulls away, she says, "Thank you so much for helping me out, young man. I really do appreciate it."

"Not a problem, ma'am."

I can't help but feel jealous of Lucy. She has a grandmother that wants nothing but the best for her. She has family that cares for her and only wants to see her do well in life. What I wouldn't give for someone to wish for the same for me.

"I hope I see you around," she says, grinning. She brushes a strand of gray hair behind her ear.

"Fingers crossed." I force a little smile and wave, heading back to my car. I don't even want to look back at Dustin because I'm sure he's probably laughing his lazy ass off. People that age only ever want to talk, and it always makes me feel strange. I don't like talking. I'd rather just sit in silence and listen to the world around me.

When I make it to my car, I lean back and close my eyes. This is almost over. Konstantin is almost out of the picture. Soon, I'll be able to put this all behind me. Disappear for a while. Not exist. Maybe I'll change everything about me. Put this in the past where it belongs. And when I come back, probably for another assignment from Mr. X, I'll never make these mistakes again.

I can't.

15

LUCY

I'm such a fucking idiot.

I should've never trusted Roman. This isn't the first time he's changed his mind. It's not even the second time. I should've known that he was going to do something like this, and yet I think this time, it's the worst of all three betrayals. Before, I wasn't head over heels for the man.

I should've listened to that little voice in my head that told me Roman wouldn't be a good idea. For the past three weeks, I let myself be convinced that this would all work out. After waiting my entire life for a moment to stop Konstantin, I thought that maybe this would be the break I needed.

The worst part is, in the most intimate moments with Roman, I forgot why we were working together in the first place. My goal was always to stop Konstantin. And now I won't be there to see it finally happen.

Bitter tears sting my eyes, and I press my face against my shoulder, trying to wipe them. Tied up in this position, it makes my arms ache, but right now, that pain is more manageable than the one in my heart. It feels like that part of me is broken completely.

I trusted Roman with my life, and he did this to me. I should be seeing red. Only, the last thing I'm feeling is rage. Sorrow weighs the heaviest on me, like I've just climbed out of the pool with all my clothes on.

Ten minutes pass, and I feel my muscles groan as I continue to struggle. The rope around my wrists burns just like it did in the bathroom at the motel, and just like then, I know that I probably won't be able to get out. Roman's good at tying knots.

The more I tug at my bindings, the more frantic I grow. I can't stay here. I don't have a story for why I'm here. People will wonder what happened to me, and I won't have any answers. I already told the police at the motel that I knew Roman. They'll wonder why I lied back then if he was actually a threat to me. And if they're still looking into the incident at the diner, they'll eventually figure out that I was the woman on camera that shot a man dead.

No, I can't stay here.

My eyes follow the bed post higher and higher, and that's when I notice that the wood gets thinner at the top. I lift my hand as high as possible, ignoring the screaming strain in my shoulders. When it's at the highest I can get it, I tug towards me. The thin post buckles, but it doesn't break. I take in a slow, controlled breath, and angle myself in a way that lets me put my weight into the next tug. To my relief, the cheap wood snaps off and I can slide the rope free.

"Yes," I whisper, nearly crying again.

I roll my shoulder in circles, wincing at the soreness. The police will be here any minute, and I have to get out of here before that happens. I repeat the same method on my other hand, jerking backwards with more strength than before. It snaps off just the same. Once again there are mild burns on my wrists, but I don't have time to worry about those.

Getting my feet untied is the hard part. I can't lift them high enough to break the posts, so I have to lean forward and undo the knots, my fingers shaking as I work. Finally, I'm free, and I roll off the bed onto my knees. When I stand, my knees are wobbly. I take a second to gain my composure and hurry to the closet.

It's been too long for me to catch up with Roman, but I can at least get the fuck out of this house before anyone shows up. I grab a large empty duffle bag and begin shoving clothes into it, fitting as many as I can inside. When I'm satisfied with how much I've packed, I hurry downstairs in search of my shoes.

I stop in the living room and grab my notepads, stuffing them in the bag as well. Roman can steal Konstantin from me, but I'll be damned if I leave this place without all the words I've written since he brought me here.

Just as I zip up the bag, there's a loud bang behind me. I spin around to find the front door knocked wide open. It bounces off the wall, and a police officer enters the living room, gun drawn. My stomach sinks, and my heart skips a beat.

"Put your hands in the air," he demands.

I drop my bag and raise my hands. "What's going on?"

"We got a call saying there was a woman tied to a bed at this address," he explains. "On your knees, now."

Part of me wants to argue, but his gun remains trained on me. As I get down on the floor, I say, "I was the woman on the bed."

"What?"

"I was tied to the bed earlier. My husband and I have this little game where he'll leave me tied to the bed and run a few errands. It's like ... It's kind of like BDSM?" It's the same excuse I used in the motel, but I'm crossing my fingers he buys it, too. "You can go upstairs and look. I got a call from a friend and had to break out of the ties."

"You stay here," he says, and he climbs the stairs, disappearing for a moment. Something inside of me says to make a break for it. I can get away and hop the fence out back before he comes downstairs again.

What if he has backup, though? What if there's someone waiting outside, prepared to shoot the very second they see a runner? Swallowing my flight response, I stay put on the ground, hands in the air. A moment later, the officer comes downstairs again.

"I'm confused about the call," he says.

"It was probably a neighbor. We live around a bunch of nosy older folks. You know how they can get," I say, forcing a laugh. "They've been weirded out by us since we moved in."

"Ah," he says hesitantly. Slowly, he puts his gun in the holster. "All right, well, I'm sorry for the interruption this morning. My recommendation is that you cover those windows before you and your husband engage in any more, uh… 'fun'."

"Oh don't worry," I laugh. "We'll make sure to buy blackout curtains before we do anything like that again."

"I'll let you get back to your day, ma'am. And sorry again for bothering you." The officer heads to the door, and I stand up, following after him.

Instead of stepping outside, though, he closes the door and locks it.

"What—"

Before I can finish my sentence, he lunges at me, grabbing for my throat. I stumble backwards and nearly trip, sidestepping his second lunge before taking off in the other direction.

"Get back here," he growls. He chases after me, managing to grab my foot as I climb the stairs. I lurch forward and slam my chin on the stair ahead of me. My head spins and I bite down hard on my tongue.

The police officer jerks backwards, dragging me down, but I grab the banister and turn over. My kick comes quick and fast, directly in the center of his face. Roaring in pain, he stumbles backwards and falls flat on his ass.

My head throbs painfully but I ignore the ache and push myself up, running upstairs. I slam the door shut and lock it, frantically looking for something to barricade it with. I run to the armoire, my muscles screaming as I slam my shoulder into it, pushing it closer to the door. Just as I approach, the door explodes open again.

The officer manages to grab me this time, and he spins me around, slamming me against the wall. The wind is knocked out of me, and I feel dizzy, my knees wobbling. When my vision stabilizes, he's glaring at me, almost as if he's taking pleasure in all of this.

He reaches for my throat, and that's when Roman's training kicks in. I move faster than him, grabbing his pinkie and thumb as his hand gets closer. He's caught off guard, and I pull backwards, trying my hardest to break his fingers. The officer recoils, cradling his hand.

"You little bitch!" he bellows.

"Fuck you!" I aim between his legs and kick him as hard as I can. Like a sack of flour, he hits the ground with a thud, groaning loudly. I don't give him a moment to recover. I kick him two more times, one in the stomach and the second in the face. When I try for a third, he grabs my leg, yanking me forward. I nearly trip as I break free, but manage to keep my balance.

Slowly, he positions himself between me and the door, and I know that the only place left to go is the bathroom. I run inside and lock the door, pressing my back to it.

"Fuck," I whisper, panic creeping over me. There's nowhere else to run. We're on the second floor, and I can fit through the window, but the fall ... I don't know if I'd be able to land without possibly hurting myself.

There's no time to reconsider other options, though.

I tear the shower curtain out of the way and stand on my toes, tugging the sliding window to the side. There's just enough room for me to get out. Standing on one edge of the tub, I hop up and begin to shimmy through when I hear the impossibly loud *bang* of a gun.

The doorknob explodes. He must have shot it from the other side. With nothing to hold it in place, the splintered door swings inwards, hanging awkwardly on its hinges. I try to quickly scramble out the window, but I don't get far before I feel hands around my waist. The cop pulls me back hard and the world spins. For a moment, I'm horizonal, but gravity catches up with me. The last thing I see is the edge of the tub speeding directly towards me before everything goes black.

༺

My vision is foggy, and I groan softly, trying to reach up to rub my hand. I immediately realize that my hands are tied behind my back. Really starting to get fucking sick of that.

"Yeah, she's awake now," I hear the officer—obviously not a real cop—say. He glances at me in the rearview mirror, a phone pressed to his ear.

"Who are you?" I demand. "Where are you taking me?"

"I'll call you back, boss," he says. He ends the call and tosses his phone into the passenger's seat. "Settle down."

I tug at the ties around my wrists, but it's useless. There aren't any bedposts I can break to escape. These knots are serious. "Please," I start.

"None of that," he says. "You nearly had me back at the house, I'll give you that. That's exactly why you can stop all of that begging. Maybe I would've been more lenient if you hadn't tried to break my fucking fingers."

"Maybe I wouldn't have tried to break your fucking fingers if you hadn't tried to grab me by my fucking throat," I spit back. "Who was that on the phone? Who's your boss?"

"You sure are a nosy little bitch, aren't you? I would've expected just a little more begging," he chuckles.

"This isn't my first time some asshole's kidnapped me," I mutter.

"You are a confusing one, Lucy. Must be that's why Konstantin wants you so badly."

My heart stops, and for a moment, I'm sure I've heard him wrong. But when I look in the mirror and meet his amused gaze, I know I heard exactly what he said.

"He's been very interested in you. Normally, I wouldn't involve myself with the Bratva, but that money sure is nice. My buddy, the guy your little boyfriend hired to watch after your grandmother, is still jealous that I got the fun job of grabbing you."

"Don't you fucking hurt her," I snarl, briefly surprised that Roman hired someone to watch my grandma and didn't let me know. I want to be grateful for that, but I'm far too angry. And now, add worry for Nana to that list.

"Relax," he sighs. "Konstantin doesn't want anything to do with the old bitch. He's only interested in you. Only has eyes for you, he said. What's so special about you, Lucy?"

"We have a history."

"Ex-girlfriend or something?"

"Something," I mutter. I'd rather not go into detail with this son of a bitch. Not when I'm caught in a trap I can't escape from. Konstantin has me. He has eyes on Nana. He probably even knows where Roman is.

We were so stupid to think that we'd do this without setting off some kind of alerts. Someone as powerful as Konstantin must have people all over the city keeping an ear to the street, listening for possible threats. And with the two of us preparing to take out one of the Bratva's biggest members, someone was bound to find out.

Shit.

I really thought that after all these years, I'd finally have the revenge I deserve, but it could never be this easy. And now it's all going to be over soon. Konstantin will probably kill me, and when he's done with that, he'll go after Roman, then Nana. No one will be left to stop him. I feel tears sting my eyes, but I squeeze them shut.

I'm not going to go out like that, sobbing in the back seat of some shady police officer's cruiser. No, I have to think. I have to plan. If Konstantin wants to kill me, he's going to have to break a sweat. He won't take me out as easily as he did Mom and Dad.

Fuck that.

16

ROMAN

A sense of calm takes over as I drive. During times like these, I find myself zoning out. It's a break from the endless plotting I do on a daily basis. I don't feel stress. I don't feel anything. Just the lack of thought. The emptiness. I don't need to worry anymore. Lucy is out of the picture. She'll hate me, but she'll be safe. All that's left to do is kill Konstantin and put this shit behind me.

I take the scenic route, looking at the city. This place is a lot different than home. Back in Russia, we lived far away from the main town. We didn't have to deal with traffic, shouting civilians, or homeless people. We had all of that, of course, but it wasn't so in your face. Here, this place is a shit show. It's a nightmare.

I've made the city a home, but if everything burned down and I had to relocate, I'd be fine with that. Nobody cares where I go. Nobody except Mr. X, that is. I doubt he'd be pleased if I suddenly moved away. Not that I would run the risk. He holds what I did to my uncles over my head all the time. Part of me fantasizes about offing him.

I could get rid of him and solve the problem of being his professional bitch. Without him around, I wouldn't have to answer to anyone or be exclusively tied to just one man. I know people all over this city want to work with me.

I've been approached by everyone and their dog. It doesn't matter how or why, but people know about my reputation. They run when they see me coming, whether it be away from me or towards me. But when they find out who I work for, they always show their disappointment.

I've had people offer seven figures for an assignment before, and I've had to turn it down. That kind of money could change a person's life, and here I am, spitting in their face. Telling them their money's no good. That I don't want to be set for life. It's fucking ridiculous.

Maybe I'll change my rates once I get done with Konstantin. I'll head back to Mr. X's spot and tell him the prices have gone up. After all, I've have just taken out a major annoyance for him. I'll have some leverage. Whether he sees it that way is another story entirely.

I glance at the fuel light and realize I need to fill up soon.

The detour is quick, and I pull into a gas station not too far away. I climb out and make my way up front to the cashier. Slapping a fifty on the table, I give him the number of the pump station I'm at, then go looking for something to eat. Nothing here is appetizing, but I settle for a bag of chips and a hot dog.

The teenage cashier scans my items, his flitting gaze falling on me a few times. He looks intimidated. Good. When I pay for the food, I grab it before he can ask if I'd like a bag or not. I stop outside by the gas pump to take a bite of the hot dog. It's nowhere near as satisfying as I want it to be, but it'll work.

I start to fill up the tank when I get a call. I dig my phone out of my pocket. The phone number is unfamiliar. No one but Mr. X and a few close acquaintants, like the one I hired to watch Lucy's grandmother, have this number.

"Hello?" I answer cautiously.

"Hello, Roman."

"Who the fuck is this?"

"You know who it is. The man you've been spending the last few weeks following."

There's no way in hell Abram Konstantin got my phone number. I don't even know how that would be possible. "What are you talking about?"

"Cut the shit," he says. "You know what I'm talking about. Mr. X sent you to kill me. I'm not particularly interested in seeing that play out. That's why I have your girlfriend."

"What?"

"Lucy Walker. Right now, she's being transported to my warehouse. She's going to be fun to have around while we wait for you. You'd better hurry up and get to me before I get bored of her. When I get bored of my toys, I have a tendency to dispose of them."

"Don't you fucking touch her, you bastard," I growl.

Konstantin only laughs. "I'll do as I please with the girl. You just worry about getting here before I finish playing with her. You'll have the address soon."

Without another word, the line goes dead. Feeling sick to my stomach, I throw the hot dog to the ground and hurry back into the car, turning on the ignition. My phone buzzes, and when I check it, I see that Konstantin has texted me the address of his location. It's far out of town, but I can be there soon.

I thought she'd be safe. That's why I tied Lucy to the bed and left her there. She was supposed to be rescued by the police and taken home. Her involvement in all of this was supposed to be minimal. She'd forget about me years down the road. Her life would go back to normal. But I've dragged her deeper. I've gotten her kidnapped. She was a sitting fucking duck because of me.

"Fuck!" I shout, slamming my fist down on the steering wheel.

It takes a few moments for me to regain my composure. I want to lash out. I want to break something. Smash it to pieces. But I can't. I have to get to her. I have to rescue her from this shit that I put her in in the first place.

I put my car in drive and speed out of the gas station, nearly clipping a car on my way out. My brain is on autopilot again, only it's different this time. It's not because I'm driving aimlessly. I now have a mission. What I planned to do later in the day has been moved forward. Konstantin isn't going to die late at night. He'll be dead by seven o'clock.

I try not to speed. The last thing I need to deal with is a bunch of fucking cops breathing down my neck, asking why I was driving so fast. It's enraging, this traffic, but I have to keep calm. I consider taking a shortcut that will get me to the warehouse faster, but I have to head back to my storage unit first. I can't go in there without weapons.

My father pops into my mind.

I haven't thought of the old coot's anecdotes in a while, but one comes back to me as I swerve through lanes, trying to get around people taking their sweet precious time.

He told me the story of how he met my mother when I was younger. I must've just started going through puberty because it was during 'the talk.'

But the story about Mom was different.

He stopped the uncomfortable jokes and looked me in the eye like a man. Like he wasn't talking to his kid. Just another adult.

He told me that he met her at a wedding for one of his friends. He wasn't interested in going, but she begged him to be there. The thing was a disaster. Everyone was late, it rained, and some drunk uncle of his friend's fell face-first into her wedding cake before they could even cut it. Everything went wrong until the moment he met Mom.

She was the one good thing about the party. Soaked through in her soft pink dress, she looked so uncomfortable that Dad almost didn't talk to her. He didn't want to disturb her when she was already having such a shit day.

But when he did go over to her, she seemed to brighten up. She wanted to know who he was and how he was connected to the family. They spent the rest of the night talking, and for the following days of the wedding celebration, they were attached at the hip.

They started as friends.

They were close, but he didn't want to do anything to fuck it up. He wanted to take his time. As he put it, he was a dog at that time. He had no problems sleeping around. In fact, he's probably where I got it from. He and Mom never slept together. For the longest time, they were just friends. They had inside jokes. They had secret handshakes. It was all so sweet that I remember groaning as a kid when he told me about it.

It took him a while to get to the point, but he eventually reached it.

He looked me in my eyes and told me that when I grew up and loved someone, I would have to protect her no matter what. It was my job to keep her safe. When it came to Mom, he would do anything. He would move mountains. He'd kill anyone that ever caused her harm. And I believed him. My dad was tough as nails, but he got soft every time he talked to Mom. The fact that he would do anything to keep her safe was the proof he needed. He realized that, and he married her as soon as he could. He couldn't run the risk of her finding someone better than his sorry ass.

After they got married, they had me.

I remember thinking his story was stupid. Girls didn't interest me. No,

I was focused on school and hunting. Still too young, just barely learning what hormones could do to a boy, I didn't get it.

I do now.

Driving through the streets, weaving in and out of traffic, I know what Dad meant.

I should've never let it get this far, but the truth is that I love Lucy. I fucking love her. She didn't ask for any of this. She didn't ask for me to kidnap her and take her to a hotel. She didn't ask to be involved like this, where her life was on the line. I have to save her, and I don't care how many motherfuckers I have to take down to do that.

When I finally make it to the storage unit, I drive in through the back, trying to reduce the amount of people that see me. Luckily, the unit is one of the furthest in the back, out of the line of sight of cameras. I park and climb out of the car.

I lift up the door and then quickly close it behind me after I'm inside. There's a small light in the unit, and I use that to start stocking up. I know that I won't have time for reloading, so I have to bring more guns than I normally might.

This is going to be a suicide mission, I can already tell that much. It doesn't matter, so long as Lucy comes out okay.

I lift up my shirt and slide a pistol into the holster I have underneath the shirt. The bigger guns and knives will have to go inside the car. I grab a blanket from the top of a few boxes and wrap two assault rifles inside.

Quickly, I hurry to my car and set the guns down in the back. I look over my shoulder, careful of anyone watching. The coast is clear so far.

When I return to the storage unit, I move on to explosives. I don't have many, but there are a few grenades. Some of them are meant for stunning people, and I make sure to pack plenty of those. I sling the backpack over my shoulder, and before I leave, I grab my shotgun. I don't know if I'll need it or how I'll carry it with everything else, but just in case.

Konstantin is going to have the place crawling with goons. People that have nothing to live for and figure it's worth the risk to kill me. They're all probably slaves to the money the same way I was. Those people, ones with nothing to lose, are the ones I have to worry about the most.

When I get back to the car, I put everything in the back seat and start to pull away. Just then, a security guard walks around the corner and approaches my car.

"Fuck," I mutter. I roll my window down when he's close enough.

"How ya doing tonight, sir?" he asks me. I see him glance into my back seat and tilt my body, trying to block his view.

"Not too bad, and yourself?"

"Can't complain. It's gonna be a long night."

"I bet," I say. I force a fake laugh, but he doesn't return it. "Is there anything I can help you with?"

"Just doing my rounds. Haven't had too many people out here this late. We're actually closed for the night."

"Oh really?" I look at the watch on his hand. It's half past six. "What time do you normally close?"

"Six on weekdays," he says.

"Ah. I had no idea. I'm so sorry about bothering you. The gate out back was opened so I just assumed."

"Yup, saw you on the cameras and figured I'd come out here and talk to you." He looks around, then down back at me. "What do you have back there?"

"Hm?"

"In your back seat, sir. You seem awfully nervous."

I look back at the blanket and say, "Just some old antiques for a friend's grandmother. She said she collects them, and I figure it'd get me some bonus points if I do something nice for her grandma. I hear women like when you're nice. Makes it easier to get in their pants."

The security guard gives a real chuckle, and I try not to roll my eyes. Of course his dumb ass would find that terrible joke funny. Idiot.

"Ain't that the truth? Listen, let me get out of your hair then. Don't wanna hold you up from getting some ass."

"You're a good man," I say, nodding at him.

When he starts to walk away, I slide my hand off the holster of my gun. He doesn't realize how close he was to being shot right. I don't have time for this shit. Luckily for him, he made the right decision to mind his own fucking business.

I wait until he walks back to the main office before I start my car again. I head to the back exit and turn left onto the street.

As I drive, I take a moment to collect myself and get my head in the game. This is going to be like the diner again. It's been a minute since I've done anything this messy, and messy it's going to be. I predict a lot of bodies. A lot of people dying for this son of a bitch. I almost feel sorry for them, but every time I do, I imagine Lucy.

She must be terrified. After all these years, Konstantin has her. He could kill her just as easily as he killed her family. I have to stop him for good. There's no way I'm going to let him touch a hair on her head.

Over my dead fucking body.

A sense of calm starts to settle over me. The closer I get to the address in the text, the more resolved I become. This is finally happening.

Maybe it's not what I planned, but the plan is still in motion. It's simple. Kill Abram Konstantin. Rescue Lucy. Get out with as few scratches as possible.

I grip the steering wheel harder and feel my heart rate start to slow. Every second I drive, I get closer to Konstantin's warehouse. Closer to putting an end to this once and for all. There's no more time left.

It all ends tonight.

17

LUCY

The ride is bumpy, and I lay back, staring at the roof of the car, waiting for the inevitable. It feels like we're starting to get closer to wherever it is this man is taking me. I thought maybe, by some kind of miracle, Roman would manage to intercept us, but he hasn't come. I don't know if he ever will.

That thought is a twisting knife in my heart. It's stupid, but I really did have feelings for him. I thought that after all of this was done, something might actually happen between us. I should be concerned with myself and with the fact that the man I've dedicated my entire life to has finally beaten me, but it's almost like... I don't care at all.

I can only think about Roman and Nana.

Who's going to take care of her if I die? Who's going to be there for her when she needs help getting in and out of the shower? Or pick up groceries? Or even just talk to her whenever she's feeling lonely? I can't imagine her living on her own, mourning the death of her last living relative. It's too painful.

All I can do is plan for how I'm going to get out of this. Konstantin has already taken so much from me. My parents. My childhood. He doesn't get to take anything else. No fucking way.

Up front, the officer says, "You're awfully quiet back there."

I don't say a word. Fuck him. He only wants to goad me into a reaction.

"C'mon, what happened to that fighting spirit, Lucy?" he chuckles.

For the rest of the ride I fantasize about killing him.

If I could manage to get my arms out of these ties, I'd jump up front and jerk the steering wheel to the left, throwing us into oncoming traffic on the highway. It would be an instant death for him, but I just might make it out alive.

If my hands were tied in front of me, I'd throw my hands over his head and use the ropes to choke him to death. That might also end in a car accident, but my probability of surviving would be much higher.

I could maybe even grab his gun and put a bullet in his head before he realized it. Quick, easy. It wouldn't be my first time shooting a man dead. It's almost scary to think that I'm the same person. Three weeks ago, the sight of the man I shot left me traumatized. Now, if I could manage to get his gun off him and empty the clip into his back, I'd be proud. I don't know who I've become.

The officer begins to slow down, and I feel my stomach sink. We're here. Time's up.

He parks and climbs out of the vehicle, slamming the door shut behind him. For a long time, nothing happens. I lie waiting, praying for some kind of miracle. Then the back door opens and a man's shadow fall over me.

"Come on," he says, reaching in. I struggle the entire time, fighting him as he tries to pull me out of the car. I even manage to roll around and throw a kick at him, only he's faster than me. He catches my foot and tugs hard, yanking me onto the pavement.

"Get the fuck up," he mutters, grabbing my shoulders. My head is slightly spinning, but I manage to stand upright.

"Where are we?"

"This is where Konstantin does all his business," he replies.

There isn't anything around for miles besides rows and rows of what look to be abandoned warehouses. I've never been to this part of town, but clearly nothing good ever happens down here. I can imagine all kinds of horrible things that Konstantin has done out here. It's secluded, and something tells me if I tried to scream for help, nobody would be able to hear me. We're all alone out here.

"Let's go," he says, pushing me forward. I take an uneasy step, but I don't have time to adjust before he gets sick of me and starts dragging me.

The warehouse inside is bustling with people, and all eyes fall on me when we enter. Most seem to look away or head back to work when they see me, but a few stop and watch, seemingly amused. Long tables full of weapons are set out, and men of all ages and races work, counting money, packing away bricks of white powder into backpacks. Konstantin is worse than I ever thought possible.

The officer pulls his phone from his pocket and makes a quick call. "We're down here."

I could make a break for it. I'm faster than this guy is, and he wouldn't see it coming. I could maybe get a few seconds of a head start. But where would I go? There's nobody around to help. I'd be running for miles, and he has a car. He'd be able to catch me without even breaking a sweat.

The officer's head tilts back, and I follow his gaze. Upstairs, there's an office with a massive window. Everyone else in this warehouse is dressed casually, but the man that I catch a glimpse of up there seems to be dressed to the nines. He opens the door to the office and crosses the catwalk down to the stairs.

As he approaches, I get a better look at him. I know him immediately. He looks so different in person, but exactly the same. Piercing brown eyes that look dark enough to be jet black. A large, straight nose. Facial hair that's perfectly trimmed. Even his suit is tailored to perfection, his jacket and the top three buttons on his white dress shirt unbuttoned stylishly.

"Well look who it is," he says. His voice is like silk, but I know what he's really about. I know the kind of man he is.

I don't reply. I glare at him instead.

"She's not so talkative," the officer smirks.

"That's okay," Konstantin says. He steps closer and tilts my head up by my chin. "We'll get her to talk soon enough."

I jerk my head to the side, shivers running through me. If I thought I could get away with it, I'd take a bite out of him.

"Take her up to one of the back rooms," he says. And just like that, he turns his attention to something else. Something more important.

I fantasize about rushing him. In some sick way, I want his attention again. I deserve his attention, after everything he did to my family. But instead, he crosses the room to talk to others, tossing me aside like I don't matter.

The officer drags me through the building, leading me through corridor after corridor. This place is huge; far bigger than it looks on the outside. Finally, he shoves me into a room and I hear him lock the door behind him.

There's not much in here. A dusty table with a chair on either side of it. A few boxes. In the corner, a pile of rags and clothes that look like they've been there for years. And on one side of the wall, something brown and crusty looks caked onto the cement. I can only imagine what that is.

I take a seat on the floor, bringing my knees up to my chest and pressing my forehead against them.

A few minutes pass and the door opens again, only this time it isn't the officer or another one of Konstantin's goons.

It's him.

"You've certainly grown up, Lucy," he says, chuckling. "I can't remember the last time I saw you. Must've been more than fifteen years ago, yes?"

"Yes."

"Normally, I'd become reacquainted on better terms, but I've heard about what you and your little boyfriend have been planning." He says it like a schoolteacher, with an air of superiority, as if he's talking to a child.

"I don't know what you're talking about."

"No?" He tilts his head and smiles humorlessly. "I don't know whether I should feel insulted or honored. Honored because I ended up on both Roman's and your hitlist. Insulted that either of you thought you could touch me."

He crosses the room and takes a seat at the table. "Did you really think you were going to get away with this, Lucy? Be honest."

I swallow down the rage and anger at his condescension. "I thought maybe I'd have a little bit of your luck and get away with murder, yes."

He nods slowly. "So, this is about what I think it is."

"If you think it's about you killing my parents, then ding, ding, ding." The bitterness drips from my words. I can't hold it back like my rage. It's already taking every last bit of control not to lose my entire fucking mind.

"You're going to have to remind me. Who were they again?"

His brevity is a slap in the face. He knows who they are. He has to remember. He just wants to make me say it, to pretend like they didn't matter to him in the slightest. "Roger and Evelyn Walker."

"Ahh," he chuckles, leaning back in his chair. "I remember the Walkers now. They were the first case I ever beat. You know, I thought it would be harder to get out of that scot-free. I guess I'm just lucky you weren't in the house. A dead kid on my hands would've been a nightmare. Thankfully, it was just your mommy and daddy that died."

He's rubbing salt in every wound I have, trying to get under my skin. He wants this to hurt more than it already does. He wants me to suffer before he finally decides to kill me. I refuse to give him any kind of outburst.

"I used to think you were my boogeyman," I say calmly.

"Am I not?"

"No." I let out a small laugh. "No, you're not as scary as I imagined. You were scarier in my nightmares. Downright terrifying. But right now, you're just a pathetic psychopath in an ugly suit. You're a coward that has everyone else do his work for him. The people I really should've been afraid of are your lawyers and lackeys. They're the ones that do all the important work."

My words dig at him. I can see that perfect blasé exterior of his crack for just a second, and I soak up every drop of his offense. Fuck him. Fuck his stupid, smarmy face. He knows my weakness, but now I know his. His insecurity.

"Are you going to have one of your little henchmen kill me, Abram?" He seems surprised that I would call him by his first name. "I've spent my entire life planning how I'd kill you, and I'd be terribly insulted if you passed the job off to someone else. Are you too much of a pussy to actually get your hands dirty?"

Konstantin stands up and stalks towards me, grabbing me by the chin. I feel my heart twist, but I can only laugh in his face. "You really think I'd kill you, Lucy?" he asks. He brushes a strand of hair from my face and drags his fingertip down my jawline, tracing it.

"Isn't that why you brought me here?"

"No, no, sweet girl," he purrs. "I brought you here so that I could get Roman. I don't have any plans for your death. You're much more useful to me..." he trails off for a moment as he looks up and down my body, drinking in my curves and my exposed skin with greedy eyes, before he finishes: "...alive."

I shudder. "What?"

"You look shocked to hear that," he grins. "He's on his way right now. All I had to do was tell him where you were and he came running. I'm sure he'll be here any minute now. And when he does arrive, I'll bring him in here and let you watch as I slit his throat. You'll get a front-row seat. Right in the splash zone."

The mental image makes my blood run cold.

"Fuck you." I haul back and spit in his face.

He recoils and pulls a handkerchief from his pocket. With a quick swipe, he cleans his cheek. "Keep fighting me," he says in a low, controlled voice. "It'll only make it that more fun when I make you mine. You'll wish I'd slit your throat too."

He leaves without another word, slamming the door behind him. The second he's gone, I press my head against my knees. This is worse than I ever imagined. I was stupid enough to think a man like Konstantin would simply kill me and not keep me around for more sadistic purposes. He would never give me a way out like that.

The fight in me almost burns out, but I can't give up.

I wipe my face on my knees and force myself to stand up. There has to be some way out of here. Something I can use to protect myself. I look around the room, desperate for a solution to this problem. In the corner with all the boxes, I start looking around, twisting my arms at an odd angle so I can open them.

The first few don't provide anything useful, but in the fourth one, I find a box knife. My heart races, and I snatch it up.

"Yes," I whisper, nearly crying again. Quickly, I slide up the blade in the tool and put it against the plastic binding around my wrists. My hands cramp as I drag the knife up and down, but I can feel it start to cut through the plastic.

Footsteps approach.

In a panic, I close the blade and hurry back to where I was sitting. I press my face to my knees again, just like Konstantin last saw me. A moment later, the door opens, and he enters the room again.

"Back so soon?" I ask bitterly.

"Do you really think I'm that much of an idiot, Lucy?"

"What?"

He approaches slowly, leisurely, and puts his hand out in front of me. I stare at it, swallowing hard. If I play stupid, maybe he'll leave me alone.

"I can't exactly give you a high five right now," I mutter.

His amused expression fades away, replaced with a stone-cold glare. "Give me the fucking knife, Lucy."

"I ..." How could he possibly know?

"Now." Reluctantly, I drop the knife. I know there's no point in trying to stab him. That'll just get me killed even faster. Konstantin bends down and grabs it, putting it in his pocket. "Did you really think you were going to get away that easily?" he asks, once again on the verge of laughing.

He turns and points to the top corner of the room. There, I see a small red light. "That's a camera," he explains. "I'm impressed, Lucy. I thought you'd given up all hope, but then that annoying fighting spirit came back again. I'm going to enjoy squashing that out."

Konstantin squats down and grabs me by the chin again, forcing me to look at him. "Get off me," I growl.

"But this is so much fun, no? You'll always be the prey, little mouse. I'll always be the cat. You had years to move on and couldn't. I'll always be chasing you, even in your memories. Even in your dreams."

The worst part is that he's right. Even when I was younger, he was always the one thing that haunted me. The one memory that chased me everywhere I went. For a moment there, working with Roman, I fooled myself into thinking that we were the cat, but I now see clearly. That role will always be Konstantin's.

He pats my cheek softly and traces his fingers over my lips. "Don't look so sad, Lucy. We'll have so much fun once I finish with Roman." He stands, adjusts his suit jacket, and heads to the door.

This time when I'm alone, I don't stop crying.

18

ROMAN

The closer I get, the stiller the night feels. It's eerie, like all the animals know I'm coming. Like they've run for cover before anyone else. I turn off my headlights as I approach, slowing the car to a creep. There are all kinds of vehicles parked outside. This place is busy.

Keeping as quiet as I can, I park the car dozens of yards away from anyone else, behind a collection of trees. I reach into the back and grab an assault rifle. When I step out, I'm careful not to slam the door. I sling the gun over my arm with the strap and approach the warehouse.

Three men are outside, two talking while the other smokes. I weigh my options. It's probably best to go for stealth, at least right now. If I go in guns blazing, they'll have time to prepare themselves. I glance at a beer bottle lying on the ground.

Scooping it up, I throw it a few feet away, hard enough to shatter. That gets their attention immediately.

"What the fuck was that?" the one of them in a hat asks.

The one with the shaggy beard shrugs. "No clue."

"Go look, dumbass."

"Why can't you look?" Beard asks, insulted.

"Because I told you to. Now go fucking look."

Muttering angrily to himself, Beard marches down to the corner of the wall. He barely registers the shattered glass before I grab him by the throat and spin him around, slamming him into the wall. The wind is knocked out of him and he gasps, unable to yell for help.

I pull a silenced pistol from beneath my shirt and place the barrel in his mouth, firing once. He slumps instantly. I drag him further away from this side of the building, around to the back. It's less visible there. Less of a chance someone might find him and alert the others.

Just as I make it back, someone turns the corner. The one with the cap on.

"What the fuck?" he says suddenly. He glances at the blood on the wall and makes a move for his gun. Lightning quick, I grab his wrist and twist hard, snapping it easily. His lips open and he starts to scream when I cup his mouth with one hand and grab the back of his head with the other. I tug his face towards my knee. There's a sick crunch. Before he has another chance to call for help, I wrap my arm around his neck and pull him close to me, squeezing the breath from his neck. He struggles, writhing and squirming, but the trauma to his nose and wrist are too much. We stand like that for much longer than I'd like. I only let him go when he's fully dead.

I grab him and drag him back to where I left Beard. When I return for the other, I don't see him anywhere. Maybe he went back inside after he finished his smoke. I hurry across the parking lot, ducking behind cars. Now directly across from the massive doors, I can see everyone inside the warehouse. There have to be at least ten of them, each doing something different.

Some of them cut and package coke. Others are lining guns up on the table. Konstantin really has the crime boss thing down pat. I grimace.

This isn't going to be easy at all. If anything, it'll take time to lure them out one by one. The quickest way would be to—

A bullet hole appears right next to the car, inches from my head. I spin around and draw my pistol to see the third man standing behind me. Before he can get another shot off, I fire two bullets into his chest and one through his head. He stumbles forward, firing once more. It's way off.

A second later, he collapses.

My heart pounds in my ears. He could've ended me right fucking there. It takes a few seconds for me to catch my breath. When I turn around, my stomach sinks. They heard the gunshots, obviously.

"What the hell is going on out there?"

"I don't know, but some shit is going down."

"Get out there and *look*!"

They come pouring out of the building like a tiny militia, guns drawn.

"Fuck," I mutter. I slip the pistol back into my holster and grab the rifle, steadying it in my hands. It's now or never. I remind myself what has to happen. No matter what, I have to stop Konstantin and get Lucy away from him. Nothing else matters besides those two things.

I pop up from behind the car and aim for the man closest to me. Five, six, seven shots land in him, from his hips and legs to his chest and shoulders. He screams and falls backwards.

Three of them turn their guns and I duck behind the car just as they fire. The clanking of bullets on metal echoes in my head. I dodge and move behind another car, breathing hard. When I stand again, I get another round of shots off, hitting two of them.

"Fuck!" one shouts. He raises his gun and shoots, just barely missing.

"Kill the motherfucker. Get him!"

They duck behind cars as well, realizing that I'm not fucking around. It's a game, a dance. I move behind their cars, peeking out to get a look at where they all are. One steps too far out from behind an SUV and I put two bullets into his knee.

"Shit!" he cries, falling forward. I empty the rest of the clip into him, watching as he dies. Then I duck down and toss the gun to the side. Should've brought two.

Out of the corner of my eye, in the reflection of the side mirror of the car I'm hiding behind, I see a man rushing towards me with a knife. I roll out of the way and grab the hand with the knife, twisting it until he lets go.

I manage to catch it with my other hand just as his punch connects with my head. The world tilts for a second, but I blink rapidly, trying to regain my composure. His second punch hits just as hard.

I can't see where he is, but I can feel him. I throw all my weight into him, pinning his body between me and the car. He tries for another punch but I twist out of the way, bringing the knife down into his chest over and over again. I don't stop until my hands are covered in his blood and his body goes limp.

My jaw aches from gritting my teeth.

I'm fucking sick of this.

I pull the backpack around and grab two of the flash grenades. I don't know how many men are left, but two are near the first few cars between me and the warehouse doors. I tear the pins from both grenades and hold them for a second. When the time is right, I roll them under the cars and turn to cover my ears.

There's a deafening bang and I hear the guys cry out in pain.

Adrenaline kicks in. They stand, coughing and blindly fumbling, and that's when I rush in. With just the knife and the gun, I take them down, slicing and shooting, like an out-of-body experience.

They're dead within seconds.

The night is quiet. I know that's not everyone, but it feels as silent as it did when I first arrived. Cautiously, I grab one of the shotguns off a dead man and creep to the door. I toss another flash grenade into the room. It explodes, but no one cries out or begins stumbling around. The first floor must be cleared entirely. Gun drawn, I inch through the warehouse on high alert.

I'm expecting someone to pop out at any moment. My finger hovers over the shotgun's trigger, just begging to pull. I start for the stairs when I hear footsteps approaching me from behind. I swing the gun around to shoot and she catches it, aiming it to the sky just as I fire.

Her leg comes out of nowhere, slamming against my exposed side. I stumble to my left but manage to grab hold of the leg, spinning her around and knocking her off balance. She tumbles to the floor in a heap.

Shit.

I don't know why I didn't expect a few women to work for him. Everything in me says that I should stick to my rules. I don't kill women. I don't hurt women. But she brushes her dark black hair from her face and glares up at me with the look of murder in her eyes and I know that she's not going to go down without a fight.

She throws herself from the floor into me, knocking me up against the wall. I see something glint off the light before she arcs her arm down. I dodge the blade just before it sinks into the drywall behind me.

Her scream is feral, and she rips the knife from the wall, preparing for another stab at me. Before she can bring the knife down again, I press the shotgun in my other hand up under her chin and pull the trigger.

The noise is deafening, and I fall to one knee, breathless, ears ringing. Fuck. *Fuck.*

I have to remind myself why I did it. I have to imagine saving Lucy, otherwise I might lose my shit right here on the warehouse floor. There's an exception to every rule. Nobody is safe as long as Lucy is in danger. Gathering my strength, I push myself up from the ground, unsteady on my feet.

I check to see how much ammunition is left and toss the gun to the floor when I see it's empty. I still have my pistol. I climb the stairs two at a time, calling out for Konstantin. "Come out here, you bastard," I say.

The second floor of the warehouse is a mess. There are rooms full of boxes that stretch towards the ceiling. Whatever he's packaging and shipping, it's huge. I go from room to room until I see one door open. The light is on.

I enter slowly, looking around. I get to the other side of the room when I hear a noise. Spinning around, I see Konstantin.

He has Lucy held tight, a gun pressed to her head. The sight makes my blood run cold.

The look of fear on her face burns itself into my mind. She looks terrified, eyes wide, nose flaring as she breathes heavily. "Let her go, Konstantin," I say. I tighten my grip on my gun. "She doesn't have anything to do with this. I was the one hired to kill you. Not her."

Konstantin chuckles and looks down at her. "Is that right? Lucy here had a lot to tell me earlier. She told me how she's always wanted to kill me. How she dreamed about me some nights. I'm certain she played as big a role in this as you did."

I want to yell at Lucy for saying anything. She should've just kept her mouth shut. But I understand. I couldn't hold back from telling Andrei and Aleksandr. I wanted to gloat. Wanted to rub it in their faces that I was the one taking them out of this world.

"Roman," she says, eyes full with tears. "You have to stop him."

Konstantin chuckles again. "He's not going to stop anything, sweetheart. He's going to do exactly what I say if he doesn't want to watch you die right in front of him."

Just the thought of it makes me sick. Death doesn't scare me. What does is the thought of Lucy being the next person I see die.

I can't shake the thought from my mind. The blood. The hollow look in her eyes. It's bone-chilling.

That's not going to happen to her.

"Konstantin, look at me."

His wild eyes fall on me. "What?"

"We can work together, okay? We don't have to be against each other."

One of his eyebrows cocks upwards. "Elaborate."

"Mr. X knows that I'm coming for you tonight. He knows that you're supposed to die. You think he's gonna stop trying to bury you, just because his first option for the job didn't get it done? No way. If I fail, more will come after me. But if you work with me, if you let Lucy go, I'll tell him you're dead. I'll let him think you're gone. You can disappear. You can move out of the city. Go somewhere else, start your businesses there. I'll deal with Mr. X on my own."

It's a solid plan. Sure, I have no fucking idea how I'm going to explain it to Mr. X, but I don't have time to think about that. I need to say anything I can to get this man to lower his weapon. I just need him to take his finger off the trigger long enough for me to shoot him dead.

"You really think I'd fall for that?"

"I know you have connections, Konstantin. You have plenty of people out there that can help you disappear. Lay low for a little while. Let me take care of Mr. X, and when it's all said and done, you can come back to town."

"You'd kill him?"

"Anything. I don't care. I don't care what it takes. If you want it, we can make it happen, okay?"

He looks as if he's considering it. I've almost got him. "What do you think?" he asks Lucy. "Should I trust him?"

"Yes," she breathes. "You should."

Konstantin smirks. He aims his gun at my feet and fires. I jump back, barely missing the bullet as it buries itself into the concrete floor, hissing. My heart races.

"Did you really think I'd fall for that, Roman? Surely you must think better of me."

Fuck.

Gritting my teeth, I steady my gun again, taking a shaky breath.

"It's not a trick, Konstantin. Anything you fucking want, you can have. Just let her go."

"I want you dead, Roman," he says, eyes glinting with psychotic glee. "I saw what you did to all of my men downstairs. I saw the carnage. I heard the screaming. You killed all of them to get up here. If I let my guard down just once, you'll be at my throat with your teeth."

He's not a stupid man. At least he has that going for him. "If you let her go, I'll walk out of here and never look back. I won't even turn around to see where you run off to."

Konstantin tilts his head. "Like you'd ever really turn against Mr. X like that."

"Fuck X," I shout. "Fuck him and anyone else I've worked for. I'm done with this shit."

He laughs, head falling back for a moment. "Is that right? You think you can just walk away? After everything Mr. X has on you?"

"What?"

There's no way in hell he knows about the blackmail. X told me he was the only one who knew. As long as he had it, he controlled me.

"You heard me, Roman. I know what you did to dear old Uncle Andrei and Uncle Aleksandr. It was vicious, but if you ask me, they had it coming. They got exactly what they deserved. I mean, killing your parents like that? How could they do such a thing?"

Lucy struggles against his grip and he presses the gun harder to her forehead.

"Who told you about that?" I demand. When he doesn't respond, I repeat myself. "Who fucking told you about that?"

"No one told me about it," he grins. His teeth practically shine, shark-like in the LED lights overhead.

"Only Mr. X knew about that. So, either he told you, or—"

"You're almost there, Roman. Think a little harder. Put the puzzle pieces together."

Finally, it clicks, and when it does, I see Lucy realize it at the exact same moment.

Momentarily, the world spins with the truth, "You son of a—"

"Finally," Konstantin muses. "You're not as smart as I hoped. Yes, Roman. I know about your uncles because I know everything. I am Mr. X. Surprised yet?"

19

LUCY

I can't breathe. I can't move. The silence that follows Konstantin's confession is oppressive, and it's hard to even think straight. None of this makes sense. Konstantin has been Mr. X this whole time. Every mission Roman worked was to help the man that killed my family. Not only has his negligence taken the lives of countless people, but he's been an active role in having others killed.

I can see the confusion on Roman's face as he tries to process this. His hand shakes and my heart sinks. I want to run to him, to throw my arms around him and try my hardest to help him figure this all out, but I can't. The cold metal of Konstantin's gun keeps me still.

"You're full of shit," Roman says.

Amused, Konstantin says, "Am I, though?" He clears his throat, and the moment he speaks again, his voice is deeper, tinged with a weirdly ambiguous accent. "Your next assignment is to take out Abram Konstantin." It's spooky; he truly sounds like a different person, nothing like the snake-oil sleaze that normally came out when he spoke.

Recognition settles on Roman's face. He must know that voice. He's probably talked to that person countless times. Roman puts a second hand on his gun, steadying his shot.

"I'm disappointed that you didn't figure it out sooner," Konstantin remarks. "I worried that you would start to add up all of the people and how they had connections to me. People that owed me money, people that pissed me off. I thought, surely, you would start to see a pattern. That's why I threw in a few random men. Men with no immediate connections to me, hardly more than slight annoyances. It's sad to see that they died for nothing, because you were too stupid to even consider the possibility that Mr. X and I might be one and the same."

He's twisted. There's no way to put it. I thought, just maybe, there was a bit of apathy that came from his privilege. That the reason he didn't care about the people who died on his properties was because he didn't know them. He didn't play an active role in their death and could rationalize that he wasn't technically responsible. But no. He's fucking sick. He took pleasure in sending innocent men to their death. He blackmailed Roman for years, used him to kill anyone he found to be a problem. He got away with it all, just because of the money and power he had.

"Roman, that pouting expression is unbecoming," he chuckles, tightening his grip around me.

"Fuck you," Roman spits.

"That's no way to talk to your boss," he says flippantly. "But I guess I understand. You're upset that you lost. You're mad that you were bested. Anyone would be cross. I get that. But I would also like to add that when I finish with you, Lucy and I are going to have a lot of fun. Aren't we, little mouse?"

His free arm slips from around my neck and travels down my chest, over my breast, and down to my hip. The feeling makes me cringe, and I try my hardest not to jerk away from him. The gun is still pressed to my temple.

"Get your fucking hands off her!" Roman shouts, taking a step closer.

Konstantin's reaction is immediate. He tugs me towards him and presses the gun even harder against my head. "Take one more goddamn step and I'll blow this bitch's brains out. Do you fucking understand me?"

I can see the rage on Roman's face and it kills me to know that I can't do anything. *He* can't do anything. He's at the mercy of this psychopath, as powerless as I am, even with his weapon.

"Put your gun on the floor," Konstantin orders. Roman hesitates. Konstantin raises his hand and strikes me with the butt of the gun.

"You fucker," Roman growls.

I feel dizzy for a moment, and a trickle of blood works its way down my cheek from my forehead. I let out a long groan and try to stay still, but everything feels off-kilter. "You asshole," I manage to get out.

Konstantin laughs in my ear. "Sorry, little mouse. I like to play rough." He turns his attention back to Roman. "Put your fucking gun on the ground *now*."

"Roman, don't," I say, surprising myself. "Don't do it, okay? Just kill him. I don't care if he kills me. Just stop him."

There's a twist of pain on Roman's face, and I feel myself fall apart all over again. I can't imagine what's going on his head. The internal conflict, whether he should stop a man who's made it so obvious that he has no respect for human life or give up and let himself die for me.

"Yes, Roman," Konstantin muses. "Take me out. You can see us both die that way."

"Lucy," he says longingly.

"Don't you dare, Roman," I cry. "I don't want to be alive if it means he has me. He's always had me. But you can free me. You can free us both."

This is the only way to keep him from hurting anyone else. I've spent my entire life planning how to hurt him. He's already taken so much from me, and I don't see a way back. I may not make it out of this situation, but if I die tonight, at least I know I'll have taken this motherfucker out with me. I'll be reunited with my parents after finally getting them the justice they deserve.

"Please, Roman," I beg, tears streaming down my face. "Please."

Roman drops the gun and I feel the worst scream tear through my chest. Roman is as good as dead. He's gone. And after that, when Konstantin takes me back to his office to have his "fun," I'll wish I was the one that died instead.

"Good," Konstantin purrs. "Kick it to me."

"Don't, Roman. You can still pick it up. Please!" Maybe I can convince him. Maybe there's still time for him to pick it up and kill Konstantin once and for all. That hope goes out the window the moment he kicks the gun towards us. It slides across the cement and stops right at Konstantin's feet.

"Don't cry, Lucy," Konstantin says softly. "It'll be okay. You'll grow to like it." He drags his fingers over my lips again.

"Fuck you," I say. "Fuck you!"

Something comes over me. I don't know what it is, but I lose it, opening my mouth and biting down on Konstantin's fingers until I taste blood.

"You fucking bitch!" he screams, slamming his gun against my head again. My skull erupts in pain, but I don't have time to stop and suffer. I'm all instinct, all reaction. He tears his hand back, and I dive to the floor, grabbing the gun. It feels heavy and foreign in my grasp, the same as it did in the diner so many weeks ago.

But I know what to do.

I flick off the safety and turn around just as there's a sudden loud pop, and I scream. It melts in with the sound of a deeper yell.

I didn't fire my gun. I know I didn't. Roman. I turn around, starting for him. I expect to see a red hole in his shirt. To see the life leave his eyes as he collapses on the cold floor. Abram got him. He got us. He killed Roman.

But when I get to him, throw my arms around him, he's still standing.

"I thought he shot you," Roman says, crushing me against him, voice hoarse.

"I thought he shot *you*," I say. I spin around, and Konstantin is still standing there, unmoved. His arm wavers, and his knee buckles. He starts to open his mouth to speak when a thick line of blood runs from the corner of his lips.

He takes a step, stumbles, and collapses face down on the floor. There's a bullet hole in his back.

Roman pulls me back into his arms. "I thought I'd lost you," he says, squeezing me tight. "I'm sorry. I just couldn't. I couldn't see another person I love go."

I want to be mad at him. The logical side of me says that he should've listened to me. He should've given me the freedom I asked for, taken the shot, and killed Konstantin. But I can't be upset. He lost everything the same way I did. He lost the only people he ever cared about, the same way I did. It wasn't fair to ask him to do that one more time.

"I love you too," I say, trying hard not to break down in tears. Konstantin is finally gone. It's finally over.

I wait for the trumpets to start playing and for the parade to begin. Only, there's nothing like that. There's no overwhelming sense of accomplishment. All there is, is the sound of Roman's heart thudding in his chest. The deafening silence that follows the echo of a gunshot.

"Wait …" I pull back and look up at him. "If I didn't shoot him, and you didn't shoot him …"

I spin around at the sound of approaching footsteps. From behind the boxes piled high to the roof of the building, I see Nana step out.

"What the fuck?" I forget all manners. I forget that I'm not supposed to curse around my elders. Because seriously, *what the fuck.*

The gun in her hand is tiny, and for a second, I think it's a toy. There's no way my sweet old grandmother has a weapon like that on her. But when she approaches us and I can see it up close. It's definitely real.

"Nana, what are you doing here? How did you even find us?"

She pauses to look at Konstantin's body, then back up at me and Roman. "Check your pocket, Roman," she says.

Confused, he digs into his jacket. What he pulls out is a tiny square. A knowing smile crosses his face, meanwhile I'm left in the dark completely.

"You didn't," he says in disbelief.

"I did," she replies, smiling as well.

"Um," I interject. "Can somebody please tell me what the hell is going on right now?"

"This is a tracking device," he says, rolling it over and over in his fingers. "I've used something like this before. You can order them online, and as long as you stay close by, you can locate the person through GPS."

"I bought a few of them online," she says. "I put one on that man you had watching me. He wasn't too friendly, but considering who he worked for, I can see why. I put one on you when you came to help me drag the recycling bin out to the curb."

I make a face. "You don't need help with the recycling. It's not that heavy."

"I know," Nana smiles. "I needed an excuse to get close to him."

"Nana, how did you even know who he was?"

"I didn't. I just had a feeling. You told me you met an old friend, and I saw the way his eyes lit up when I mentioned that my granddaughter helped me with the trash. I knew right then and there that he was someone you knew. Did you really expect me to believe you were working on a writing gig for that long, sweetheart? I know you're impulsive, but you're not impulsive enough to quit your job and disappear for weeks at a time."

I blush and look away, embarrassed because I really did think Nana believed the story. There was no way she'd question me about this gig because she always pushed me to do more writing in the first place. Little did I know, she was working on a plot of her own.

I rush towards her and throw my arms around her, squeezing her tight. I'm still trying to process the fact that she was the one that saved us in the end, but I'm more than happy to see that she's here. Moments ago, I was sure I'd never see her again.

"Whose gun is that?" I ask after the hug.

She lifts it up and examines it. "It was your grandpa's. He said we'd only use it to protect the family, and that's what I did. I couldn't let that bastard take another one of my babies from me."

I could cry. In my anger at Konstantin, I blindly forgot that Nana also suffered. She might have been the one trying to move on, but that never meant she still didn't hurt. That she still didn't carry the same burning rage for Abram Konstantin that I've spent my entire life harboring. I hug Nana again, this time squeezing her tighter than before.

"I love you, Nana."

"I love you too, sweetheart. When I said I'd never let anything bad happen to you, I meant it." She looks into my eyes with her own striking blue ones.

She's been my rock. The one thing in this world, above work and my friends, that's kept me sane. I don't know what I'd do without her, and I don't want to think about it. Right now, the only thing that matters is that we're together, and we've stopped Konstantin.

I turn around to look back at his body. "You know," I start. "If this were a movie, he'd get one last shot at us while we're not expecting it."

Roman leans forward and grabs the gun from beside his body. He fires two more shots into Konstantin's back, then wipes the gun and tosses it across the room. When he looks up at us, he says, "Good thing this isn't a movie."

~

Nana says she's going to wait in her car for us, and I give her one last hug before she heads downstairs, stepping over all the bodies and all the carnage. I can hear her clicking her tongue at all the mess Roman and the others have made.

"That woman is something else," he says, shaking his head at me.

"I'm glad you got to formally meet Nana. For a second time, I suppose," I say with a smile. I look around at the warehouse, suddenly aware of just how quiet it is. Without all of Konstantin's men working or talking, it's eerily silent.

"What now?" I ask.

This place is going to be swarming with police soon. We may be pretty far away from the city, but eventually people are going to start to wonder. I'm sure others know where Konstantin works, and I don't want to be here when they come looking for him.

Roman pulls me into him and kisses me again, long and hard, before reluctantly drawing back, leaving me giddy. "Thank God you're okay."

"You left me tied to a bed," I begin, still angry even though there's nothing better than being back in his arms, knowing he's safe.

"I'll pay for that later." He runs his fingers lightly through my hair, lingering, before kissing me once more. It doesn't even occur to me to stop him, even if I'm pissed off. Finally, he steps back. "I wish we had time for more of that, but I have to clean up this mess."

I follow Roman downstairs, unsure what "clean up" means exactly. I'm careful to stay out of his way, but I do watch in the background as he unloads his car of all the guns he brought. He tosses them around the factory, staging the entire thing.

He positions certain people in a way that makes it look like they turned their guns on each other.

Roman then heads up to Konstantin's office, sitting at his computer and typing away.

"What are you doing?" I ask quietly.

"Pointing all the evidence back to Konstantin," he says. I watch as he pulls up Konstantin's email, double-clicking on one particular. A quick scan shows that he was having a conversation about having someone offed a few weeks ago.

"Won't that lead back to you?" I ask.

"Burner email. I'm always careful about that kind of thing."

"The police are going to find this, right?"

"If you can convince them to come, they will."

"Me?" I ask.

"I don't know who's going to pick up that phone. Konstantin had men all over the place. Police officers were always in his back pocket. They might recognize my voice if I pick up. I've met with plenty of them before. But if you call, they won't have a clue."

I guess that makes sense. Roman pulls a cheap flip phone from his pocket and hands it to me.

"Tell them you heard a lot of shooting and yelling. Tell them you were driving by but didn't stop because you were scared. Then hang up immediately," he instructs.

With a hard swallow, I dial the three numbers and wait for the operator to pick up. When she does, I tell her exactly what Roman said, trying my hardest to sound as terrified as I can. Before the woman asks for my name, I hang up the phone and hand it back to Roman. "How'd I do?" I ask with the slightest of smiles.

"You did perfect." He stands up and pulls me in for a kiss.

We get back to his car and find Nana waiting for us, her windows rolled down. "Come back to my place when you're done," she says.

I wave goodbye to her, and after she returns the gesture, she heads home.

∼

In Roman's car, I turn to him and look at him carefully. "Did you really mean it?" I ask.

"Mean what?"

"What you said back in the warehouse. That you love me."

Roman looks out the window for a moment, hands frozen on the steering wheel. Just when I think I've done something wrong by bringing it up, he says,

"I did. I do love you. It just ... terrifies me."

"Why?"

"You know why, Lucy. When you love something, it becomes your weakness. I don't want to lose you like everyone else. That's why I didn't want to care about you. But when that bastard called me and told me you were in danger, I didn't think. I didn't question going back. I knew that I had to save you. I knew that I loved you."

I reach forward and place my hand on top of his. I rub my fingers over his knuckles, slow and soothing. "I love you too, Roman. More than I've loved anyone else."

He gives me a smile, a rare sight, and turns the car around, leaving the warehouse behind.

We both fall silent as he drives, one hand on the steering wheel, the other in mine. I look back at the warehouse, watching it get smaller and smaller until it finally disappears, gone from my life for good.

Just like Konstantin.

I sit back in my seat and smile to myself.

It's finally over.

20

ROMAN

I drive Lucy back to grandmother's house, and the drive is quiet. Neither of us talks, but neither of us needs to.

Hearing Lucy beg me to shoot Konstantin tore a hole in my heart. I could see me, years ago, so desperate to kill Andrei and Aleksandr that I would've done anything to make them suffer. I would've gone down with them if it meant they paid for what they did.

Staring at Lucy in the warehouse, I saw that same determination. I just couldn't let her go down that road. I couldn't let her die for my mistake. Konstantin was right. I should've put it all together. Stepping back, anyone could see that all the crimes were tied together. Every man I killed was connected to Abram Konstantin in one way or another.

But now the Bratva has taken a hit I don't know if they'll recover from.

Serves those fuckers right.

I glance at Lucy and watch as her eyes grow heavy. Her blinking slows and she begins to fall asleep. As she drifts off, her muscles relax, and I see the tension disappear.

I drive through the city streets slowly, looking at everything. It's interesting how different the world looks when I'm not planning which escape route to take, mapping everything out, figuring out when the best time is to step from the shadows and stick someone with a syringe. It's kind of beautiful, this shithole of a place.

For the first time in years, I'm free. Nobody's blackmailing me any longer. That secret died with Konstantin. Now, I'm free to do as I please. It's a strange feeling.

We make it back to the house thirty minutes later. I'm reluctant to wake Lucy, but I know that she'll want to talk to the old woman. They probably have plenty to discuss. Her grandmother isn't like any woman I've ever met before.

I thought she was some kindly old lady. She could barely manage the recycling bin, and she loved to stay and talk because nobody else was around to talk to. But like her granddaughter, she surprised me.

If Konstantin had been able to get the shot off, I don't think either of us would be sitting in this car now. She's as big a hero as her granddaughter, and she has my respect in a way that not many others do.

Slowly, I open my car door. Immediately, Lucy sits up and rubs her eyes. "Are we home?" she asks.

"Yeah."

She yawns loudly and opens her door, climbing out. When we get inside the house, her grandmother is in the kitchen, stirring something on the stove. Lucy runs into the kitchen and gives her a hug.

"I thought you two got lost or something," she chuckles, rubbing Lucy's upper arm.

"Were we gone that long?"

"Just a little while," she says. "I thought you two might be hungry, so I warmed up some leftover chili."

"I'm starving," I say.

She grabs two bowls from the cabinet and fills them. When I try to help, she shoos me away and tells me to sit down. Lucy giggles, and I smile with embarrassment. A few moments later, Lucy's grandmother places two bowls of chili in front of us and sprinkles a handful of cheese on them.

"I'm going to head to bed now, darling. Come wake me up if you need something, okay?"

"Okay, Nana. Love you."

"Love you too." The two of us share a nod before she heads back to her bedroom and I start to dig in. This must be the best food I've had in years, because I can barely stop eating to talk.

"That woman is a great cook," I say.

Lucy nods. "She cooked for me every night when I was younger. Didn't matter what I wanted, or how long it took, she was going to make whatever I was in the mood for."

The two of us eat quietly, occasionally making small talk. She mentions how she's going to write a killer climax to her book after what happened tonight. She's even thought of another book that she wants to work on soon. It's strange, watching her disappear into the world of her own creation.

She talks about her characters like they're real people. Like they can make their own decisions and lead the story in ways she has no control over. And I can see she'll use those characters to help her work through the hell she went through tonight.

Finally, I speak. "I'm sorry for lying to you, Lucy."

There aren't many people I apologize to. I've lived my whole life doing whatever it took to survive. Lying. Stealing. Cheating. It didn't matter, as long as it benefitted me in some way. But I've lied to Lucy more times than I should have, and it's fucking me up inside.

"Why did you do it?" she asks.

"You told me you were scared of who you would become if you went through with this. You said you might become as bad as me. You might lose your humanity. That made me change my mind. I couldn't let you go down that road. I know it would've felt good, killing Konstantin, especially after what he did to your folks, but …"

I shrug. "I tied you up because I wanted to keep you away from him. I thought you were safe at the house. And I'm sorry. If I hadn't done that, you wouldn't have been in danger."

She smiles sadly. "I've been in danger my whole life, Roman. Konstantin's been this bad dream in my life for so long that I started to get used to him. I felt comfort knowing that I could always hate him when life got too hard for me. I forgive you, though. For lying to me."

Relief hits me hard. I can't believe how much power this tiny woman holds over me. She leaves me on my knees more times than I'm comfortable saying, and yet she uses her power for good. She's never manipulated me or tried to sway me with how much I care about her.

"Fuck, I love you," I say.

Lucy laughs softly and reaches a hand across the table to hold mine. "I love you too."

We finish eating, and after, I help her do the dishes. It's like we're back at the safe house again. She dries and I wash, a perfect team. When we're done, I pull her into my arms. "This is a lot to talk about right now, but I think we should start preparing for the future. New names, identities, all that."

"What are you talking about?"

"We can't stay here, Lucy," I explain. "Konstantin's men are bound to find out that we were the ones that killed him. If we stay here, we'll always be in danger. We'll always have a target on our backs. But if we disappear and start over, we'll be harder to track down. Harder to find."

This won't be my first time becoming someone else. After killing Aleksander and Andrei, I moved, and decided to become who I am now. Learning English was difficult, but it came eventually. I grew more and more fluent, adopted the name Roman, and began working for Mr. X. Konstantin figured out who I was thanks to his ties to Russia, and that's when he blackmailed me.

This time, I'll be more careful. *We'll* be more careful.

"Do we really have to?" she asks, chewing on her bottom lip. "I just don't want to stress Nana out with money. Moving, becoming someone else ... I don't want to put any more pressure on her when she's been sick lately."

"I'll take care of everything," I say. "I have more than enough money for us to live comfortably. Konstantin may have been a piece of shit, but he paid well. Money isn't an issue."

That seems to calm her down some. I know Lucy struggled before she met me. I know she worked at that diner because she needed to pay the bills and keep the lights on. She did what she had to do, same as me. But this is different. We have a way out now. We don't have to work for anyone else. We can do what we want.

"We should call ourselves Bonnie and Clyde," she teases.

"We are definitely *not* calling ourselves that," I say. It's hard to keep a straight face, and I end up smiling at the idea. I like the spirit behind those names, but we'll need something much more unassuming. Something that makes it easy for us to blend in with the crowd.

"I just want to add," Lucy says, running her fingers up and down my arm, "If you ever leave me tied to a bed and drive off again, I'm going to change my name to Lorena Bobbitt."

"Ouch," I say, stealing a kiss from her.

"I mean it, Roman. I've done my research. I know lots of different ways to kill a man. Don't mess with me."

"Okay, okay," I say, pecking her lips again. "The next time I tie you up, it will be consensual. How does that sound?"

She makes a soft *mm* sound and kisses me back, her tongue passing my lips and brushing against my own. There are so many filthy things I could do to her right now, but I have to behave myself. We're in her grandmother's house. If we get too wild, she could come out at any moment and see us. After saving our lives, I doubt that's the kind of thanks she wants to receive.

"We should go somewhere," I say between kisses.

"Like where?"

"Somewhere private. I don't want to disturb your grandmother."

Lucy snickers softly. "When did you become such a gentleman?"

"It's a recent development," I reply.

Lucy nods and crosses the room to grab her jacket from the hook hanging by the back door. She pulls it over herself and pulls on her shoes. "Lead the way," she says, gesturing to the front door.

In the car, I decide that I can probably take her to a hotel or something nearby. I have enough cash on me to pay for a month, so we're not bothering her grandmother. I'd consider the safe house, but if Konstantin's men know where that is, I'll have to get rid of the property.

After driving around for a while, Lucy turns to me and says, "Actually, can we make a detour?"

"Sure. Where to?"

"Do you know where the Jefferson Cemetery is?"

"I do."

When we arrive at the cemetery, Lucy looks hesitant, like she might change her mind and ask to go back to the hotel. I don't blame her. This has to be hard. Visiting my parents' and brothers' grave for the last time before I left Russia was the hardest thing I'd ever done. I wanted to stay there. I wanted to die and be buried next to them. But I had to go. I had to move on from the past and try to make a new life for myself.

I know that's what Lucy's parents would want for her too.

I lace my fingers through hers, offering some kind of reassurance. It seems to work. Lucy leads me through the rows and rows of headstones. Part of me wonders who all is here. What their stories are. Who remembers them.

For a long time, neither of us say a word. Then Lucy stops in front of her parents' gravestones and runs her hand over them. I want to comfort her. I want to pull her into my arms and tell her how proud of her they'd be. But I know what this moment feels like. I know how personal it all is. She wants me here for moral support and nothing more.

Lucy brings her hand up to her face and wipes her eyes, and the sight breaks my heart. I've always understood her pain, but seeing it on display tonight is something different. It's more than just the knowledge. It's the sight of how bad this tragedy still is. How broken she is, even after all these years. What Konstantin did to her can never be undone. Even if he is dead, he's left his mark on her forever.

After fifteen minutes, Lucy stands up. Her eyes are rimmed in red. She gives me a sad smile. I pull her into my arms, and she presses her cheek against my chest.

"I've got you," I say softly. "I'm here."

Lucy starts to cry again, but she looks up into my eyes. "Thank you," she whispers. "For everything."

"No. Thank you."

She doesn't know how much she's changed me. She doesn't understand that she's pulled me away from the deep end. I may have helped her stop Konstantin, but she made me into someone else. Someone ready to give up this life. Someone that I don't despise. I want to be better because of her.

Hand in hand, we start to walk back. Lucy looks over her shoulder once and smiles. When she looks at me, I smile as well. It's hard not to fall in love with this woman all over again.

So why resist? This time, when I feel my heart leap, I don't stop myself.

Once again, I fall hard for Lucy Walker.

EPILOGUE

ROMAN

I still haven't gotten used to California weather. In New York, the rain and snow were common. It was familiar. The constant sunshine and warmth in San Jose feel foreign. It's strange. I like it.

Lucy laces her fingers through mine as we walk. This has become a morning routine for us. She likes to just walk around with me. For so long after Konstantin, we lived in hiding. No one could find out who we were. No one could know the truth about us.

That's why she suggested we come up with new identities. Roman and Lucy had to disappear, and two other people had to take their places. Chris doesn't suit me, I don't think, but Lucy says it's a fine name. Unassuming. I have to agree with her there.

Daisy suits her, I think.

She's bright like the flower, and it's close enough to her actual name that she doesn't completely ignore it whenever I call out for her when we're in public.

These past few months have felt like a dream I don't deserve living.

The move from New York to the other side of the country was easier than I thought it would be. Lucy told me she had Nana and everything else was expendable. She didn't need anything from home. I made a few calls, withdrew a large amount of cash, and we disappeared. Just like that.

I don't know if we'll ever go back. I don't know if I even want to. New York was good for business, but Lucy's pressuring me to hang it up. She keeps reminding me of what I told her in the safe house. How I wanted to protect people instead of kill them. How I should focus on doing more of that.

I give her the answers she wants, but the truth is, I don't know if I'll ever go back to that. I can't say for certain. I know about killing. I've spent my entire life doing it, even from a young age. I know more about that than anything else in my life. And there might always be that pull. It's guaranteed money, and I'm good at it.

So far, I've kept my word to her. If I wanted, I'm sure I could make a few calls and find a client here in California. Only, I don't really want to.

I like things how they are now.

Lucy drops her head on my shoulder, and I come back down to earth. I look at her, run my fingers down the two braids she wears on either side of her head. She's tanned since we moved, and her freckles are even darker.

She's the perfect distraction.

Without her, I'd spend every second preparing for Konstantin's men to come. I know they're out there. Most of them were busted when the police found evidence of his crimes, but I'm sure there are people on his payroll that managed to avoid getting caught. The roaches of organized crime. Maybe one day they'll come for us. That's why I have to stay ready.

But when Lucy squeezes my hand and makes me remember that I should be enjoying time with her, I drop my guard just a little.

"Have you heard back from any agents?" I ask.

"Nothing serious, yet. I did have one agent tell me I should revise some parts of the book and send it back to her when it's complete."

"Are her revisions good?"

Lucy shrugs. "They're all right. I don't think they're necessary, but if I get a lot of agents saying that I need to work on that aspect, I'll reconsider. It's just getting so tiring. No one ever told me it would take this long. That writing the damn book was the easy part."

I smile at her frustration and drape my arm around her thin shoulder. "I believe in you. It's gonna take time, though."

She sighs. "I know. I'm just impatient. You know how I get."

Our trip through the city leads us back to the house, and I'm almost disappointed it doesn't last longer. Today's a beautiful day, one we wouldn't ever get back in New York. We should be out soaking up the light.

Lucy has work to do, and I need to start looking for a job.

We've been living off the money I have in my account, which is plenty, but I don't like the idea of sitting around the house all day. I need to do something. I need to be productive or I'll lose my fucking mind.

Lucy stops by Nana's room to check in on her when we get home. It's like looking at a completely different woman. The therapist and doctors we've hired have made a big improvement on her. Just last week, she was able to go shopping at the grocery store by herself. In New York, that was something Lucy had to do.

"You both worry too much about me," she says, passing us and heading into her bedroom. With the whole left wing of the house to herself, she's made this place like a home of her own.

"Where are you going?" Lucy asks.

"Me and some of my girlfriends are going to the Olive Garden for lunch and our book club meeting." She pulls her coat on and reaches for the romance novel on the table. It looks like something from the eighties, a man lounging on a bed with a busty redhead in his arms. I crack a smile. My mom read books like that when I was a kid.

"Don't stay out too late, okay?" Lucy says.

Nana gives her a look. "Girl, don't you go bossing me around. I'll stay out as late as I'd like."

"You tell her," I smirk.

Lucy's eyes go wide and she looks between us. "Wow, so now you're both ganging up on me? I see how it is."

Nana leans forward and kisses her on the cheek, giving her a quick hug. "I'll be back before you know it."

Once she's gone, Lucy turns to me. "So, I'm pretty hungry… Think I could seduce you into making me some breakfast?"

I suppress a smile. "Depends on what you're offering, miss."

She looks down shyly as one of her hands rises to the buttons on her flannel. "Well," she demurs, sliding the button free. A flash of skin, tan and creamy and smooth, appears where the fabric parts. "Maybe this will get me some coffee?"

I nod, slowly. I can feel my stiffness in my pants, starting to strain against the fabric. "Just coffee?"

She pushes another button loose. Now, I can see the gentle swell of her breasts. She's not wearing a bra. I want to run my tongue over them, trace kisses down the flat expanse of her belly to the edge of her denim shorts. To explore everything below and between. "How about this?" she asks, her eyes darting up to meet mine for a moment, a slow smile spreading across her face.

"I could maybe do some eggs, for that."

She wrinkles her brow as if she's deep in thought. "I am *very* hungry, though, sir. I don't think just eggs will be enough." With that, she undoes the last button of her shirt and slides it off of her shoulders. It falls to her feet in a soft puddle, but my eyes are fixated on the curve of her shoulders to her breasts to her hips. Her body is screaming for my touch, but I force myself to stand still, leaning against the countertop in the kitchen, hands trapped in my pocket.

I feel that familiar heat, that familiar hunger, that hasn't changed since the first time I saw Lucy. Since the night in the motel when I pinned her beneath me and wanted her more than I'd ever wanted anything in my entire life.

But I make myself play out this game a little farther.

"Well, bacon seems reasonable, now," I add in a husky voice.

Lucy bites her bottom lip, and my cock jumps at my zipper. It wants out. It wants her.

Her hands slip down her belly and she hooks her thumbs in her jean shorts. She tugs down a little, revealing the frilly edge of a pair of pink panties. My breath catches in my throat, but I don't let her see the war erupting inside of me. My face is calm and smooth.

"Pancakes are going to cost you, ma'am."

"Oh?" she whispers. "This much?" She undoes the button of her shorts.

I shake my head. "A little more."

"This much?" she repeats. She pulls the zipper down. I can see the upper rim of a damp patch in her panties. She's soaked through. She is fighting the same battle in her head that I am – temptation versus teasing – and I see that she's on the verge of losing, just like me.

My stomach is churning with need – for Lucy, for her warmth, for her touch. Almost there, almost there.

"Just a bit more."

She wriggles her hips and pushes the jeans down the tan length of her legs, stepping out of them towards me, one foot stepping delicately in front of the other. She has only the panties on now, and I let my eyes rove up and down her body. This is my woman, my love. The light of my world. The flower of my life.

And I am dying with the urgent need to fuck her senseless.

"Very close to complete," I say. "But the price for syrup just went up."

She smiles again. I'm squeezing the marble countertop behind me, white-knuckling it, and I'm half-afraid it is going to snap off in my hands. Lucy closes the last few feet between us with slow, careful steps, eyes locked on mine the whole time, until she's inches away from me, looking up into my gaze. I watch her soft lips move as she whispers, "I hope this can cover the difference."

She brushes her mouth against mine. It's a soft, chaste kiss at first.

But that is all it takes to push me over the edge.

I push my tongue past her lips, opening our jaws up wide to mingle our lips and our heat together. With one hand, I yank her into my embrace, so our chests are flush together. With the other, I scoop her up and wrap her legs around me. She hooks her ankles behind the small of my back as I spin around and set her on the countertop.

She gasps and giggles at the cold sensation on her bare skin. I lace my fingers through the roots of her hair and pull back softly, exposing her throat to my nipping kisses. I bite and suck easily down to her collarbone while my fingers play with the edge of her panties where they meet her inner thighs. She squirms towards and away from my touch, not sure if she's ready yet for it, teasing me to go farther, challenging me.

I put my lips to her nipple and draw in. She gasps again, putting her hands on the back of my head and hugging me to her.

"Roman..." she hushes.

I smile and push her back. She obliges, falling backwards until she's laying on top of the counter. I reach across her, pluck the biggest chef's knife from the wooden block that houses them, and lay the cold flat of the blade against her thigh. She freezes.

"You better not!" she warns.

"Oh? Are you telling me what to do, princess?"

"I'm telling you, Roman, if you..."

I grin as I slip the blade under the thinnest part of her panties and slice outward. The fabric falls away from her hip. I pull the rest of it away, leaving her completely naked before me. Exactly how I want her. Exactly how I always want her.

"You bastard!" she shrieks playfully. "These were my favorite."

"You should've known better than to tell a hitman not to use a knife."

She kicks me in the side. I just laugh and pin her ankle against me as I lean forward and press my mouth against her hot center. The words fall dead in her mouth as I start to lick slowly and delicately. I build pressure, circling the tip of my tongue around her clit, darting in and out of her. I can feel her body around me, tensing and relaxing in waves, while little whimpers of pleasure slip out from between her lips.

"You, you..." But nothing she says makes sense anymore as I add my fingers to the mix, pushing into her slowly but firmly. Her walls contract around my touch. I speed up the lashes of my tongue.

Outside, cicadas chirp and the sun is beaming, but in here, all that matters is the growing rod in my pants and the warmth emanating from Lucy as I lick her into a thrashing, screaming orgasm. She bucks in my grasp as it takes her. Her fingers claw into my upper arm, holding on for dear life. I press the heel of my hand against her center and let her ride the wave against it. It is a long minute before she comes down. When she does, she leans up and looks at me.

Her hair is a wild mess, and her eyes shine through the loose bangs that have fallen over her face. They're bright and thirsty. She bites her lips. "Is breakfast over?" she asks, teasing.

"Just getting started," I assure her.

I unbutton and unzip my pants. At long last, my cock springs free. I've made myself wait for what feels like a fucking eternity. Now, it's time.

I pull Lucy towards me and push her thighs apart as I line myself up with her entrance. She grinds against my tip for a minute before shooting up onto her elbows.

Fixing me with a fiery stare, she says, "Wait a minute there, mister. I want my eggs scrambled, not fertilized."

I laugh out loud. I've been doing a lot more of that lately than I ever used to. It feels incredible. "I think this will be a good meal for both of us, this way," I say cautiously.

Lucy tilts her head and bites her lip. "Are you sure?"

I know what she's asking. Am I sure that I want to be with her? Am I sure that this is the life for me? Am I sure that I can leave all my demons behind? Am I sure that we can have a future – a happy one – one that a child would be blessed to be born into, not cursed like she and I were?

The first, uglier part of the truth is that I'm not sure. They are impossible questions. We'll never have certain answers. It'd be a lie, and a disgraceful one, to pretend that I knew for sure how to say yes to all of those questions.

But the second, more beautiful part is that I want to find out. I want it as bad as I've ever wanted anything. I want to find out – with Lucy by my side. My teammate, my woman, my partner in crime. The only one I want with me. Now, and forever.

So I hesitate for just a brief second before nodding. "I am sure."

Lucy's face splits into a sunbeam smile. I pull her face up towards mine so I can kiss my woman as I slide my length deep into her.

I keep her pinned close to me with my hands on her thighs as our tongues thrash and our hips rock together. It's slow, gentle strokes at first, just exploring each other, accommodating each other. The sensation of hot, wet, tight heat on my cock is nearly enough to make me come right away, but I force myself to savor the moment instead.

Lucy's mouth finds my ear. Her breath rattles seductively as I start to slip in and out of her faster. When our hips meet now, there is a fleshy slap that echoes in the kitchen, the hard, whimpering thrust of lover meeting lover.

Her ankles tighten behind me. Her hands dig into my skin. Her teeth lock down on my earlobe, enough to draw a growl of half-pain and half-pleasure from me as I speed up again.

I'm going as fast as I can now, fucking into her with all the force I can muster. I hear her begging for more, more, as I push deep into her. She squeezes around my length and holds onto me like she's riding out a storm.

"I'm almost there, Roman," she pants. I am, too, coasting right on the edge of unleashing.

Three, two, one more thrust, and then I can't hold it anymore, and neither can she, and we both go tumbling down over the edge of our orgasms. I let loose inside of her. She lets loose around me. Neither one of us lets go.

The tremors coursing through each of us take a long time to recede. When we've finally relaxed, I slide myself out of her with a regretful wince. I put my fingers under her chin, tilting her gaze up to meet mine, then plant a kiss on her. "Breakfast is served," I say softly.

She laughs. "You aren't getting out of it that easily, buster. I want *real* breakfast." She nips another soft kiss before hopping down and sashaying towards the bathroom to clean herself up. As she disappears down the hallway, I hear her call out over her shoulder.

"Oh – and wipe that counter off, first!"

I can only laugh.

~

One thing I wanted in this new house was a big kitchen. The little one from my safe house back home wasn't good enough. This one is practically the size of the master bedroom, which is big on its own. Freshly showered and dressed only in my shirt with nothing underneath, Lucy takes a seat at the table and opens her laptop, typing away while I cook. Like always, I find myself singing, only Lucy doesn't laugh at me this time. She sings too. Much better than I can.

I make pancakes, something easy that I know she'll love. Half the batch of batter is for regular ones, and the other half is for blueberry pancakes. While I wait for one side to cook, I think back to mornings with my parents.

Mom would always cook breakfast for me, Ivan, and Gedeon. She sang in Russian, but those songs are now just distant memories. I remember helping her clean up after we ate. My brothers ran off to go play with their toys, but I stayed back to help. She would turn to me, cup my face between her hands, and tell me that she appreciated all my help. Then she'd kiss me on the nose and tell me to go play. She had it under control.

The memory is heavy, and normally, I'd think of something else. Today is different. I want to think about those times. Times when I was happy. Before all the shit with my uncles. Before I lost them all. Being with Lucy brings that same kind of happiness in a way that I never thought a woman could.

When I serve her, she closes her computer and perks up, blue eyes growing big. "This looks delicious!" she exclaims. She doesn't wait for me, either. She dives in, practically scarfing it all down.

"Slow down before you choke," I warn, laughing at her enthusiasm.

"I'm ravenous," she says, her mouth full. "*Someone* made me work extra hard for my breakfast this morning."

∼

Three Months Later

"Roman," Lucy says, tapping me on the shoulder. It's early morning. I can see the sun peeking through the slats in the blinds. I'd be asleep, half-mired in a dream that made no sense in the light of day.

"Mm?" I grunt.

"Wake up, I need to tell you something."

I bolt up and immediately reach for the gun I keep tucked behind my nightstand.

"No, no, no!" she laughs, pushing me in the chest back down to the bed. "It's nothing like that; relax." She sees the gun in my hand and frowns. "And we'll need to talk about *that* later, mister. You told me you kept all the weapons in the gun safe."

"It's – uh," I babble. I'm still half-asleep. "Nevermind. What do you have to tell me?" I lay back down and let the adrenaline in my veins recede.

"I don't want you to get mad or anything, so I've been putting it off." She's nervous, chewing on her fingernails and twirling her hair over and over again. She won't look me in the eye, either.

This doesn't sound good. "What's wrong?"

"Nothing's wrong," she says carefully. "It's just ..." Lucy trails off thoughtfully. She has a faraway look on her face.

"Lucy."

She doesn't say anything as she pulls something from under the covers. She opens her hand and shows me what's in her palm. I immediately recognize it as a pregnancy test.

There are two pink lines.

"Is this ..."

She nods. "It is. I'm pregnant."

I'm at a loss for words.

I want to say something profound, or just something at all, but all I can do is look at the test in her palm. Those two lines. She's pregnant. It hits me at once. First, the joy. She's going to have my child. The family she's always wanted. The family I never thought I would have.

Fear is second. What if I fuck this up? I told myself I would never bring a kid into this world and expose them to the shitty people that inhabit it. Too many people die. School shootings, kidnappings, sex slavery. I could never do that to another person. I could never run that risk.

But then the resolve comes last.

This is what I've wanted, deep down. This is it. I told Lucy I would give her anything in the world, and this is what she's wanted for so long. I push myself up from the pillows and pull her into my arms, spinning her around. When she pulls back to look at me, she's crying. She's never been more beautiful.

"Fuck, Lucy," I say, shaking my head. "I can't believe this."

"I can't either!" She wipes her eyes and laughs. "I found out yesterday, but I didn't know what to say. I was so scared you'd be upset."

"Never. Never in a million fucking years." I mean it, too. As fucking terrified as I am about this news, I know that she'll be an amazing mother. She'll give this kid all the love he or she deserves. We'll make this work, I know we will.

I pull her in for a kiss, but it turns into multiple kisses. She giggles and kisses me back. "You taste like you," she whispers against my lips.

"And you taste like you," I reply. I roll on top of her. She lets out another giggle, but that disappears the moment she watches me move down her body.

She spreads her legs for me, rocking on her hips to help as I pull down her panties and push the shirt of mine she likes to sleep in up higher. I still can't get enough of her body. I run my fingers through the small patch of hair just above her center, teasing her clit with a few nudges before I get started. She's already soaking wet.

I drag my tongue in slow strokes over her pussy, listening to hear her reaction. It happens immediately. She lets out a soft groan and a hand falls to the back of my head. She doesn't need to say anything. I got the message loud and clear.

I work my tongue against her again, harder this time. She tastes just as good as I remember, and I'm hungry for her. I lap at her, over and over, relishing in the noises she makes. She squirms beneath me too. I place both hands on her thighs and squeeze them, keeping her in place.

"Tell me this is mine," I instruct her, looking up. She meets my gaze. Her face is flushed, pink across her nose and cheeks, and her eyes are wide.

"It's yours, Roman," she says. "It's all yours."

I could listen to her repeat that all day. It is mine. *She's* mine, just like I'm hers. I kiss my way up to her clit, taking my time. I want her practically melting for me. I tease and flick it, even venturing to lightly tug with my teeth. It all makes Lucy whimper with pleasure. Her body grows warmer by the second.

When I work my fingers inside of her, her head falls back. "Fuck, yes, Roman," she cries. Lucy squeezes at her breasts, twisting her nipples.

I can tell she's getting close. The moment she starts playing with herself, I know that her orgasm is right around the corner. My tongue is relentless, with a mind of its own. Over and over and over, I taste her.

"I-I'm close," she stutters.

I curl my fingers inside of her, rubbing against the spot I know that tears her to pieces. When I find her g-spot, she practically screams, that noise melting into a laugh. "Fuck, yes," she whimpers, rutting her hips down against my fingers and tongue. "Yes!"

I feel her whole body vibrate as she comes, but I don't pull away. I continue to eat her out, sloppy, greedy to taste every last drop of her juices. She squeezes my head with her thighs, and a deep animalistic groan rumbles in the back of my throat. Fuck, she's sexy when she gets like this. When she stops playing nice and holds me in place, riding out her orgasm with me.

Finally, I sit back, wiping my mouth. Lucy begins to push herself up when I put my hand on her chest and press her back into the wooden table. "I'm not done yet," I tell her.

Her eyes are wide for only a moment, then a darker look crosses her face. "What's next?" she asks.

"I'm going to fill you up," I tell her. Her bare foot drags down my chest, then back up, where she knocks against my chin.

"I wanna feel it all, Roman."

I grab both of her legs and roughly part them, stepping between. "You will, baby. I promise."

I free my throbbing cock, slapping it down on her hot pussy a few times. She bites down on her lip and spreads her legs wider. "Don't tease," she grins.

I take hold of myself and press into her deep, all at once. Her face contorts. She lets out a delicious moan, and I don't give her a second chance to calm down before I slide out and bury myself inside her again.

"Jesus," she cries, her back arching.

My movements are rough and quick. She wants to play naughty, and I'm going to give it to her that way. Her walls constrict around me, hot and wet, and I shudder, pressing my palms flat against the table.

Each thrust feels like heaven, and I hear our bodies connect every time. It's a perfect fit, like two puzzle pieces. "Fuck, you're so wet for me," I grunt. I take hold of the shirt she's wearing and pull it up over her head, stripping her completely.

With her chest free, I lean in and suck on her nipples, using the same force and enthusiasm I used on her clit. Lucy takes me as best she can, a steady stream of moans and whimpers falling from her lips. She brushes the hair from my face and meets my gaze.

"Show me I'm yours," she says.

As if I weren't already fucking hard enough.

I put my hand on her neck. It brings me right back to that night in the motel so long ago. The first time I touched her. The first time she ever made me rock hard. That alone seems to be all she needs, because Lucy's lips part and she slips a hand between the two of us.

I add just enough pressure to her throat, squeezing only a little. It's enough. In mere seconds, she's crying out again, making a mess on my cock once more.

Her second orgasm is what pushes me over the edge. Her entire body clenches, and the walls of her pussy practically drain my cock. I double over on top of her, cursing loud, thrusting powerfully between her legs. Lucy wraps her arms around me and grinds against me, both of us riding out this ecstasy together.

I haven't come that hard in a long time.

Reluctantly, I slide out of her, but I don't pull away. We stay like that, my weight on top of her, both of us panting.

Lucy reaches up and runs her hand through my hair, and I lean into it. Her hand cups my cheek, and she smiles up at me. "What do you want?" she asks. "Boy or girl?"

I hadn't thought that far ahead. I'm still reeling from the news that she's actually having a baby. "I don't know," I admit. "A girl would be nice. My mother only had boys."

Lucy cracks a smile. "Mine only had a girl."

"Do you only want one?"

"For now," she says. "I don't want to have to split my attention between two little monsters. With one, we can give them all our love and make them the center of our worlds. And then maybe down the line, we can have more."

The idea of more than one kid scares and excites me. Lucy was where my world stopped, but now there will be even more love to share. I can already see it all. The tiny clothes. Lucy designing the bedroom until it's just perfect. Teaching the little tyke how to ride a bicycle and how to swim. How to hunt, like my father taught me.

It's too sweet for me to handle. Who am I becoming? What happened to Roman the hitman? He's still there, deep inside me, but he doesn't come out as often anymore. He doesn't need to, and I think that's probably for the best. He'll never be gone for good; the speed with which I grabbed the gun from the nightstand proves that beyond a shadow of a doubt. And there are some things I still need that side of me for.

To keep my family safe, first and foremost.

But I'm learning – slowly – that that doesn't always require force. Brute strength and violence can keep you safe in this world, but they can also make things more dangerous. Those things change you when you let them. Hurting others can hurt yourself just as badly. I have only to close my eyes and picturing Konstantin's ugly, twisted scowl to understand that the things we do are done to us, in a perverse sort of way. I have only to remember my family's history to remember that violence stains forever.

I want to spare my child – or my children, rather – from ever having to go through what I went. I can never truly abandon the life I've led, but I can protect them from it all the same.

I couldn't protect Lucy from it, not fully. But I can already see the shadows fading from her soul. A little bit more every day. Me, I'm scarred for life. And that's fine. That's what I chose. But she deserves better. Brighter. Freer.

I can give her that. I can give my children that. So that's exactly what I'll do. I'll be the barrier between their light and the world's darkness. I'll protect them from the things they should never have to see. In that way, I can honor my past and embrace my future. I can make their world a good one to live in, full of laughter and love and the bright, shining eyes of their mother.

I look down at Lucy and know that I've made the right choices – for once in my life.

"Don't get ahead of yourself," I chuckle, kissing her neck. "We'll have as many as you want, but only if we get to keep practicing our technique on how to make them."

She clings to me again, turning her head and exposing more of her neck to me. "Seems fair to me." Then her tone changes to more serious. "You know you're the best thing that's ever happened to me, right?" she asks.

I pull back and look into her eyes. She's so full of hope and sunshine. My woman. My daisy.

"Yeah?"

"Yep. And in a few months, you'll lose that role to this little thing." Lucy places her hand on her bare stomach.

Slowly, I kiss my way down towards it. I press a longer kiss to her stomach. "I'm happy to give that up." For this kid, I'd give up anything.

THE END

Thanks for reading! But don't stop now – there's more. Click the link below to receive the FREE extended epilogue to <u>STOLEN BY THE MOB BOSS</u>. You'll also get a free sneak preview of another bestselling mafia romance novel.

So what are you waiting for? Click below!

www.bookfunnel.com/StolenbytheMobBossEpilogue

SNEAK PREVIEW (BROKEN VOWS)

Keep reading for a sneak preview of my bestselling mafia romance, BROKEN VOWS!

∼

She's my fake wife, my property… and my last chance at redemption.

She's beautiful. An angel.

I'm dangerous. A killer.

She's my fake bride for a single reason – so I can crush her father's resistance.

But marrying Eve brings me far more than I bargained for.

She's fiery. Feisty. Won't take no for an answer.

She makes me believe that I might be worth redemption.

Until I discover a past she's been hiding from me.

One that threatens everything.

Now, I know that our wedding vows are not enough.

I need to make sure she's mine for good.

A baby in her belly is the only way to seal the deal.

In the end, the Bratva always gets what it wants.

Luka

Their fear tingles against my skin like a whisper. As my leather-soled shoes tap against the concrete floor, I can sense it in the way their eyes dart towards and away from me. In the way they scurry around the production floor like mice, meek and unseen in the shadows. I enjoy it.

Even before I rose through the ranks of my family, I could inspire fear. Being a large man made that simple. But now, with brawn and power behind me, people cower. These people—the employees at the soda factory—don't even know why they fear me. Other than me being the owner's son, they have no real reason to be afraid of me, and yet, like prey in the grasslands, they sense the lion is near. I observe each of them as I weave my way around conveyors filled with plastic bottles and aluminum cans, carbonated soda being pumped into them, filling the room with a syrupy sweet smell.

I recognize their faces, though not their names. The people upstairs don't concern me. Or, at least, they shouldn't. The soda factory is a cover for the real operation downstairs, which must be protected at all costs. It's why I'm here on a Friday evening sniffing around for rats. For anyone who looks unfamiliar or out of place.

The floor manager—a Hispanic woman with a severe braid running down her back—calls out orders to the employees on the floor below in both English and Spanish, directing attention where necessary. She doesn't look at me once.

Noise permeates the metal shell of the building. The whirr of conveyor belts and grinding of gears makes the concrete floors feel like they are vibrating from the sheer power of the sound waves. A lot of people find the sights and smells overwhelming, but I've never minded. You don't become a mob underboss by shrinking in the face of chaos.

A group of employees in blue polos gather around a conveyor belt, smoothing out some kink in the production line. They pull a few aluminum cans from the line and drop them in a recycling bin, jockeying the rest of the cans back into a smooth line. The larger of the three men—a bald man with a doughy face and no obvious chin—flips a red switch. An alarm sounds and the cans begin moving again. He gives the floor manager a thumbs up and then turns to me, his hand flattening into a small wave. I raise an eyebrow in response. His face reddens, and he turns back to his work.

I don't recognize him, but he can't be in law enforcement. Undercover cops are more fit than he could ever dream to be. Plus, he wouldn't have drawn attention to himself. Likely, he is just a new hire, unaware of my position in the company. I resolve to go over new hires with the site manager and find out the man's name.

When I make it to the back of the production floor, the lights are dimmed—the back half of the factory not being utilized overnight—and I fumble with my keys for a moment before finding the right one to unlock the basement door. The stairway down is dark, and as soon as the metal door slams shut behind me, I'm left in blackness, my other senses heightening. The sounds of the production floor are but a whisper behind me, but the most pressing difference is the smell. Rather than the syrupy sweetness of the factory, there is an ether, chemical-like smell that makes my nose itch.

"That you, Luka?" Simon Oakley, the main chemist, doesn't wait for me to answer. "I've got a line here for you. We've perfected the chemistry. Best coke you'll ever try."

I pull back a thick curtain at the base of the stairs and step into the bright white light of the real production floor. I blink as my eyes adjust, and see Simon alone at the first metal table, three other men working in the back of the room. Like the employees upstairs, they don't look up as I enter. Simon, however, smiles and points to the line.

"I don't need to try it," I say flatly. "I'll know whether it's good or not when I see how much our profits increase."

"Well," Simon balks. "It can take time for word to spread. We may not see a rise in income until—"

"I'm not here to chat." I walk around the end of the table and stand next to Simon. He is an entire head shorter than me, his skin pale from spending so much time in the basement. "There have been nasty rumors going around among my men."

His bushy brows furrow in concern. "Rumors about what? You know we basement dwellers are often the last to hear just about everything." He tries to chuckle, but it dies as soon as he sees that I'm not here to fuck around.

"Disloyalty." I purse my lips and run my tongue over my top teeth. "The rumbling is that someone has turned their back on the family."

Fear dilates his pupils, and his fingers drum against the metal tabletop. "See? That is what I'm saying. I haven't heard a single thing about any of that."

"You haven't?" I hum in thought, taking a step closer. I can tell Simon wants to back away, but he stays put. I commend him for his bravery even as I loath him for it. "That is interesting."

His Adam's apple bobs in his throat. "Why is that interesting?"

Before he can even finish the sentence, my hand is around his neck. I strike like a snake, squeezing his windpipe in my hand and walking him back towards the stone wall. I hear the men in the back of the room jump and murmur, but they make no move to help their boss. Because I outrank Simon by a mile.

"It's interesting, Simon, because I have reliable information that says you met with members of the Furino mafia." I slam his head against the wall once, twice. "Is it true?"

His face is turning red, eyeballs beginning to bulge out, and he claws at my hand for air. I don't give him any.

"Why would you go behind my back and meet with another family? Have I not welcomed you into our fold? Have I not made your life here comfortable?"

Simon's eyes are rolling back in his head, his fingers becoming limp noodles on my wrist, weak and ineffective. Just before his body can sag into unconsciousness, I release him. He drops to the floor, falling onto his hands and knees and gasping for air. I let him get two breaths before I kick him in the ribs.

"I didn't meet with them," he rasps. When he looks up at me, I can already see the beginnings of bruises wrapping around his neck.

I kick him again. The force knocks the air out of him, and he collapses on his face, forehead pressed to the cement floor.

"Okay," he says, voice muffled. "I talked with them. Once."

I pressed the sole of my shoe into his ribs, rolling him onto his back. "Speak up."

"I met with them once," he admits, tears streaming down his face from the pain. "They reached out to me."

"Yet you did not tell me?"

"I didn't know what they wanted," he says, sitting up and leaning against the wall.

"All the more reason you should have told me." I reach down and grab his shirt, hauling him to his feet and pinning him against the wall. "Men who are loyal to me do not meet with my enemies."

"They offered me money," he says, wincing in preparation for the next blow. "They offered me a larger cut of the profits. I shouldn't have gone, but I have a family, and—"

I was raised to be an observer of people. To spot their weaknesses and know when I am being deceived. So, I know immediately Simon is not telling me the entire story. The Furinos would not reach out to our chemist and offer him more money unless there had been communication between them prior, unless they had some connection Simon is not telling me about. He thinks I am a fool. He thinks I will forgive him because of his wife and child, but he does not know the depths of my apathy. Simon thinks he can appeal to my humanity, but he does not realize I do not have any.

I press my hand into the bruises around his neck. Simon grabs my wrist, trying to pull me away, but I squeeze again, enjoying the feeling of his life in my hands. I like knowing that with one blow to the neck, I could break his trachea and watch him suffocate on the floor. I am in complete control.

"And your family will be dead before dawn unless you tell me why you met with the Furinos," I spit. I want nothing more than to kill Simon for being disloyal. I can figure out the truth without him. But it is not why I was sent here. Killing indiscriminately does not create the kind of controlled fear we need to keep our family standing. It only creates anarchy. So, reluctantly, I let Simon go. Once again, he falls to the floor, gasping, and I step away so I won't be tempted to beat him.

"I'll tell you," he says, his voice high-pitched, like the words are being released slowly from a balloon. "I'll tell you anything, just don't hurt my family."

I nod for him to continue. This is his only chance to come clean. If he lies to me again, I'll kill him.

Simon opens his mouth, but before he can say anything, I hear a loud bang upstairs and a scream. Just as I turn around, the door at the top of the stairs opens, and I know immediately something is wrong. Forgetting all about Simon, I grab the nearest table and tip it over, not worrying about the potential lost profits. Footsteps pound down the stairs and no sooner have I crouched down, the room erupts in bullets.

I see one of the men in the back of the room drop, clutching his stomach. The other two follow my lead and dive behind tables. Simon crawls over to lay on the floor next to me, his lips purple.

The room is filled with the pounding of footsteps, the ring of bullets, and the moans of the fallen man. It is chaos, but I am steady. My heart rate is even as I grab my phone, turn on the front facing camera, and lift it over the table. There are eight shoulders spread out around the room, guns at the ready. Two of them are at the base of the stairs, the other six are spread out in three-foot increments, forming a barrier in front of the stairs. No one here is supposed to get out alive.

But they do not know who is hiding behind the table. If they did, they'd be running.

I look over at one of the chemists. They are not our family's soldiers, but they are trained like anyone else. He has his gun at the ready, waiting for my order. I nod my head once, twice, and on three, we both turn and fire.

One man falls immediately, my bullet striking him in the neck, blood spraying against the wall like splattered paint. It is a kind of artwork, shooting a man. Years of training, placing the bullet just so. Art is meant to incite a reaction and a bullet certainly does that. The man drops his weapon, his hand flying to his neck. Before he can experience too much pain, I place another bullet in his forehead. He drops to his knees, but before he falls flat on his face, I shoot his friend.

The men expected this ambush to be simple, so they are still in shock, still scrambling to collect themselves. It makes it easy for my men to knock them off. Another two men drop as I chase my second target around the room, firing shot after shot at him. He ducks behind a table, and I wait, gun aimed. It is a deadly game of Whack-a-mole, and it requires patience. His gun pops up first, followed shortly by his head, which I blow off with one shot. His scream dies on his lips as he bleeds out, red seeping out from under the table and spreading across the floor.

There are three men left, and I'm out of bullets. I stash my gun in my pocket and pull out my KA-BAR knife. The blade feels like an old friend in my hand. I crawl past a shivering Simon, wishing I'd killed him just so I wouldn't have to see him looking so pathetic, and out from behind the table. I slide my feet under me, moving into a crouch. The remaining men are wounded, and they are focused on the back corner where shots are still coming from my men. They do not see me approaching from the side.

I lunge at the first man—a young kid with golden brown hair and a tattoo on his neck. It is half-hidden under the collar of his shirt, so I cannot make it out. When my knife cuts into his side, he spins to fight me off, but I knock his gun from his hand with my left arm and then drive the knife in under his ribs and upward. He freezes for a moment before blood leaks from his mouth.

The man next to him falls from multiple bullets in the chest and stomach. I kick his gun away from him as he falls to the floor, and advance on the last attacker. He is hiding behind a metal table, palm pressing into a wound on his shoulder. He scrambles to lift his gun as I approach, but I drop to my knees and slide next to him, knife pressed to his neck. His eyes go wide, and then they squeeze shut as he drops his weapon.

The blade of my knife is biting into his skin, and I see the same tattoo creeping up from beneath his collar. I slide the blade down, pushing his shirt aside, and I recognize it at once.

"You are with the Furinos?" I ask.

The man answers by squeezing his eyes shut even tighter.

"You should know who is in a room before you attack," I hiss. "I am Luka Volkov, and I could slit your throat right now."

His entire body is trembling, blood from his shoulder wound leaking through his clothes and onto the floor. Every ounce of me wants this kill. I feel like a dog who has not been fed, desperate for a hunk of flesh, but warfare is not endless bloodshed. It is tactical.

"But I will not," I say, pulling the blade back. The man blinks, unbelieving. "Get out of here and tell your boss what happened. Tell him this attack is a declaration of war, and the Volkov family will live up to our merciless reputation."

He hesitates, and I slash the blade across his cheek, drawing a thin line of blood from the corner of his mouth to his ear. "Go!" I roar.

The man scrambles to his feet and towards the stairs, blood dripping in his wake. As soon as he is gone, I clean my knife with the hem of my shirt and slide it back into place on my hip.

This will not end well.

Eve

I hold up a bag of raisins and a bag of prunes a few inches from the cook's face.

"Do you see the difference?" I ask. The question is rhetorical. Anyone with eyes could see the difference. And a cook—a properly trained cook—should be able to smell, feel, and sense the difference, as well.

Still, Felix wrinkles his forehead and studies the bags like it is a pop quiz.

"Raisins are small, Felix!" My shouting makes him jump, but I'm far too stressed out to care. "Prunes are huge. As big as a baby's fist. Raisins are tiny. They taste very different because they start out as different fruits. Do you see the problem?"

He stares at me blankly, and I wonder if being sous chef gives me the authority to fire someone. Because this man has got to go.

"You've ruined an entire roast duck, Felix." I drop the bags on the counter and run a hand down my sweaty face. I grab the towel from my back pocket and towel off. "Throw it out and start again, but use *prunes* this time."

He smiles and nods, and I wonder how many times he must have hit his head to be so slow. I motion for another cook to come talk to me. He moves quickly, hands folded behind his back, waiting for my order.

"Chop up the duck and make a confit salad. We can toss it with more raisins, fennel—that kind of thing—and make it work."

He nods and shuffles away, and I mop my forehead again.

At the start of my shift, I strode into the kitchen like I owned the place. I was finally sous chef to Cal Higgs, genius chef in charge at The Floating Crown. After graduating culinary school, I didn't know where I'd get a job or where I'd be on the totem pole, and I certainly never imagined I'd be a sous chef so soon, but here I am. And now that I'm here, I can't help but wonder if it wasn't some sort of trick. Did Cal give into my father's wishes easily and give me this job because he needed a break from the insanity?

I've been assured by several members of staff that the dishwasher, whose name I can't remember, has been working at the kitchen for over a year, but he seems to be stuck on slow motion tonight. He is washing and drying plates seconds before the cooks are plating them up and sending them back out to the dining room. And two of the cooks, who were apparently dating, decided that the middle of dinner rush would be the perfect time to discuss their relationship, and they broke up. Dylan stormed out without a word, and Sarah, who should be okay since she was the dumper, not the dumpee, is hiding in the bathroom bawling her eyes out. I've knocked on the door once every ten minutes for an hour, but she refuses to let me in. Cal has a key, but he has been shut away in his office all night, and I don't want to go explain what a shitshow the kitchen is, so we are making do. Barely.

"Sarah?" I knock on the door. "If you don't come out in five minutes, you're fired."

For the first time, there is a break in the crying. "You can't do that."

"Yes, I can," I lie. "You'll leave here tonight without your apron. Single and jobless. Just imagine that shame."

I feel bad rubbing salt in her wound, threatening her, but I'm out of options. I tried comforting her and offering her some of the dark chocolate from the dessert pantry, but she refused to budge. Threats are my last recourse.

There is a long pause, and I wonder if I'm going to have to admit that I actually can't fire her—I don't think—and tell the staff to start using the bathrooms on the customer side, when finally, Sarah emerges. Mascara is smeared down her cheeks, and her eyes are red and puffy from crying, but she is out of the bathroom. As soon as she steps through the doorway, one of the waitresses darts in after her and slams the door shut.

"I'm sorry, Eve," she blubbers, covering her face with her hands.

I grab her wrists and pry her palms from her eyes. When she looks up, her eyes are still closed, tears leaking from the corners.

"Go to the sinks and help with the dishes," I say firmly. "You're in no state to cook right now. Just focus on cleaning plates, okay?"

Sarah nods, her lower lip wobbling.

"Everything is fine," I say, speaking to her like she is a wild animal who might attack. "You won't lose your job. Cal never needs to know, okay? Just go wash dishes. Now."

She turns away from me in a daze and heads back to help the dishwasher whose name I can't for the life of me remember, and I take a deep breath. I've finally put out all the fires, and I lean against the counter and watch the kitchen move around me. It is like a living, breathing machine. Each person has to play their part or everything falls apart. And tonight, I'm barely holding them together.

When the kitchen door swings open, I hope it is Makayla. She has been a waitress at The Floating Crown for five years, and while she has no formal culinary training, she knows this kitchen better than anyone. I've asked her for help tonight more times than I'm comfortable with, but at this point, just seeing one, capable, smiling face would be enough to keep me from crying. But when I turn and instead see a man in a suit, the tie loose and askew around his neck, and his eyes glassy, I almost sag to the floor.

"You can't be back here, sir," I say, moving forward to block his access to the rest of the kitchen. "We have hot stoves and fire and sharp knives, and you are already unstable on your feet."

Makayla told me a businessman at the bar had been demanding macaroni and cheese all night between shots. Apparently, he would not take 'no' for an answer.

"Macaroni and cheese," he mutters, falling against my palms, his feet sliding out from underneath him. "I need macaroni and cheese to soak up the alcohol."

I turn to the nearest person for help, but Felix is still looking at the bags of raisins and prunes like he might seriously still be confused which is which, and I don't want to distract him lest he ruin another duck. I could call out for help from someone else or call the police, but I don't want to cause a scene. Cal is just in the next room. He may have hired me because my father is Don of the Furino family, but even my father can't be angry if Cal fires me for sheer incompetence. I have to prove that I'm capable.

"Sir, we don't have macaroni and cheese, but may I recommend our scoglio?"

"What is that?" he asks, top lip curled back.

"A delicious seafood pasta. Mussels, clams, shrimp, and scallops in a tomato sauce with herbs and spices. Truly delicious. One of my favorite meals on the menu."

"No cheese?"

I sigh. "No. No cheese."

He shakes his head and pushes past me, running his hands along the counters like he might stumble upon a prepared bowl of cheesy pasta.

"Sir, you can't be back here."

"I can be wherever I like," he shouts. "This is America, isn't it?"

"It is, but this is a private restaurant and our insurance does not cover diners being back in the kitchen, so I have to ask you—"

"Oh, say can you see by the dawn's early light!"

"Is that 'The Star-Spangled Banner'?" I ask, looking around to see whether anyone else can see this man or whether I'm having some sort of exhausted fever dream.

"What so proudly we hailed at the twilight's last gleaming?"

This is absurd. Truly absurd. Beyond calling the police, the easiest thing to do seems to be to give in to his demands, so I lay a hand on his shoulder and lead him to the corner of the kitchen. I pat the counter, and he jumps up like he is a child.

I listen to the National Anthem six times before I hand the man a bowl of whole grain linguini with a sharp cheddar cheese sauce on top. "Can you please take this back to the bar and leave me alone?"

He grabs the bowl from my hands, takes a bite, and then breaks into yet another rousing rendition of "The Star-Spangled Banner." This time in falsetto with accompanying dance moves.

I sigh and push him towards the door. "Come on, man."

The dining room is loud enough that no one pays the man too much attention. Plus, he has been drunk out here for an hour before ambushing the kitchen. A few guests shake their heads at the man and then smile at me, giving me the understanding and recognition I sought from the kitchen staff. I lead the man back to the bar, tell the bartender to get rid of him as soon as the pasta is gone, and then make my way back through the dining room.

"She isn't the chef," says a deep voice at normal volume. "Chefs don't look like *that*."

I don't turn towards the table because I don't want to give them the satisfaction of knowing I heard them, of knowing they had any kind of power over me.

"Whatever she makes, it can't taste half as good as her muffin," another man says to raucous laughter.

I roll my eyes and speed up. I'm used to the comments and the cat calls. I've been dealing with it since I sprouted boobs. Even my father's men would whisper things about me. It is part of the reason I chose a path outside the scope of the family business. I couldn't imagine working with the kind of men my father employed. They were crass and mean and treated women like possessions. Unfortunately, the more I learn of the world beyond the Bratva, the more I realize men everywhere are like that. It is the reason I'll never get married. I won't belong to anyone.

I hear the men's deep voices as I walk back towards the kitchen, but I don't listen. I let the words roll off of me like water on a windowpane and step back into the safe chaos of the kitchen.

The kitchen seems to calm down as dinner service goes on, and I'm able to take a step back from micro-managing everything to work on an order of chicken tikka masala. While letting the tomato puree and spices simmer, I realize my stomach is growling. I was too nervous before shift to eat anything, and now that things have finally settled into an easy rhythm, my body is about to absorb itself. So, I casually walk over to where two giant stock pots are simmering with the starter soups for the day and scoop myself out a hearty ladle of lobster and bacon soup. Cal doesn't like for anyone to eat while on service, but he has been in his office all evening, and based on the smell slipping out from under his door, he will be far too stoned to notice or care.

The soup is warm and filling, and I close my eyes as I eat, enjoying the blissful moment of peace before more chaos ensues.

The kitchen door opens, and this time it really is Makayla. I wave her over, eager to see how everyone is enjoying the food and whether the drunk patriot finally left the restaurant, but she doesn't see me and walks with purpose through the kitchen and straight to Cal's office door. She opens it and steps inside, and I wonder what she needed Cal for and why she couldn't come to me. Lord knows I've handled every other situation that arose all night.

I'm just finished the last bite of my soup when Cal's office door slams open, bouncing off the wall, and he stomps his way across the kitchen.

"Eve!"

I shove the bowl to the back of the counter, throwing a dish towel over top to hide the evidence, and then wipe my mouth quickly.

"Yes, chef?"

"Front and center," he barks like we are in the military rather than a kitchen.

Despite the offense I take with his tone—especially after everything I've done to keep the place running all night—I move quickly to follow his order. Because that is what a good sous chef does. I follow the chef's orders, no matter how demeaning.

Cal Higgs is a large man in every sense of the word. He is tall, round, and thick. His head sits on top of his shoulders with no neck in sight, and just walking across the room looks like a chore. I imagine being in his body would be like wearing a winter coat and scarf all the time.

"What is the problem, Chef?"

He hitches a thumb over his shoulder, and Makayla gives me an apologetic wince. "Someone complained about the food, and they want to see the chef."

I wrinkled my forehead. I'd personally tasted every dish that went out. Unless Felix managed to slide another dish past me with raisins in it instead of prunes, I'm not sure what the complaint could be. "Was there something wrong with the dish or did they simply not like it?"

"Does it matter?" he snaps. His eyes are bloodshot and glassy, yet his temper is as sharp as ever. "I don't like unhappy customers, and you need to fix it."

"But you're the chef," I say, realizing too late I should have stayed quiet.

Cal steps forward, and I swear I can feel the floor quake under his weight. "But you made the food. Should I go out there and apologize on your behalf? No, this is your mess, and you will take care of it."

"Of course," I say, looking down at the ground. "You're right. I'll go out there and make this right."

Before Cal can find another reason to yell at me, I retie my apron around my waist, straighten my white jacket, and march through the swinging kitchen doors.

The dining room is quieter than before. The drunk man is no longer singing the National Anthem at the bar and several of the tables are empty, the bussers clearing away empty plates. Happy plates, I might add. Clearly, they didn't have an issue with the food.

I didn't ask Makayla who complained about the food, but as soon as I walk into the main dining area, it is obvious. There is a small gathering at the corner booth, and a salt and pepper-haired man in his late fifties or early sixties raising a hand in the air and waves me over without looking directly at me. I haven't even spoken to the man yet, and I already hate him.

I'm standing at their table, staring at the man, but he doesn't speak to me until I announce my presence.

"I heard someone wanted to speak with the chef," I say.

He turns to me, one eyebrow raised. "You are the chef?"

I recognize a Russian accent when I hear one, and this man is Russian without a doubt. I wonder if I know him. Or if my father does. Would he be complaining to me if he knew my father was head of the Furino family? I would never throw my family name around in order to scare people, but for just a second, I have the inclination.

"Sous chef," I say with as much confidence as I can muster. "I ran the kitchen tonight, so I'll be hearing the complaints."

His eyes move down my body slowly like he is inspecting a cut of meat in a butcher shop. I cross my arms over my chest and spread my feet hip-width apart. "So, was there an issue with the food? I'd love to correct any problems."

"Soup was cold." He nudges his empty bowl to the center of the table with three fingers. "The portions were too small, and I ordered my steak medium-rare, not raw."

Every plate on the table is empty. Not a single crumb in sight. Apparently, the issues were not bad enough he couldn't finish his meal.

"Do you have any of the steak left?" I ask, making a show of looking around the table. "If one of my cooks undercooked the meat, I'd like to be able to inform them."

"If? I just told you the meat was undercooked. Are you doubting me?"

"Of course not," I say. *Yes, absolutely I am.* "It is just that if the meat was undercooked, I do not understand why you waited until you'd eaten everything to inform me of the problem?"

The man looks around the table at his companions. They are all smiling, and I can practically see them sharpening their teeth, preparing to rip me to shreds. When he turns back to me, his smile is acidic, deadly. "How did you get this position—sous chef? Surely not by skill. You are pretty, which I'm sure did you a favor. Did you sleep with the chef? Maybe—" he moves his hand in an obscene gesture —"'service' the boss to earn your place in the kitchen? Surely your 'talent' didn't get you the job, seeing as how you have none."

I physically bite my tongue and then take a deep breath. "If you'd like me to remake anything for you or bring out a complimentary dessert, I'm happy to do that. If not, I apologize for the issues and hope you will not hold it against us. We'd love to have you again."

Lies. Lies. Lies. I'm smiling and being friendly the way I was taught in culinary school. I actually took a class on dealing with customers, and this man is being even more outrageous than the overexaggerated angry customer played by my professor.

"Why would I want more food from you if the things you already sent out were terrible?" He snorts and shakes his head. "I see you do not have a ring on. That is no surprise. Men like a woman who can cook. Men don't care if you know your way around a professional kitchen if you don't know your way around a dinner plate."

The older gentleman is speaking, but I hear my father's words in my head. *You do not need to go to culinary school to find a husband, Eve. Your aunties can teach you to cook good food for your man.*

My entire life has been preparation for finding a husband. The validity of every hobby is judged by whether it will fetch me a suitor or not. My father wants me to be happy, but he mostly wants me to be married. Single, I'm a disappointment. Married, I'm a vessel for future Furino mafia members.

Years of anger and resentment begin to bubble and hiss inside of me until I'm boiling. My hands are shaking, and I can feel adrenaline pulsing through me, lighting every inch of me on fire. This time, I don't bite my tongue.

"I'd rather die alone than spent another minute near a man like you," I spit, stepping forward and laying my palms flat on the table. "The fact that you ate all of the food you apparently hated shows you are a pig in more ways than one."

In the back of my mind, I recognize that my voice is echoing around the restaurant and the chatter in the rest of the room has gone quiet, but blood is whirring in my ears, and I can't stop. I've stayed quiet and docile for too long. Now, it is my turn to speak my mind.

"You and your friends may be wealthy and respected, but I see you for what you are—spineless, cowardly assholes who are so insecure they have to take their rage out on everybody else."

I want to spin on my heel and storm away, making a grand exit, but in classic Eve fashion, my heel catches on the tablecloth, and I nearly trip. I fall sideways and throw an arm out to catch myself, knocking a nearly full bottle of wine on the table over. The glass shatters and red wine splashes across the tablecloth and onto the guests in the booth like a river of blood.

I pause long enough to note the old Russian man's shirt is splattered like he has been shot before I continue my exit and head straight for the doors.

I suck in the night air. The evening is warm and humid, summer strangling the city in its hold, and I want to rip off my clothes for some relief. I feel like I'm being strangled. Like there is a hand around my neck, squeezing the life out of me.

Breathing in and out slowly helps, but as the physical panic begins to ebb away, emotional panic flows in.

What have I done? Cal Higgs is going to find out about the altercation any minute, and then what? Will he fire me? And if he does, will I ever be able to get another chef position? I was only offered this position because of my father, and I doubt he will help me earn another kitchen position, especially since I'm no closer to finding a boyfriend (or husband) since I left for culinary school.

Despite it all, I want to call my dad. He has always made it clear he will move heaven and earth to take care of me, to make sure no one is mean to me, and I want his support right now. But the support he offered me when a girl tripped me during soccer practice and made me miss the net won't apply here. He will tell me to come home. To put down my apron and knife and focus on more meaningful pursuits. And that is the last thing I want to hear right now.

I pull out my phone and scroll through my contacts list, hoping to see a spark of hope amidst the names, but there is nothing. I've lost touch with everyone since I started culinary school. There hasn't been time for friends.

This is probably the kind of situation where most girls would turn to their moms, but she hasn't been in the picture since I was six years old. Even if I had her number, I wouldn't call her. Dad hasn't always been perfect, but at least he was there. At least he cared enough to stay.

I untie my apron and pull it over my head, leaning back against the brick side of the restaurant.

"Take it off, baby!"

I look up and see a man on a motorcycle with his hair in a bun parked along the curb. He is waggling his eyebrows at me like I'm supposed to fall in love with him for harassing me on the street, and the fire that filled my veins inside hasn't died out yet. The embers are still there, burning under the skin, and I step towards him, lips pulled back in a smile.

He looks surprised, and I'm sure he is. That move has probably never worked for him before. He smiles back at me, his tongue darting out to lick his lower lip.

"Is that your bike?" I purr.

He nods. "Want a ride?"

My voice is still sticky sweet as I respond, "So sweet of you to offer. I'd rather choke and die on that grease ball you call a man bun, but thanks anyway, hon."

It takes him a second to realize my words don't match the tone. When it hits him, he snarls, "Bitch."

"Asshole." I flip him the bird over my shoulder and start the long walk home.

∽

Click here to keep reading BROKEN VOWS.

MAILING LIST

Sign up to my mailing list!
New subscribers receive a FREE steamy bad boy romance novel.

Click the link below to join.
http://bit.ly/NicoleFoxNewsletter

ALSO BY NICOLE FOX

Kornilov Bratva Duet

Married to the Don

Til Death Do Us Part

Heirs to the Bratva Empire

*Can be read in any order

Kostya

Maksim

Andrei

Tsezar Bratva

Nightfall (Book 1)

Daybreak (Book 2)

Russian Crime Brotherhood

*Can be read in any order

Owned by the Mob Boss

Unprotected with the Mob Boss

Knocked Up by the Mob Boss

Sold to the Mob Boss

Stolen by the Mob Boss

Trapped with the Mob Boss

Volkov Bratva

Broken Vows (Book 1)

Broken Hope (Book 2)

Other Standalones

Vin: A Mafia Romance

Printed in Great Britain
by Amazon